HAPPY

David Cook was bor[...]
trained as an actor, a[...]
television, repertory a[...]
ated the part of Trevor in John Bowen's *Little*
Boxes, and spent a year as the host of a TV programme for children with his side-kick, Bungle
the Bear.

He began writing in 1969, and has published
five other novels – *Albert's Memorial, Walter*
(Hawthornden Prize), *Winter Doves, Sunrising*
(Southern Arts Fiction Prize) and *Missing Persons*.
Several of his television plays have been nomi-
nated for awards; his series *A Place Like Home*,
for BBC Schools, won the Writers' Guild Award
in 1977, and the film of *Walter* which he scripted
was chosen for the Opening Night of Channel 4,
received the Jury's Special Award at Monte Carlo
and was runner-up for an International Emmy.
He has also written the script for the television
film of *Missing Persons*.

He lives in London and near Stratford on
Avon, and does his writing in both places and at
local Public Libraries.

David Cook

HAPPY ENDINGS

ARENA

FOR MY MOTHER AND FATHER

An Arena Book
Published by Arrow Books Limited
62–65 Chandos Place, London WC2N 4NW

An imprint of Century Hutchinson Limited

London Melbourne Sydney Auckland
Johannesburg and agencies throughout
the world

First published in Great Britain by The Alison
Press/Martin Secker & Warburg Ltd 1974
Reprinted 1975
Arena edition 1989

Typeset by Input Typesetting Ltd, London
Printed and bound in Great Britain by
The Guernsey Press Co Ltd
Guernsey, C.I.

ISBN 0 09 958300 3

Contents

Interfering

May 1951

The Lion and the unicorn were fighting for the crown.
The Lion beat the unicorn all around the town.
Some gave them white bread, and some gave them brown,
And some gave them syrup of figs, and beat them out of town.

'How old are you?'

Morris said he was twelve.

'When is your next birthday?'

Morris said, 'November the fifth.'

'Guy Fawkes Night?' Morris was not sure if this was a question, so he did not reply.

He was standing before a large table. On the table was a bottle of water, and on top of the bottle, presumably keeping out dust, was a glass tumbler. Behind the table sat three people, one man and two ladies. One of the ladies was small, but the other, who sat in the middle and was asking him questions, was large, so large that, even though she was sitting down, he had to look up at her. Except that he couldn't look at her. Instead he looked at the large coloured badge which was fixed to the wall above her head. The lion and the unicorn were supported by a shield between them. Neither of them seemed interested enough to fight for the crown which was above the shield.

'Come here, and talk to me, Morris.'

Morris took two paces forward.

'Come closer. We're not here to bite you. Are we?' The large lady was asking the people on either side of her, but neither of them replied. Morris's mother had been removed from sitting

7

beside where he stood, and had been asked to sit directly behind him. Morris supposed that this was to prevent her from telling him what to say. He attempted a look at his mother before moving any closer to the table, but the large lady was asking him another question, and he must concentrate on giving the right answer. The question was an important one. It was, 'Why did you do it?'

'Why did you do it, Morris?' Some gave them syrup of figs, and beat them out of town. Had the lion won the crown? It would have suited the unicorn best, for the spiral horn of the unicorn would have kept the ring-shaped crown in place.

'Why did you do it, Morris?' He knew there were lots of people behind him, staring at the back of his head. There was the man who had brought them from the Waiting Room. There were two women dressed like policemen. There were four young women sitting at the back of the court, and with them was Miss Edge. There were at least four other men, including a proper policeman. There was his mother, and, sitting three chairs away from his mother, there was his father.

'It says here that you are a quiet boy, always polite. That the neighbours think of you as a proper little gentleman. That you run errands for them, and never accept money for doing so. That you have run a lot of errands for Mrs Richards, and that is why she trusted you. So what could have made you do it?'

Mrs Richards always bought her blouses at Marks and Spencer's. They were always nylon, and always had plunging necklines. Morris would stand at the bottom of the back-door steps, and Mrs Richards would bend down to tell him what she wanted.

'Half a pound of margarine.' Morris would long to grab inside the plunging blouse, and swing on Mrs Richards' tits.

'A pound of smoked bacon. Lean.' He would grab. He would swing. 'Make sure it's smoked. And lean.' He would swing. He would squeeze. 'Two pints of gold top, and you'll need a carrier bag.' Swing! Squeeze! Swing! Squeeze! As Mrs Richards leaned towards him, Morris would be hanging on to her tits, and skimming over the back-door step. 'Don't forget the dividend tea: I've nearly got my card full. There's no need to give you a list, is there? You never forget anything of mine.' Morris never forgot anything of hers. Mrs Richards straightened her

8

back, and Morris would have a final swing before she went indoors. He closed his eyes.

'You do know what we're talking about, don't you?' Morris wondered why the large lady said 'we'. Only she had spoken, except for the man who sat to one side of the table, and had read out to Morris from a paper what Morris was said to have done, and had asked Morris if it were true or not. *'Morris, it says here that on the afternoon of. . . and that you then Interfered with Angela Richards, and that you were found in the act of Interfering by Angela's mother. . . What do you say to that, Morris? Is it true?'* And Morris had said that it was true, and the large lady had asked what exactly the Interference was said to have consisted of, and a policeman had written something down on paper and passed it to the large lady, who had read it and passed it to the small one, who had read it and passed it to the man on the large lady's other side.

'Now, Morris, we're talking about what you did to Angela. I don't want to go into too many details, because it's only embarrassing for all of us, isn't it?' Morris agreed that it was. He could not look at the people in front of him, so he looked either at the water jug or at the badge on the wall above them. When he looked at the water jug, the small lady turned the paper from which she had been reading face downwards, so that if Morris had been able to read upside down, he would not know what had been written about him. Some of what had been written about him said that he could hardly read at all, even when the writing was right way up.

'I have here your School Report, and it tells me you're not really a bad lad. Quite the reverse.' Morris frequently had a daydream of which he was ashamed. The dream involved owning black slaves, and had been inspired by the film of *Sanders of the River*, which Morris had seen at the age of eight at the Rialto, Ridgemont, which specialized in old films at cheap prices. All the slaves were beautiful and naked, and they stood in line for his inspection.

'It tells me you could easily learn to read and spell if you'd only put your mind to it.' He would walk along the line, touching and prodding them, and finally he would force them to touch and prod each other while he watched.

9

'You're good at general knowledge, and you like acting. Is that true?'

'Yes, miss.' When Morris's father had found out about Angela, he had called Morris a dirty-minded bastard, and it was true. Morris looked again at the unicorn's horn, and imagined a crown around it. It was unfair that lions should always win: unicorns were far more beautiful.

To Morris, lots of people were beautiful, and he knew that this was wrong.

'I'm afraid it also says that you're a whiner, and that you don't mix.' It was all right having a dirty mind, as long as people didn't notice. In his mind, Morris enjoyed physical contact. In real life, he avoided it. But now people knew about his mind. They would be able to guess what he was thinking.

'It says that you let other boys hit you. You won't hit them back, but you complain. Is that true?'

'Yes, miss.' Even when Mrs Richard was hitting him around the head, screaming at him and making Angela scream, he had been looking at Mrs Richards' tits, and holding them in his mind.

'When a boy as big as you are Inferferes with a little girl, a girl who is only five—that's not much more than a baby, is it?'

'No, miss.'

'—we have to find out why. And you don't seem able to tell us.' The large lady waited for a reply. Morris wanted to say, 'Because I've got a dirty mind,' but he couldn't say it. Instead he cried.

'Do you know what we mean by "Interfering", Morris?'

'No, miss.'

'We mean taking Angela's clothes off, Morris and putting Ludo counters into her private parts. We mean hitting her and bruising her. Do you know how babies are born, Morris?'

Morris didn't know, and didn't answer.

'Does he know how babies are born, Mrs Cowley?'

'I don't think so, madam.'

'Well, let's just say, Morris, that you could have frightened Angela in a way that might make it difficult for her to have babies when she's old enough to do so. Her mother says you've frightened Angela so much that she refuses to take her clothes off any more. Now that's going to be very inconvenient, isn't it?'

'Yes, miss.'

'Then you realize the seriousness of your actions?'

'Yes, miss.'

'What do you think we should do with you?' There was a master at school who always asked this question before he hit you with a ruler. Morris said he didn't know what they should do with him.

The large lady whispered to the two people sitting beside her. The words Morris heard were, 'Needs a strong hand. . . No question. . . punishment. . . father. . . useless. . . mother unreliable. . . toughen him up. . . needs. . . shock. . . Assessment.'

'We're going to send you away to an Assessment Centre. We think you need to be Assessed. You're a weak boy, Morris; it's not entirely your fault, but there it is. One of the problems anyone dealing with you is going to have to face is how to make a man of you before it's too late. You'll go to Stonebridge Assessment Centre, and when you've been thoroughly Assessed, we'll know what next to do with you. You may sit down now. Do you understand that, Mr and Mrs Cowley? He's to go to the Assessment Centre, and then we'll see him again.'

Morris turned and saw his mother crying. Then he looked further, and saw his father crying. His mother was crying with her face turned away, but his father was crying and looking straight at him. The look said, 'See what you've done. You've made me cry.' Morris was aware that his dirty thoughts had shamed them all, the whole family, not just himself. There was no way of explaining about all the thoughts he had managed to keep inside with no harm done, no way of making them understand the awfulness of pretending to be 'a little gentleman' so that no one should suspect what was going on inside his head. He hadn't liked running errands, refusing tips, standing up at concerts and saying poems. Now he was to be Assessed, and his father was crying. They had not taken into consideration the fact that he had won a Talent Contest, and a Fancy Dress Contest, and also his painting was improving. They had insinuated that he was a coward, and made his father cry. Morris had

11

never seen his father cry before, and it frightened him. No one had said how Angela had teased him, asked him to examine her, and had wanted to feel inside his trousers.

'Mr and Mrs Cowley, will you come up here, please?' Morris's parents stood, as he had done, in front of the large lady.

'Now, I think it's disgraceful what's been going on at your house.' Neither of Morris's parents answered.

'Well, let me put it this way. I believe you have a lodger. Is that correct?'

Morris's mother said, 'Yes.'

'What position does he hold in your household?'

One of the policewomen giggled, and had to leave the court. Morris's mother said that she was afraid she didn't understand. The two parents were standing well apart, and through them Morris could see the large lady's face, which seemed to be getting very red. The small lady took a drink of water.

'I don't think we should beat about the bush, Mrs Cowley. I have in front of me a report made by the Children's Welfare Officer after visiting your house.' The Children's Welfare Officer was Miss Edge. She had been to see Morris, and talked to his parents. 'Now do you know what I'm talking about?' No one answered.

'Is it not true that there were three people in one double bed at four in the afternoon?' Morris knew that of course it was true. His mother and father and Mr Henderson would always be in bed on a Sunday afternoon. On a weekday, Mr Henderson would be at work. At this point, the man at the side table, who had read out what Morris was said to have done, interrupted the large lady, and said, 'With respect, ma'am, I think the boy should leave the court,' and the large lady took a lace handkerchief from the top pocket of her lace blouse, and said, 'Oh, my Goodness! Yes, of course. Thank you, Mr Simmonds.'

The man who had brought Morris in from the Waiting Room took him back there, but not before he had heard his father say, 'That woman had no right to peer in at the window.'

While Morris was out of the court, an argument developed as to whether Miss Edge had knocked at the front door before peering in at the bedroom window and whether she was within her rights in visiting them on a Sunday, a day of rest. The argument became heated, and was stopped by the large lady's banging the small lady's glass tumbler on the table, spilling some of its contents. Apologies were then offered by Miss Edge and Morris's parents. The large lady instructed Mr and Mrs Cowley to sit, so that the matter might be discussed calmly, and told them that she was not there to judge their morals. Their morals (she told them) were for their consciences alone, but it was her job to decide whether they were fit persons to look after Morris, and in the light of what she had heard, she was of the opinion that if he stayed at home Morris would run some danger of moral corruption. She asked them to consider evicting their lodger, at the cost of whatever temporary financial hardship, and living what the world would consider to be a more respectable life, so that, whatever might be decided, at some future date they would stand a better chance of having Morris home again.

Assessment

'This is Morris. Are you the Reception Boy?' A boy wearing a white coat rose from the chair he was sitting in, and admitted reluctantly that he was. Miss Edge sat down, and rested her hand on the chair beside her to indicate to Morris that he should sit also.

'This is the Reception Boy, Morris. When you've had your interview with Mr Radcliffe, it will be this boy who will show you around.' After that no one spoke. Morris looked at the Reception Boy. The Reception Boy looked at Morris, then at Miss Edge, then back at Morris. Morris looked at Miss Edge and then at the ground. Looks had been exchanged all round, except for Miss Edge who never looked at anyone.

They were sitting in the Entrance Hall of the Assessment Centre. It was very large. Tubular steel chairs had been placed round a table with tubular steel legs and a Formica top. They had come by bus, and walked in through a large gate that no one seemed to guard. To Morris the Centre looked like just another housing estate. Some of the buildings had been built of corrugated iron, and some of brick. The brick buildings were tall and had lots of windows.

Morris wondered who would be the first to speak. Surely they were not waitng for him. Morris's teeth were clenched together. His bottom teeth fitted inside his upper teeth, and he pressed his jaw up towards the roof of his mouth as hard as he could. He knew that if he opened his mouth he would cry.

'What's he done, miss?' Morris remained as still as he could. He was leaning forward with his elbows on his thighs, his left hand cupped tightly inside his right. He was looking at the highly polished floor. At any moment, the world would know what he had done.

'It's all right; you can tell me, miss. I've *been* assessed.' Morris looked again at the boy who had been Assessed. He looked unhappy. Resentful. He played with a blister on the back of his hand. All his fingers on both his hands bore the marks of scars and blisters. (Was this because he had been Assessed?) His knuckles stood out, white and bony. At any moment, this boy would know what Morris had done. Morris felt tired. He was sinking. He wanted to sleep. If only he could fall asleep quickly enough, he wouldn't have to listen to Miss Edge describing to the boy what he had done. She would use the word they had used in the Children's Court—'Interfering', as though Angela had been a piece of machinery or a jigsaw puzzle. But the boy would know what 'Interfering' meant. He would stop being resentful for a moment, and he would laugh. He would look at Morris again, this time differently. Morris was not sure in what way the look would be different, but he did not wish to remain awake long enough to find out.

'It's not my job to inform you of what Morris has or has not done. If you wish to ask him yourself when I've gone, you'll have lots of opportunities, I'm sure.'

Morris closed his eyes. If a woman as large as Miss Edge was afraid to tell the boy with blisters what he had done, when she was not even obliged to stay here and listen to people laughing, how could he be expected to tell?

He could not now think of a better word than 'Interfering' to describe what he had done. If he said, 'I played with this little girl, and her mother caught us,' that would not be a proper answer, because although what he had done had seemed natural enough at the time, its effect on Angela's mother had not been natural, and when they came to describe it in Court, it had been written down on a piece of paper, and handed to the Magistrate. 'Interfering' was not right, but it was what they had called it, and Morris could not think of a more suitable word.

Morris opened his eyes. At the other end of the hall, a tall thin woman and a very small boy had come out of what sounded like a kitchen. The woman also wore a white coat, and was supervising the small boy, who pushed a long pole before him. At the end of the pole was a polishing pad. 'Rub it!' For a while,

15

the boy did pretend to rub the floor, but as soon as the woman turned her back he did a little dance in front of Morris, using the pole first as a May Pole and then as a partner. Miss Edge coughed loudly twice, and the tall woman turned, grasped the very small boy by the scruff of his neck, and said, 'Right. Now we'll do the pans.'

Whereafter Miss Edge was sent for, to talk with the unseen Mr Radcliffe, leaving Morris alone with the Reception Boy. And when she returned, it was to leave Morris altogether, for she was the Child Care Officer, and did not belong to the Centre: she had brought Morris to be Assessed, but was not required to do it herself. She bent down towards Morris as she left him, and for a moment he was afraid that he was in some danger of being kissed, but all Miss Edge did was to whisper to him, 'It'll be easier here. There aren't any little girls about.'

Mr Radcliffe had left his home that morning in a cloud. The cloud was heavy and dark grey. It was hanging above him, and clinging around him, and seeping inside him. It had accompanied him from one of the Staff Houses in which he lived with Mrs Radcliffe. It seemed to have the property of expanding to fill whatever space he occupied. At present it filled the Interview Room.

It had started as a mere puff, with a remark made by Mrs Radcliffe the night before: 'I wonder if I can interest you in any way.' Mr Radcliffe had replied, 'I shouldn't have thought so,' and immediately the puff had taken on depth and darkness and damp.

The reply had been unnecessary. It was true, but it was unnecessary. Margaret Radcliffe had left the room, in order to be found half an hour later, lying spread out on the carpet of the Spare Room. She was pretending a faint: it was a ritual. And what annoyed Mr Radcliffe more than the inconvenience of a ruined evening—one of the few he spent off duty—was that these fake fainting fits, always in a different place, dated back almost to the day on which one of the boys had started having them, and he himself had described the boy's attention-getting device to his wife. It showed a marked lack of invention on Mrs Radcliffe's part, all the more so in that she was quickly running out of new and interesting places to drop. The Spare

16

Room had been used before, except that this time, instead of lying on the bed, she lay beside it, her arms and legs spread-eagled as if she were inviting someone to rape her. Which, in a sense, she was.

Mr Radcliffe had looked down at her, wondering how one human being can start so high in the estimation of another, and, in the space of a marriage, sink so low. He was forty years old, and could look forward to perhaps three times as much resentment, anger and frustration. He had then descended to the revival of Mrs Radcliffe, who had clung to him, bitten him in several places, and finally fallen asleep where she lay on the carpet of the Spare Room. Luckily, the places where Mrs Radcliffe had placed her love-bites were all below the line of his collar, so that they would not show when it was fastened.

He was forty years old. He had lifted himself up from the carpet of the Spare Room, gone downstairs, and spent the rest of the night in the kitchen. By morning the cloud which he now carried above, around and within him was as dark and heavy as it would ever get.

For the ritual was not yet over. At some time during the middle of the morning, he would receive a phone call from his wife. The switchboard operator would listen to it, and by lunchtime the senior members of Staff would know of it.

Meanwhile, there was a boy sitting in front of him. Morris Cowley—what a name to land a child with! The boy's eyes leaked distrust at every corner, and spoke sorrowfully of his having been put down in a world that was too big, too uncertain, too unkind. Well, the boy's eyes were right on all three counts. The boy's folded arms spoke of a wish to please, and promised obedience. The boy's tightly closed legs and knees pushed together, heels out, toes in, indicated a passive dreamer who had difficulty keeping awake.

'Do you wet the bed, Morris?'

Morris thought before answering. Mr Radcliffe was reading from a large folder on the desk in front of him. Morris knew that every paper in that folder was about him. He coughed, and whispered, 'Sometimes.'

'Say "sir", Morris.'

'Sometimes, sir.'

17

'Enuresis. Empty your pockets, and put what you've got on the desk.' Morris took everything from his pockets, and laid it out beside the putty-coloured folder. Mr Radcliffe continued reading.

'You haven't been assessed before, have you?'

'No, sir.' Morris had no idea what being Assessed meant. But he knew that he had been sent to this place to be Assessed, and since what he had done was so very wicked he knew that Assessment must be some kind of punishment. He remembered that the hands of the Reception Boy had been covered with scars and blisters, and *he* had been Assessed. Punishment was not new to Morris: he had been hit in his time by angry teachers. But no special place was needed for punishment of that sort, and here there were buildings for it of corrugated iron and brick. Being Assessed must be a very special sort of punishment, probably long-lasting and certainly painful.

Mr Radcliffe told him that he would not be allowed to smoke until he was sixteen, and asked him if he already did so. Morris said, 'No.'

'Good. What's it like at home, Morris?'

Morris did not know how to answer this question. When he thought about home, he found that he was in great danger of crying, so he said quickly, 'All right, sir,' but by this time it was already too late, and both his eyes had filled with tears.

'What colour are your eyes, Morris?'

'Don't know, sir.' They were flooding now, tears running down his face. His nose was running too.

'Don't know? Haven't you ever looked in a mirror?'

'Yes, sir.' Mr Radcliffe leaned forward across the desk; and examined Morris's eyes.

'I'd say they were hazel. Will you agree to that?'

'Yes, sir.'

'Good. We're making contact.' The boy was clearly about to cry, and had better be comforted. 'I'm not sure you should be here at all. As far as I can see, you haven't done anything so terrible.'

Had Miss Edge not told him? Had she been unable to bring herself to say it, just as she had not told the Reception Boy? It must be written down on one of those pieces of paper in the putty-coloured folder, but then Mr Radcliffe had not finished reading it. There were a great many pieces of paper in the folder, and perhaps the one that said 'Interfered with Angela Richards' was at the bottom of the pile.

'Do *you* know why you've been sent here, Morris?' Morris sniffed. He had stopped crying now, and had managed without using his handkerchief, which still lay with his other possessions on Mr Radcliffe's desk. There was no other way of saying it; he was going to have to use that word. If he tried to pretend he didn't know why, Mr Radcliffe would be even more angry. He opened his mouth, and said carefully, 'Sir, it's because I. . .' pausing before the word itself, trying to remember how the Clerk had said it in Court, and in that pause the telephone rang.

At first Mr Radcliffe did not answer it. He left his desk quickly, moved to the window, brought a packet of cigarettes from his pocket, tore at the cellophane which kept them airtight, pulled at the red tab in order to take one cigarette from the packet, and spilled all but two on the floor. Meanwhile the telephone continued to ring.

Mr Radcliffe realized that Morris was watching him, lit one of the two cigarettes which had not fallen, took a deep drag, and returned to his desk to answer the telephone.

Morris could hear the voice at the other end. He could not hear what the voice was saying, but knew that it was female. The effect it seemed to have on Mr Radcliffe was to make him sweat. Sweat formed around the corners of his nose, on the tip of his unshaven chin, and in the hollow parts of his neck. The stubble on the underside of his chin was brown and grey. Mr Radcliffe rubbed his chin and the side of his neck, and Morris noticed that there was a small mark there like a bruise. He considered it odd that a man in Mr Radcliffe's position was not wearing a tie. Mr Radcliffe, seeming to notice the direction of Morris's gaze, fastened the top button of his shirt, and this looked even more odd.

The female voice went on and on, while Mr Radcliffe interjected, 'Right,' and 'Fine,' and 'I'm sure you will,' 'No,' and 'Look! I must go now,' and 'Can we talk about that tonight, Margaret?' Morris thought that Mr Radcliffe put a great deal of force behind the name 'Margaret'. Finally the receiver at the other end was replaced, but Mr Radcliffe held on to his own telephone for a moment until he had heard the receiver of the extension phone also being replaced. Then he sat for a long time in silence, staring down at the putty-coloured folder. Then he thumped his left fist hard down on the folder, picked up a glass ashtray with the right, and threw it hard in the general direction of the window and filing-cabinet. As luck would have it, the ashtray chose the filing-cabinet to hit, and made a dent in the A to K drawer.

It was clear to Morris that Mr Radcliffe must now have come across the word 'Interfering' in the file, and that this was the reason for his outburst of rage. He waited for Mr Radcliffe's next move. He would scream if he were hit. He would scream and then faint. The tightness with which his arms were folded was making it difficult for him to breathe. He was finding it difficult to keep Mr Radcliffe in focus. He would like to have closed his eyes, but he dared not, because he must watch out for the furious blow to come. He was about to be Assessed. He could see two Mr Radcliffes sitting behind Mr Radcliffe's desk.

Both Mr Radcliffes lifted their heads at the same time, and both smiled at Morris, like a pair of hungry tigers. 'Do you know what I mean when I say we are going to assess you?' Morris said, 'Yes, sir,' quickly. It was always better to tell a teacher that you knew you were going to be punished, and deserved it. If you argued or pretended innocence, it gave him longer to prepare the blow.

'Not that it matters. You'll find out soon enough.' Mr Radcliffe's manner had changed. He spoke quickly, and without conviction or any of the force which had made a dent in the to drawer. He told Morris that lunch was in five minutes, and that the Reception Boy would take him there, and on to the Sick Bay afterwards. He remarked, without ever using the word 'Interfering', that this was in most respects an open school, but that there were one or two small children who belonged to the staff, and that if Morris were to be found anywhere near these small children he could only expect to be whisked away and locked up before he could say 'knickers'. 'We all have problems with our sex lives, Morris.' Mr Radcliffe picked the eighteen cigarettes off the floor, and lit one for himself. He replaced the ashtray on his desk. 'Once you've had a few games of football,' he said, 'showers, that sort of thing, got to know one or two of the other boys really well, I'm sure that'll take your mind off it.'

The interview was over, and however close he may have come to it, Morris had not yet been Assessed.

Lunch was mince. Under the mince there were two heavy dumplings, and beside the dumplings there were mashed potatoes and mashed swedes. There would be jam sponge afterwards. Usually each boy collected his own food from the serving hatch. The name of a House would be called, and a group of boys would stand, slide their chairs under the table with a scraping sound, and wait, each behind his chair, until the master in charge gave the command to move.

Since Morris was new, and did not know the routine, it was the Reception Boy's job to bring him his meal. Morris whispered that he did not feel like eating, but the Reception Boy brought the meal anyway. When Morris shook his head, and pushed away the mince and dumplings, the Reception Boy shot his hand into the air, looked at the master in charge, was given a nodded permission, and piled mince, dumplings, swede and potatoes on to his own plate.

The extra mince overflowed the plate, and the Reception Boy scooped it up with his pudding spoon and shovelled it into his mouth. Morris concentrated hard on his own fingernails, but he could not help hearing the conversation of the six other boys at the table, who were discussing in detail the kind of worms the Reception Boy might be suffering from. One suggested that he might have a snake inside him, and another laughed and said that he had seen its one eye. A boy named Pearce was alleged not only to have seen the snake, but sucked it. The mention of Pearce so amused the Reception Boy that he laughed with his mouth full of food, much of which spilled back from his mouth on to the plate, where it became mixed with the snot that flowed liberally from his nose. The master in charge ordered the removal of the plate, which was done by another boy, who bore it back to the kitchen at arm's length, getting a laugh. Morris asked for permission to leave the room.

The Reception Boy, who had been refused jam sponge, was sent with Morris to show him the way, and to stand outside the door. Once inside the bog, for which there was no lock,

Morris knelt down, and was sick. From outside the Reception Boy told him not to hurry, as he was smoking a tab. Morris allowed his head to hang well into the stained toilet bowl. The stains around it, and the smell of his own sick, assisted him to heave. While heaving he cried, and his head buzzed with pain and longing. He longed for the feel of his grandma's taffeta dress and the smell of her mothballs, which she sometimes mistook for Mint Imperials. He longed to be at home; he longed for sleep and warmth. Finally and most desperately he longed to be lying in a warm bath and to watch and listen while his mother came into the bathroom and sat on the toilet to pass water.

The Reception Boy finished his tab, opened the door of the bog to watch Morris, who remained where he was, listening to his mother pass water and noticing the old blood-stain on her knickers. He could hear someone asking him if he were finished, but he did not wish to move. His knees were beginning to hurt, and the back of his neck ached, but he wished to stay exactly as he was.

After a while, the Reception Boy said, 'Cor!' and pulled the chain. Some of the water splashed against Morris's face. Two hands were placed underneath his armpits, and slowly he was dragged out of the bog.

And still he had not been Assessed.

The visit to the Sick Bay began the process by which Morris was absorbed into the routine of the Centre.

At the door, shoes had to be removed, and left on the mat. No reason was given for this: it was not the habit of the nurse in charge to supply reasons. Morris was instructed to strip down to his underpants, but since he had no underpants he stripped down to his vest, and wrapped it round his waist. The nurse searched in his ears, his mouth, his hair, and between his toes. She told him that on no account must he contract foot-rot, and that the best way of avoiding this was to dry his feet thoroughly, and not to splash about in the water on the floor of the shower-room. She manipulated each one of his limbs in her strong hands, pulling it backwards and forwards to satisfy her curiosity that each limb worked separately and to her requirements. She unwrapped the vest from around his loins with a 'Tut! Tut!' and

22

felt his genitals with her fingers, squeezing both balls (perhaps to make sure that there were two) and his penis for no reason that Morris could guess. Then she gave him a glass tube, and told him to pee into it.

Only when this had been completed to her satisfaction, and the examination was over, did she ask Morris why he had been sick and if he now felt all right. Morris replied that he did not know why but that he did now feel better. The nurse said, 'Good.'

Morris was assigned to a House. He was to be in Blair House. He was assigned to a bedroom, which he was to share with three other boys. The oldest was called Jenkins. He had the beginnings of a blond moustache, and was the Group Leader. The other two were called Korky the Cat and Angel.

Korky, as he explained to Morris, was not really called 'Korky the Cat'; his real name was 'Bewlay', but it did not suit him. He was proud of his nickname, which had come from *The Dandy*, a comic favoured by the boys of the Centre, who read comics when there was nothing else to do, which was quite often. (Therefore there was a cupboard specially devoted to the storing of comics.) Korky did look like a cat. His ears stuck out, and he had high cheekbones and a very round face. One of the ears had little black marks on it, like the muddy footprints a bird makes on white concrete. Korky also had several teeth missing, and much of his body seemed to be covered in either bruises or scabs. Morris wondered if he had been Assessed.

The other boy, Angel, was quiet and seldom spoke, in contrast to Korky, who was noisy and excitable. Morris liked him. Angel had straight ginger hair, and a bald patch which had, he explained, been caused by a scald. He wore very large spectacles, and would sit for hours in one position, his hand always covering his mouth, because he was embarrassed by the colour of his teeth, which were green. Angel was shy and dreamy. If anyone asked him a question, he would put on a voice, and say, 'I'm thick.' He also had freckles.

The House Mother of Blair House gave Morris a sweater and jeans, which looked exactly like those the other boys wore. However, this was not a uniform, because not all the sweaters were of the same colour. He was also issued with underwear, shirts, and special clothes for games. And a pair of new black shoes was taken from a box and presented to him. Unlike the games clothes, those shoes might be taken away with him when he left the Centre, and that was a good reason, said the House Mother, for keeping them clean.

However, the shoes had first to be 'named'. The Reception Boy took Morris across the yard to where the Odd Job Man was mending a padlock. He was an old man, precise with tools. He took a mallet and a small chisel, and indented, 'MORRIS COWLEY' carefully on the side of each heel.

'Your dad must have had a sense of humour calling you that.'

'He said they were reliable.'

'Well, you weren't, were you?'

Morris and the Reception Boy left with the shoes. The Reception Boy said, 'It's all right them saying you can take them home with you, but supposing I was sitting at a dance with my feet up, and somebody noticed I'd got my name on the side of my shoes. They'd know right away where'd I'd been, wouldn't they?'

And still Morris had not been Assessed.

None of the boys spoke of having been Assessed. Morris assumed that it was too dreadful to speak of, nor could he know if it was something which happened to everyone, since some boys seemed to live almost permanently at the Centre, while others came and went. Certain special boys had to go to the Sick Bay three times a day, but that was not to be Assessed; that was for pills. Korky was one of these boys. His excitability had to be controlled, because it led him into accidents. The black marks on the side of his right ear were stitches from his last accident, waiting to be removed.

Morris was given a Jam Ticket, which was a yellow Ludo counter, to be used for jam for the whole week. Next week he would get a green one. Two boys tried to persuade him to fetch them a skirting-board hammer and some tartan paint, but Morris said it was not his job to fetch and carry for them, and that if they wished tartan paint and a skirting-board hammer they would have to get these things for themselves. He was taken on the Assault Course, wearing his newly issued plimsolls and football shorts, where he scaled a high wall, climbed through a rubber tyre which hung by a rope from a tree, and swung by another rope over a square of water. When the rope had come to the end of its swing, Morris had been frightened to jump off, and had slid down instead, burning the palms of his hands and landing in muddy water up to his waist. And he had appeared naked in front of other boys.

He had never liked undressing in front of other people, and had always managed to avoid it. Even his grandma had never seen him without clothes on. Only his mother did that. Changing before the Assault Course, he had noticed that at least three of the other boys kept their underpants on under their football shorts, and decided to do the same, alleging that he had—as they had—a weak bladder. But after the Assault Course, when he was muddy, with mud in his hair (which had been thrown at him) and having been told comfortingly by the master in charge that he had done very well, then showers were to be had, and even the boys who had worn their underpants now took them off.

Three boys were allowed into the shower at any one time. Morris sat with a towel round his waist until it was his turn, and then ran in quickly, while the master stood at the entrance, watching them and shouting, 'In! Soap! Rinse! Out!' Neither of the boys, one of whom was Korky, seemed at all interested in Morris's nakedness. Instead Korky asked him a riddle, 'Why was the boss-eyed teacher no cop?' The answer to this was, 'Because he had no control over his pupils.'

In the evening before bedtime, the boys wore pyjamas, dressing-gowns and slippers, and played table-tennis, or snooker, or dominoes, or draughts, or read comics. Morris had never worn a dressing-gown before, and rather liked it. Nobody asked him to play any of the games, so he sat and read of how Desperate Dan got his next meal of cow pies, of how Pansy Potter, the Strong Man's daughter, made a machine to help improve her football, and of how the machine went wrong, and ended by kicking her up the backside. He read of how Korky the Cat tried to catch a bulldog in order to ride it in the Derby, fell through the roof of a greenhouse, was hit by the bulldog with a mallet as large as Korky himself which said 'CLONK! ! !' on impact, hung from a drainpipe, slid down the inside of a chimney (which was cleverly cut away so that the reader could see Korky descending), was run over by a steamroller, emerging from underneath it as a flattened strip, and finally did succeed in winning the Derby after all, riding a sausage-dog which had wandered on to the racetrack by mistake.

Next morning at seven, the housemaster walked down the corridors and banged on the door of every room to get the boys out of bed. Pyjamas were removed at speed. Each new boy at the Centre had to learn by copying the others. Morris watched to see what the other three wore, and copied them. Consequently he was last to report for the morning duty which had to be performed before breakfast. It was the duty of every new boy to spend the first week cleaning out the showers, wash-room, and toilets.

With a large bar of strong-smelling soap, Morris set to work on the showers. He remembered that the nurse had told him not to contract foot-rot by splashing about in the water on the floor. He wondered what there was lurking in the water on the floor of the Shower Room that could rot his feet. He knew what rot looked like. Old Fred, who had lodged with his grandma, had once shown Morris the root of a brussels sprout stalk which had been lying under some dead leaves. The root had been black and squashy. Maggots crawled in and out of it, and a small mushroom, in which Fred had been particularly interested, was growing from within the root.

His black plimsolls would protect his feet from rot, but if he were to clean out the shower trough, he must kneel down. A line of numbered towels was hanging in the wash-room on either side of the row of wash-basins. Morris's towel was number 26. Morris chose number 13 as a kneeling-mat to protect his knees from rot. He did not choose it at random, but because he had noticed it to be the property of a boy smaller than himself.

He cleaned the toilets simply by pulling the chain. One of them had been blocked for two weeks, but boys in need had continued to use it. Morris closed the door with no lock, and left it.

When the plugs of the wash-basins were pulled, the water did not go down a pipe and into the ground as it did at home. There was a pipe, but it ended about a foot off the floor, and the water splashed on into a trough, which served all ten basins.

26

So that when all ten (or indeed more than four) were in use at the same time, the trough overflowed and flooded the floor. Morris discovered that this also happened when someone had swivelled the pipe round so that it no longer pointed at the trough, but at the feet of anyone letting water out of the basin. His plimsolls were by now thoroughly wet. He tried to dry them with towel number 13, and then used it to mop some of the wash-room floor. By then it was time to change for breakfast. He rinsed the small boy's towel quickly under the hot tap, and hung it back on its hook. All the other boys were already changed, and four were playing snooker with cracked cues.

After breakfast there were lessons—if they *were* lessons. If they were lessons, they were like no lessons Morris had ever had before.

He was in a room with some of the newer boys. The teacher took off his wristwatch, and placed it on the desk before him. Each of the boys was given a piece of paper with sixty circles on it. They had to turn the circles into faces, starting when the teacher said 'Go!' and stopping when he said 'Stop!'

The teacher said 'Start!'

Morris looked at the circles. It was not easy to make faces out of them, because faces were not circular. Even Korky's face, which was the roundest Morris had ever seen, was not a complete circle. And to draw sixty faces, all looking like different people, would take a lot of time. He wondered how long the teacher intended to give them. The other boys seemed to be working quickly, jabbing at the paper with coloured pencils. Morris gave the first circle a pair of eyes. He gave the eyes eyeballs, eyelashes and eyebrows. He gave the circle hair and a mouth with lips. He gave the circle nostrils and a nose around them. He decided that the circle was a lady, and began to shade her cheeks. The teacher said 'Stop!'

At the bottom of the paper was printed the question, 'How many will you do next time?' The teacher drew the boys' attention to this question, and asked them to write in the answer. Since Morris had not yet finished his first face, and thought it better not to overestimate, he wrote in '0' in the box provided, making a sixty-first circle on the page. The teacher said he would now give them another thirty seconds, and said 'Start!' again.

27

Morris finished off his lady, giving her ears and a neck. Then he started on the second circle, which he intended to turn into an old man. The wrinkles took time, and when the teacher called 'Stop!' again, Morris had completed one and a half faces. When the teacher picked up Morris's paper, he said 'Very interesting', and Morris took this to be a compliment on the work.

The next piece of paper had a drawing of a ladder, with the spaces between the rungs numbered from one to ten. This was called the Admiration Ladder. In the top space, each boy must write the name of the person he liked best, and in the bottom space, the name of the person he liked least. Somewhere on the ladder he must write his own name. Beside each name must be the reason why that name was in that place. And afterwards each boy had to tell where he would be on the ladder in six months' time, and what he intended to do to get there.

Morris put his grandma at the top of the ladder, with the reason that she was dead. In the space at the bottom, he wrote the letter 'M', with enough space after it for the M to become 'Mum' or 'Morris' or 'Me'. While he was still trying to decide which of these it should be, the teacher collected his paper. Morris wondered whether he would lose marks for incomplete work.

The next question asked him whether he ever thought about the future.

That night, after all the lights had been switched off by the House Mother, and all talking was supposed to have ceased, Korky began whispering to Morris. He wished to know how Morris had got on in class, and whether what Morris had been asked to do was what he himself had done three weeks earlier. He asked how many faces Morris had drawn, and Morris replied that he could not remember. He asked about the Admiration Ladder, and wished to know whose name Morris had written along the top rung. Morris answered that he had written his Grandma's name, and added that she was dead. This seemed to satisfy Korky, for he was silent for a while, but then he said, 'I wrote Angel's name, but that was before you got here.'

Morris could not think why Korky had said that, nor why his having said it should make Morris himself feel uneasy. After another long silence, Korky said, 'Do you like me?' and Morris felt even more uneasy. He considered for a moment. There was only one answer he dared give, and that was 'Yes', yet if he were to say, 'Yes,' he was not sure what that would imply, and what thereafter might follow. Korky seemed eager for a quick answer, and kept repeating, 'Eh? Do you? Go on, you can say,' so eventually Morris replied, 'Yes, I think so,' and Korky whispered, 'Good. You've got to like someone here. That's important.'

Fresh in the confidence of knowing that he was liked, Korky continued to whisper. He enjoyed talking, and since he always found it hard to get to sleep, this was the time he talked the most. Some of what Korky whispered Morris found incomprehensible, but provided that he could keep awake and that he himself was not called upon to break the rule of silence too often, he had no objection to listening, for it took his mind off home and his mother.

Korky spoke of thoughts and of dreams. He said, 'When you've forgotten something, it goes up into the sky, and then comes down into someone else's head. I'll bet you didn't know that.' Morris admitted that he didn't.

Korky said, 'Did you know your thoughts were all written down by God before you were born? He writes them all with pencil on a tiny piece of skin inside your head. The writing's so small that even with a magnifying glass you wouldn't be able to see it. If everything you think was decided all that time ago, you shouldn't be punished now if you had bad thoughts, should you?' Morris said, 'No.'

'I mean, it's not your fault, is it? You see, I don't understand some of my thoughts, so I reckon they can't really be mine. Do you see what I'm getting at?' Morris said, 'Yes.'

'It's as if they belong to a stranger, and they've got inside my head by mistake. It could happen.'

A door at the end of the corridor banged as it was closed and then locked. Korky stopped whispering, and said, 'That's the House Mother going home to her old man.' Morris considered the thoughts that were written down inside his head, and wondered whether the dirty ones which had got him here were his own or whether they had really belonged to someone else, and a mistake had been made. He turned his face to the wall and closed his eyes, and tried not to think anyone's thoughts. In the morning he would clean the showers and toilets, and there would be more faces to be drawn and more questions to be answered.

'When somebody looks at you, why don't you feel it?' Morris turned over to face Korky's bed. 'I was looking at you then, but you didn't know. You'd think you'd feel something on your face, but you don't.' Morris was not sure whether Korky was offended at his having turned away, or whether this was just another of Korky's observations. In order to change the subject, he replied, 'I used to think that birds brought you dreams. When they flew over your house at night, they dropped a dream, and you dreamt it. Some of my dreams were dirty, and I never looked at birds in case they recognized me.'

Korky found this confession very funny, and, covering his face with a pillow, he kicked his legs in the air. When he had regained his breath, he said, 'Dreams are inside your head all the time, didn't you know? It's only when you go to sleep that they come out, and bang themselves against the walls.'

Jenkins, who had been woken by Korky's laughter, got out of bed, and crossed the room to the bed in which Angel was pretending to be asleep. Jenkins was naked. He pushed his hand under the bedclothes, and locating Angel's private parts, he said, 'Come on, kid. Let's be having you.'

Angel went through the performance of pretending to wake up. Then he climbed out of bed, put on his spectacles, and shuffled to the door. Jenkins said, 'You too, Cowley. Come on.' Then he followed Angel down the corridor.

Morris remained where he was. Korky leaned over and whispered, 'He just wants you for look-out.'

Morris remained as still as he could, but Korky pulled back the bedclothes and shook him. He said, 'They're in the bog. Go on. He'll only come back and get you if you don't.'

Morris got out of bed, and then moved to the door. Korky said, 'If he tries it with you, have a coughing-fit.'

In the Wash Room, Angel was bending over, his hands holding a wash-basin. Jenkins untied the cord which held Angel's pyjama trousers up, and they fell to the wet floor, and rested there around his ankles. Morris stood by the door, looking down the corridor. At the first sign of the Night Watchman's flashlight, he was to warn Jenkins.

Jenkins turned on the hot-water tap, and moved the red carbolic soap about in his hands under the running water. His own pyjamas had been left with a pillow under the sheets on his bed to form a bulge which might, at a distance, be mistaken for Jenkins' body.

As Morris watched, Jenkins spread the thick lather from his hands on to his cock: he might have been washing it, but was not. Methodically he used first one hand then the other, rubbing the lather round and over, and pushing back the foreskin. The cock seemed very large to Morris, and was so. Its size was one of the reasons why some of the older boys referred to Jenkins as 'Trigger, the Wonder Horse'. The other reason was because on Jenkins' arrival at the school he had been seized and mounted by an older boy whose name happened to be Roy Rogers. In fact Roy Rogers had ridden Jenkins regularly once a night for three weeks, and the riding had only stopped because the older boy had been moved to another school. But Morris did not know either of these facts at this time.

Angel remembered that he was still wearing his spectacles, removed them for safety's sake, and placed them next to the carbolic soap. Then he bent over again, and Jenkins placed what remained of the lather on Angel's bottom. Then Jenkins used his hands to pull Angel's buttocks apart, and aiming carefully for the right spot, he thrust his hips forward. Angel lifted his right hand from the wash-basin in his habitual gesture of covering his mouth. But this time it was not for the purpose of concealing his green teeth. Instead he placed his ink-stained thumb between those teeth, and bit hard.

After that Angel bent lower over the sink like a small dog being mounted, while Jenkins reared up and over him, pushing his pelvis backwards and forwards as he repeated this rhyme:

> 'Solomon Grundy,
> Born on Monday,
> Christened on Tuesday,
> Shagged on Wednesday,
> Split on Thursday,
> Died on Friday,
> And that was the end of Solomon Grundy.'

When the rhyme was at an end, Jenkins began to grunt and

31

to move his hips more quickly. Then he gave one last desperate thrust, drew in breath sharply as if something had touched a nerve in one of his teeth, and sagged over Angel, weighing him down.

Angel wriggled to get out from under this heavy weight, and Jenkins' cock came out, making a noise like a cork being drawn. Then Angel walked shakily towards one of the cubicles, and sat down on the bowl without lowering the seat. Jenkins turned on the hot-water tap, and began washing the dangling, but still large, cock.

By the time Angel came out of the cubicle, Jenkins had managed to make his cock stand up again, and had begun to apply more lather. He said, 'It's ready for some more.'

Obediently Angel removed the spectacles he had only just that moment put on, and placed them by the soap. Jenkins picked them up again and handed them back. He said, 'Put them on. It's your turn to be watchdog. Cowley's got a hole, hasn't he?'

Angel took up Morris's position at the door, and Jenkins gripped Morris by the arm, and led him towards the wash-basin. He said, 'Haven't seen your hole yet, have we? See it a little better when it's been stretched.'

Taking Morris's hand in his, and bending the fingers back to show what tortures might follow if Morris didn't comply, Jenkins slapped Morris's hands down on the edge of the sink, and kicked at the inside of each ankle to force Morris's legs further apart. Then the pyjama cord was untied, and the trousers slid to the floor. Taking Morris's penis and balls in one hand, he began fingering and rubbing them. With his other hand, he applied more soap to his own cock, and some to Morris's bottom. He said, 'God, this is tight. I've got myself a virgin. I was one once.' Morris said, 'No.'

'No what?'

Morris said, 'No. Please. Don't.'

'Stop me, then. Go on.'

Morris began to cough. At first no sound came out, because he had been holding his breath, fighting to keep back tears. But as he felt the sharpness of a fingernail being pushed into his bottom, he screamed, and the scream turned into a cough, and he began to choke.

Suddenly Korky rushed through the door, grabbing and shaking Angel by the lapels of his pyjama jacket as he came, and hissing, 'You stupid four-eyed git! There! There! Didn't you see the light?'

Jenkins quickly placed his erection under the cold-water tap. Then he darted into one of the cubicles, and sat down. Morris pulled up his pyjama trousers, and Angel led the way back to their room, leaving Jenkins sitting.

Back in the room, Morris whispered, 'Are they here?' and Korky shook his head. He placed an arm round Morris's shoulder, and then slid the arm downwards and, touching him in the centre of his bottom, he said, 'Did Jenkins get it?' Morris shook his head.

Korky, 'You like me now, don't you?'

During the afternoon of the next day, Jenkins took all Korky's personal belongings from his untidily kept locker, laid them out on the floor of their room, and urinated on them. He did this, he said, as an example to Morris and a reminder to Korky that boys at the Centre should keep the contents of their lockers tidy at all times, and that, as Group Leader, he was responsible for the tidiness of the room.

Korky was, as has been said, an excitable boy, who was given pills to control his excitability. Since he did not like taking pills, and avoided going for them when he could, his excitability was not always controlled. When he discovered what Jenkins had done he became very excited, and not long before Tea, Morris saw him climbing out through one of the top-floor windows, crying, swearing, and carrying five dinner knives.

Morris did not yet know all the rules at the Centre. He sensed that it would be against the rules to climb through a top-floor window, but he also sensed that it would be wrong to report what he had seen, and particularly wrong if Korky was taking his leave of the Centre. In any case, he owed Korky a favour. It did not occur to Morris to wonder why anyone should take his leave by way of the roof, when the gates were not locked, because Korky had been at the Centre longer than he, and must know more about how to escape. As for the five knives, Morris thought that they were just objects, easy to carry and easy to sell. Either that, or Korky was taking them to spite the cook.

Morris went thoughtfully down to Tea, and when the house-master asked where Korky was, he remained silent. Shortly afterwards a dinner knife dropped past the window behind the housemaster and landed with a clatter on the concrete path. The housemaster asked Jenkins to walk over to the Sick Bay, and see whether Korky was there. Through the window, Morris could see a boy from one of the other Houses, a ginger-haired boy who had falling-down fits and had been at the school for three and a half years, throwing stones at the roof. Suddenly it came to him that he should have reported what he had seen, and he shouted, 'He's on the roof, sir.' Through the window, the ginger-haired boy could be heard shouting, 'Get down, you silly bugger,' as he continued to throw stones upwards, and the noise of the stones rolling down the roof could be heard in the room.

Tea was left, as the boys rushed outside. In the rushing, Morris was pushed aside. He did not want to go outside and see the boy on the roof, yet if he stayed indoors it might be thought that he had something to hide. Through the window, he could see Matron approach the stone-thrower from behind, grab him by the hair, and lead him away, probably towards a cold shower. Morris wished that Korky had not climbed out on to the roof, or at least that he himself had not seen Korky do so. Without having made a decision, Morris found that he was standing outside with the others, staring upwards.

'Pissing bloody Jenkins! Rotten sodding pissing bloody Jenkins!' Korky sat astride the corner of the chimney stack, with tears pouring down his face. He dared not look down at the spectators, because he had discovered that he did not care for heights.

'Come down, lad, or you'll kill yourself.' Matron had returned to talk with the boy on the roof. Her turn of phrase was a practical one.

'Piss on Jenkins,' Korky screamed towards the sky. Large heavy drops of rain began to fall; the slates would get wet and slippery. One of the masters, who was known to have climbed mountains, had been sent for. Someone else had gone for a ladder. Soon it would be dark. Korky clutched the four knives he had left in one hand, and grasped the corner of the chimney stack with the other.

'Drop the knives down the chimney, boy. They're no good to you.' Korky closed his eyes. If he did drop the knives, he would have two hands with which to grip the stack. But then he would have carried them all this time for no reason.

Morris found that he was standing next to Jenkins. All the other boys, on hearing that Jenkins was the indirect cause of their evening's excitement, had moved away.

'Mr Smith is bringing a rope, Korky. I think we should talk about Jenkins in my office.'

The mention of Jenkins reinforced Korky's sense of grievance; without it, he would have no justification at all for being on the roof. 'What's the good of talking? He pissed on my going-home trousers. I need them on Friday.' The home-visit he was due had now been put in jeopardy. Reminded of this, he burst into renewed tears. Down below, he could just make out the figure of Jenkins standing beside a smaller boy. With some difficulty he transferred three knives to his left hand, and threw the fourth. It missed. The effort had taken a lot of concentration, and left Korky feeling giddy, and had done no good.

The knife landed at Morris's feet. Korky had thrown a knife at him, and might have cut his head. Did Korky believe that Morris had betrayed him and become Jenkins' friend? Or did he wish him to pick up the knife and stab Jenkins with it? Morris left the knife where it was, and moved away from Jenkins.

Mr Smith, the mountain-climber, emerged from the window Korky had used. It was unknown whether the guttering would hold a man of his size, but sensibly he had tied a rope around his waist, and secured it inside the building. He reached the gutter, and spoke calmly to Korky. He was not going to come any closer until Korky dropped the remaining three knives down the chimney. He pointed out that the nights were drawing in, and this felt as if it might be a cold one. His guess was that by morning Korky would be offering to pay to be helped off the roof, but at this minute he was prepared to perform the service free of charge, provided Korky disarmed and promised total cooperation.

'Can I go home on Friday, sir?'

'That's something we can only decide when you're down.' At least it was not an outright refusal. Korky dropped the knives down the chimney, and several boys rushed indoors to see them drop into the hearth. Morris decided that when Korky had been brought down, he would help him keep his locker tidy.

Mr Smith had reached the point of the roof, and was edging along it. From the ground, he looked like a large bulldog, creeping up on Korky.

'Hey, Korky!' The boys inside had collected the knives, and were now shouting up the chimney; he did not at first realize where the sound was coming from. 'Why don't you climb down the chimney like a real Korky? Then you'd be as black as he is.'

The Korky on the roof started to laugh. He shifted so as to try to see down the chimney and shout back at the boys who were shouting up at him. He thought one of them was Morris, and he shouted 'Morris!'. Then he lost his balance, and began to slide down the slates. 'Sir!' he said, 'Sir!' He was held for a moment by the guttering, and Morris saw a round terrified face staring down at him, and shoes which scrabbled on the slates, before the guttering gave way, and Korky fell three floors on to the concrete path, bouncing once, and ending with his smashed face upwards.

Shocked and frightened, the boys gave way, while Matron came forward quickly to see to the body. Only Morris remained where he was, unable to move, gazing at Korky. Blood ran slowly from the sockets of Korky's eyes, which were staring. His nose had been pushed back and his teeth had snapped in his mouth. In one ear, the marks of stitches still showed, and his face was dirty with dust and blood and tears. Korky the Cat had fallen off the roof, but he had not won the Derby.

Inconsequential

Yes, Stephen liked his feet. They were beautiful. The big toe leaned towards the smaller ones like a mother comforting her children. Next to the mother stood a perfectly straight toe. This was the eldest child. The responsibility of setting a straight example caused it to be thinner than the others, and gave it a pathetic look. Next came the studious toe, its nail too long, knobbly and bent, as if over a book. Then the clown toe, curled and giggling; its nail all askew, it bent round the studious toe, and rubbed at its side. Last the baby toe, fat, red, and crying, 'Wee! Wee! Wee!' all the way home, with its nail the size of an orange pip. Feet have character. His had. Placed together on the side of the bath, they matched perfectly. A pair. One mirrored the other, even in the way the nails had been cut. Two households, both alike in dignity.

He liked them, not just because they were the most splendid part of him, but also because they were strong; they had often gone on walking when the rest of him would have stopped. When his mind cried, 'Cease! No more!' and his back ached (his back was not strong), his feet would walk on, unblistered, unperturbed. In all their thirty-three years of life, neither left foot nor right had had a day's illness—one couldn't count the occasional chilblain: chilblains were like flu, arriving once a year, usually in time for Christmas, staying for a day or two, and then disappearing until the next year.

His knees he liked also. The brave knees he saw before him in the bath were not like Morris's knees, which, Stephen remembered, had knocked, and from the age of seven to eight

37

Morris had visited an Infirmary, and done exercises to stop them knocking. Morris himself had not minded the knocking, since they made no noise, but other people had minded, and had said, 'Did you know Morris's knees knock?' and Morris's mother (Stephen remembered) had taken him to a lady, who made him press them outwards and walk round the room looking bandy. Until one day the lady had said, 'Morris has done very well with his knees, to have lost the knock so quickly. You needn't come again.' So knees, as it seemed to Stephen, could better themselves. Stephen approved of anything that tried to better itself.

Now that he had been studying his knees for three minutes, the bones in them seemed to jut out, making them look weak and vulnerable. If Stephen stared at anything for long enough, after a while he stopped being able to see it as it was, and saw it only in terms of its sharp or soft edges, its bone formation, its texture. Now he was inside the structure of his knees, feeling the space around him. They were no longer knees, but caverns.

Eventually he moved out from the hollowness of his knees to the roundness of his thighs. They were a little thick. That was all.

He supposed his balls to be standard, like eggs. Except that 'standard' in eggs nowadays meant small. Now they reminded him of two chicken breasts, plucked and waiting to be buttered for the oven. If he pulled gently at the sparse hairs, tiny white speckles appeared, just as they do when feathers are pulled from a bird. They were standard and not small, though he often worried that they were a little loose, slacker than balls he had seen hanging in the Changing Room. But then the Changing Room had always been cold, and balls when cold hang in a beautiful tight pouch. Far more pleasing, and easier to draw.

There were lots of jokes about one ball hanging lower than the other. But was it always the left one? Was there some medical reason why his left ball should be heavier than his right? It was not a question he could put to his doctor, since his doctor already considered him a hypochondriac. No, he must do his own research, study all the paintings and sculpture he could find that depicted male nudity, and do a census. Perhaps he should give it to 4C as a project.

Always when he was lying in the bath, his cock would lie on

its left side, pointing to the window, displaying itself in the northern light. Bobbing up and down gently, or swaying from side to side, its pink toadstool-like head, so brutally circumcized, rested on the skin of his stomach. No beauty here. No self-improvement. Just a resting wrinkled cock-head, the size of a large india-rubber. At least it was a *large* rubber.

His belly-button was a crater, designed to collect fluff. . .

'Are you all right, Stephen? I couldn't hear you splashing.'

Stephen turned on the hot water. 'If I do splash, you accuse me of masturbating.'

'All right, then. Don't be long.' Stephen's mother descended the stairs, and opened the front door. In the kitchen she opened the window and began to fry two slices of bread. While the bread was frying, she smoked a cigarette. By the time Stephen came down, all trace of the fried bread and the cigarette would have been eaten or wafted out into the morning air.

Crossing the landing wrapped in a towel, Stephen practised his deep-breathing, and caught a lungful of what he identified as Craven A Filter mixed with best beef dripping. Come November, he would invest in a dressing-gown. It could be a birthday present from his mother. He would allow her to think she had chosen it, and they would buy the one he had already seen and wanted.

Stephen studied the vinyl-cork notice-board that he had nailed to the west wall of his room to see if he had left himself a message from yesterday. There was no message. But the word for the day which he had chosen from the *Readers' Digest* to improve his word-power was 'inconsequential'.

Drying his toes carefully on a towel, Stephen tried to think of ways to work 'inconsequential' into the Common-Room chatter. Some of the *Readers' Digest*'s words for the day had defeated him. He had spent the whole of two free periods trying to introduce the word 'coagulate' into a discussion on the forthcoming pantomime, and when at last he had managed to bring up the question of blood during the battle between King Rat and the pirates, the Domestic Science mistress had shouted in a voice that belied her size, 'Blood or costumes. You can't have both.' The producer had calmed her by saying hastily that there was no question in his mind which was most needed. And so 'coagulate' had been added to the list of Stephen's undigested words.

Inconsequential. . . 'I'm sure that what you say is by no means inconsequential, but. . . ' There was a great deal that was inconsequential about the grey-haired, grey-suited, grey-skirted, dog-eared educationalists who sat about the Common Room in groups, exchanging disappointments and guarding each other from the slightest possibility of enthusiasm. In a school of thirty teachers, if one didn't go around in a group, one would automatically be assumed to be on the transfer list.

Stephen sat on the floor and tucked his toes under the bottom of his bed. Clasping his hands behind his head, he lowered himself into a lying position. Then he brought the top half of his body up to the vertical: it was important, while doing so, to keep his legs straight. The iron frame of the bedstead cut into his leg: he was sure it was doing him good. He had graduated to Exercise Thirteen in *The Penguin Book of Physical Fitness*; it had to be performed thirty-six times. Stephen did a thirty-seventh pull-up to prove himself superior to Messrs Penguin, and then lay panting and looking at the ceiling.

After a while, he rose, and started running on the spot. He found it impossible to count how many times his feet touched the floor, so he ran until his heart felt as though it were floating on the wrong side of his chest. Then he touched his toes, with arms outstretched. Then he twisted from the waist, again with arms outstretched. Then he sat on the edge of his bed until the room stopped revolving.

Another week, and he would be on Exercise Fourteen. Stephen wished he did not feel so light-headed in the mornings; but it was impossible for him to refuse bread and potatoes in the school canteen without the passing of snide remarks from the other male members of staff, most of whom flaunted their bellies, as though in a hurry to change sex and become the most favoured and largest handmaidens of some Arabian sheikh.

Sitting on the foot of his bed and pulling on his corduroy trousers, Stephen looked out of the window over the rooftops of Black Chapel Street and Black Cambridge Street, over the roof of the Twisters' and Dyers' Association, and over the roof of the Paradise Working Men's Club. It would be a fine day. He would not need a cardigan.

His trousers were on. He would wear a check Viyella shirt and knitted tie. As he buttoned his shirt, Stephen saw, as he always saw at this time of the morning, the painting above his bed. The painting was in students' oils on hardboard. One looked down into it from where the moon would be, down into a village of grey houses, resting among dark green hills against a night sky which was red and purple. Squares of yellow light shone from the taller buildings, and were reflected by paler squares of light on the concrete paths which ran from one building to another. On the top of the tallest of the buildings stood a black cat. The cat had been painted before the red of the sky, so that the red paint had run, separating the cat from its tail, and giving its right ear a torn look, as if the cat had been in a fight. Also a brush which was too thick for the work had been used to paint the cat's whiskers, and one of them sagged at the end. The cat's neck stretched up towards Stephen, so that its face, and particularly the mouth, was much larger than life. The mouth was enormous: its pointed teeth were white, and shone, and its pale pink tongue and gums were wet and shiny. The cat had been caught in mid-scream. Its green eyes bulged with fear, and seemed to reflect light.

Morris had painted this picture when he was thirteen.

On the wall to the right of Morris's picture, there was a view of the River Ribble in watercolour, pen and wash. The river was seen from a hill overlooking the Ribblesdale Valley. The sky, which took up a good half of the picture, was what Stephen called a 'Biggles Sky', with a great deal of blue, and pillow-like clouds, round and comforting white ones at the front, and pale grey ones behind. Nothing threatening, nothing sinister. They were the sort of clouds which move around fast, and fulfil their first promise of a fine day.

On the banks of the Ribble, which twisted and turned exactly as the Ribble is wont to do, three picnickers had laid out a square white tablecloth, and painted on the cloth in careful detail were a pink thermos and a plate of triangular sandwiches of brown bread. A fourth picnicker was bathing in very shallow water, so that his limbs showed as wavy lines. In the distance, a town had been painted, with a particular reference to what was there. Town Hall, church, high-rise flats, gasometer—all placed so that they could be immediately identified by any inhabitant of that district. But although the sky was blue, the clouds white, the town grey, the grass the usual colour of grass, the river itself was pink. It was the only fault in an otherwise perfect picture.

Stephen had painted it during his final term at the Preston School of Art, and without the pink river it would have won him a prize. If he were to paint it again now, he would of course take more trouble with the river, painting it as it really was, green where it was deep and a rusty brown where it was shallow. Now he would get it right.

But nowadays, of course, Stephen never did paint pictures.

He descended the stairs carefully, his head buzzing with good health. 'I'm not sure what time I'll be home, but it won't be very late.' His mother looked at him sideways from the stove.

His mother preferred to have an exact time. Stephen preferred to have a little leeway. 'I can't give you an exact time,' he said. She was stirring milk in a pan. Slowly.

'Why are you boiling milk?' She showed him by pouring the hot milk over the cornflakes which filled the bowl in front of him. 'Thank you.'

Standing at the sink with her back to him, she began noisily to wash the cup and saucer she had used for her own breakfast. This she did whenever she wished him to know that she was upset. On the days when nothing was wrong, she sat opposite him, talking and watching him eat.

'Am I to guess what has upset you?'

Lifting the gold-rimmed china cup above her head, she flung it down into the sink with enough energy to smash it into very small bits. Then she was shaking, controlling her need to cry, to scream, to hit him, to see him injured, to know that he had changed his mind and taken notice. Stephen finished his cornflakes. When he had done so, he stood, placed the bowl on the draining-board beside her, unclasped her hands which were gripping the sink, took them in his own, and led his mother to a chair. She sat down, and he placed both her arms around his waist, and leaned his hips towards her, so that she could rest her head against the zip of his trousers, and cry.

'I'll have to go soon.'

'You haven't drunk your tea.'

42

'That's all right. I'll take a flask. Did you manage to pack me any sandwiches?'

'I'll do them now. It won't take a minute.' She unwrapped herself from around him, and moved towards the cupboard she kept for tinned food.

'I've got an idea. Why don't I take these?' Stephen lifted three pieces of buttered sliced bread from a plate on the table. 'And these three bananas. I can make the sandwiches just before I eat them. That way they'll be nice and fresh.'

'Are you sure you wouldn't rather have luncheon meat or tuna fish?'

'No, I like bananas. And I'll put some ice in the flask with the orange squash.'

By the time he was ready, she had rinsed her face under the cold-water tap, and was waiting to be kissed. Stephen asked her if she was all right to be left, hoping desperately that she would say, 'Yes,' and not turn away, or, worse still, start crying again. Instead she nodded, and gave him a caramel she had been keeping in her apron pocket.

'We'll talk about it tonight.'

Clay

Stephen sat at his desk in the Art Room with the lights out, slicing his banana with a clean palette-knife, and laying the rounds of over-ripe banana in a circular pattern on the slightly curling sliced bread.

What did she want? His mother never broke crockery unless she wanted something from him.

The light from the corridor fell in a shaft across the room, and illuminated the wall opposite. A still life, depicting a pair of old tennis shoes and a school tie, was the main object to gain advantage from this. Grouped around it were three shapely bottles, a piece of driftwood, the plaster figure of a footballer, and a mobile made out of coils of cardboard. In the Science Room next door, the cleaners could he heard trying to dissuade the young children they had brought with them from turning on the Bunsen burners and sniffing the hissing gas. Soon they would leave, and his pot-throwing ladies would arrive.

Stephen gazed gloomily at the still life, and what his mother was campaigning for became clear. Uncle Leonard. He remembered noticing a letter propped up on the mantelpiece: it had been left there for him to notice. He remembered the neat round schoolboy handwriting on the envelope, and the absence of the word 'Mrs' before his mother's name.

He finished his banana sandwich, placed the skin in a paper bag, and opened the door of the Art Room. Outside he found one of the cleaners' children using the recently polished corridor as a slide. He handed the bag to the child, and said, 'Give this to your mother.' The child looked into the bag, expecting a gift, and finding only a banana skin, burst the bag, and placed the skin on the floor outside the Science Room. Stephen closed the door of the Art Room quickly, and switched on all the lights. From a tea-chest he selected four pliable dollops of clay, and began kneading each one in turn, pressing his fingers into the grey mass, and thumping it down against a wooden board. From outside he could hear the louder noise of a bucket rolling down the corridor in confirmation that the first cleaner had happened upon the banana skin.

By now his mother would have cleaned the entire house in a way that he would not be able to escape noticing. She would have prepared him something special for supper, and she would be sitting waiting for him, with her hair washed and still damp so that he could curl it. This was the campaign, and it always followed the same line of attack. First, the enemy must be made aware that something is wrong: the gold-rimmed china cup had been sacrificed for that. Then embarrass him by overconsideration and thoughtfulness. Stephen threw down a dollop of clay so hard that it knocked over and broke the three shapely bottles.

Sooner or later he would have to notice the letter on the mantelpiece. If he did not, his mother would take it down and read it aloud.

She would have spread the front doorstep with red Cardinal Polish, because she disliked the smell of it, and because she disliked her doorstep's losing its individual identity and becoming the same colour as all the other doorsteps in the street. She would have spent the entire day doing things she disliked, changing the sheets and remaking the beds. And tonight she would allow him to pin her hair in tiny circles all over her head. She would go to bed with her hair still damp, and endure the discomfort of a sleepless night so that, in the morning, Stephen might take out the grips and brush it into a style she hated since it reminded her of the sickly-sweet child called Bubbles in the advertisement for Pears' soap. She would allow this because it was the only style Stephen could manage, and she knew it gave him pleasure.

Four members of the Evening Class arrived, wrapped themselves in overalls, and began sandpapering their ashtrays and decorating their decorative tiles. Mrs Langton threw one of the dollops of clay on to a wheel, started to pedal, and exclaimed that if she didn't make something this week she intended to change course and learn Russian. The clay spun off the wheel

45

and Mrs Langton got down on all fours to retrieve it from under a desk usually occupied by Mary Whittaker, who had clear blue eyes and a skin so pale that it was almost transparent. Stephen had often wished that Mary Whittaker's clothes were transparent instead of her skin, and, looking at Mrs Langton ill-treating clay, he thought again of Mary, thought of what might lie under the unfortunately non-transparent clothes, and moved quickly on to his next pupil.

At no point would his mother ask him for money: she knew he would offer it. He would offer it because she had pulled herself together, because she had tidied the house and made his supper. He would offer it because she had not asked. Most of all, he would offer it because, if he didn't, his weekend would be in jeopardy.

The letter on the mantlepiece *was* from Uncle Leonard.

Uncle Leonard visited Stephen's mother once a month, usually for the weekend. He would stay at the Traders' Arms, since he was not allowed to enter the house. In wet weather, he would stand at the front gate, waiting for Stephen's mother with a soggy copy of the *Sun* covering his head, and they would go off to the pictures together or to somewhere in the town where they could be together in the dry. In fine weather, Uncle Leonard would be invited into the tiny front garden, and would be given tea. Stephen's mother had argued fiercely with Messrs Duckworth and Hanson, solicitors, to gain this concession.

When Stephen's father died, it was discovered that he had been saving secretly for years, and had gradually managed to buy the house they were living in. It was also discovered that he had made a will, which made Stephen's mother surprised and angry, since property, after all, should naturally come to the next-of-kin. She was even more angry when she learned the terms of the will. The house had been left to Stephen, not to her, and only on the condition that Uncle Leonard never entered it. If this condition were broken, the house was to be sold, and the money put in trust, and inherited by Stephen's eldest legitimate child at the age of twenty-one. Whether the child were a boy or a girl, it should be named 'Leslie', after Leslie Howard. So far no legitimate children had been born to Stephen

46

(or any children as far as he knew), and so far Uncle Leonard had never entered the house.

Stephen disliked Uncle Leonard. He disliked him for his cheesy smell and for his loose damp nicotine-stained hands, which he could not keep to himself, since he required his hand to be shaken in a manly way as proof of friendship. He disliked Uncle Leonard for his round greasy face, and his pot-belly and his ludicrous bow-tie. He disliked hearing Uncle Leonard wheeze and cadge cigarettes, and make jokes. He disliked the jokes themselves, which would usually be about queers or Sambos. Uncle Leonard's imitations of these queers were so real as to be frightening. Stephen did not know many queers, and none of the ones he did know were as real as Uncle Leonard's imitations. It was these queers who were keeping Uncle Leonard out of work, and their number was growing every day. If Uncle Leonard were to be believed, Leeds (which was where he lived) was peopled entirely by queers and Sambos. Stephen disliked having to travel on a bus with Uncle Leonard. Perhaps in Leeds it was all right to shout, 'Hey, Sambo! Ring dat bell!' but it wasn't all right in Rossendale.

Most of all did Stephen dislike Uncle Leonard's collection of country lore, which was considerable for a man living in Leeds. *'A ring round the moon, it will rain very soon!'* Most country lore had to do with rain. A toad crossing the road was a sign of rain, and moles threw up more earth than usual, and geese always gaggled on the pond: it was not clear where in Leeds one ever saw a goose, except hanging upside down with its throat cut in a poulterer's shop, and even then not often, since most poultry of any kind nowadays came frozen solid in a plastic wrapping. When old cats played, that meant rain, and you should never trust a July sky, and if it was the ash before the oak, we'd surely have a soak, and the further the sight, the nearer the rain. And you should never offer your hen for sale on a rainy day. As far as Stephen could gather from Uncle Leonard, there wasn't a single manifestation of nature (except a red sky) that *didn't* foretell rain, so it was a miracle any hens ever got offered for sale at all.

Weather and animals! *A winter fog will freeze a dog. . . Children and chicken must always be a-pickin'. . . They as brings up the cows should be one-legged and dumb. . . If in doubt, sow Square-Head*

47

Masters. . . Stephen had wondered whether 'Square-Head Masters' was the name of a man, some down-to-earth country character like Harry Wheatcroft who had given his name to a seed with which it was impossible to fail, like the dwarf 'Amateur' tomatoes, or whether square headmasters were to be planted, in which case his own headmaster (with whom Mrs Langton was friendly so perhaps it would be better if she didn't change to Russian) might be in danger. *When in doubt, sow Square-Head Masters. . .* He saw them as a kind of potato. Mrs Langton pumped away at the foot-pedal of her wheel, and dug her fingers into what looked like a rotating clay boomerang. Most of the other members of the Evening Class had cleared away their projects, washed their hands, and gone home.

Stephen looked at his watch. 'What's it going to be, Mrs Langton?'

'Too soon to say, but I think I've got the hang of it.' The top half of the boomerang hung over the side of the wheel, and as Mrs Langton pressed her foot down harder to gain more speed, it broke and rolled across the floor.

'Do you know any Russian, Stephen?'

Stephen said, 'When in doubt, sow Square-Head Masters.'

Of course Uncle Leonard wasn't really Stephen's uncle.

'Why can't he come, then?' Adjusting his mother's position in the armchair, and pulling at the towel to stop the water on her hair from running down her neck, Stephen formed the pin curls into circles similar to the circles he had made with the sliced banana.

'He says he can't afford to stay at the pub. He's lost his job again, and he's not a chicken any longer.' The rest of what she had to say was said between sobs and while fighting back real tears—tears she had held on to all day. She would not be left alone this weekend. If Stephen left her alone, she wouldn't trust herself, and he had better be willing to accept responsibility for whatever happened. It was no good him counting on Whist Drives, because there weren't any, and in any case she would rather be seen dead than to turn up at Saint Margaret's on her own, when only three weeks ago she had been accused of cheating.

'Revoking.'

48

'What's the difference?'

'Revoking may be an accident, even in your own favour. Cheating means that you broke the rules in order to win.'

'You didn't even notice the front doorstep.' Stephen had noticed the front doorstep, because his mother, believing that the longer you left polish on the more good it did, had forgotten to take it off, and the soles of his shoes were still sticky with it. But he told his mother that he had been so surprised by the brightness of the doorstep that he had tried to get his key into the lock of their neighbour's door. His mother was not amused by this joke.

In any case, Stephen did not feel like making jokes. His weekend was in jeopardy. But to be serious with his mother when she was in this state would only exaggerate and prolong the state until he promised something he would later regret. He decided to read Uncle Leonard's letter, which explained the reason why Uncle Leonard had become unemployed. Uncle Leonard, as Stephen and his mother knew, sold scrubbing-brushes from door to door: they were of real bristle, and exceptional value. Unfortunately the housewives had moved from scrubbing-brushes to foam-rubber mops with long handles, and these were difficult to carry from door to door without a car, and Uncle Leonard hadn't got a car. It was to do with the queers. Since the women of Leeds now had to compete with pansies for their husband's favours, they had decided to look as if they never worked, instead of glorying in spotlessly clean kitchens scrubbed so by manual labour. Consequently the scrubbing-brush with real bristles of exceptional quality was doomed. Uncle Leonard had tried travelling in rubber gloves, but for some reason he found the housewives suspicious.

In the postscript to his letter, Uncle Leonard had worked out in detail what it would cost him to come for the weekend. Stephen told his mother that he would send Uncle Leonard a postal order for the full amount. There was no fear of Uncle Leonard's not coming, provided that the G.P.O. delivered the letter by Friday, since in Uncle Leonard's mind there would be the possibility, once he got here, of a non-returnable loan.

Sarah

Sitting by the window in the Buffet on Blackpool North Station, Stephen watched the other passengers arrive and leave. Today he had managed to catch an earlier train. Every other Friday for the last four years, he had packed a holdall with some weekend clothes, and caught the same train to come and visit his wife. Always when he arrived in Blackpool, he phoned his wife to warn her. But today he was early. He would not ring until his usual train arrived. That was only fair.

Outside the buffet, a man had taken his boots off, and was hopping around on the concrete as if it were hot. The man hopped round and round in a circle, holding first one foot then the other, gasping sharp breaths, and making a noise as though his feet were on fire. Stephen watched. A crowd gathered around the man, and finally a policeman picked up the hopping man's boots, and guided him away, still hopping.

There was always something to see here. Stephen wondered whether the Blackpool Corporation paid local eccentrics to come to the station and entertain holiday-makers. Several times, and always at the same time while waiting to phone his wife, Stephen had watched a particular woman, who never seemed to travel anywhere, but came into the station, carrying two suitcases, and walked to the bench in the middle of the Entrance Hall. If the bench were occupied, as it often was, the woman would say, 'Excuse me. Excuse me,' over and over again until the surprised occupant moved. Then she would place the suitcase on the bench, and proceed to unpack and fold the garments contained in one suitcase, and repack them in the other. While she did this, she would speak aloud, and what she said would always be, 'He's gone on a boat, you know. Yes, he's gone on a big boat. Mind you, the Germans stopped the last boat he went on. So you never know.'

Stephen had heard this speech seven times in all. At first he had thought he must be watching a Happening or a shock advertisement for whatever play was being performed at the Grand Theatre, but since then a porter had volunteered the information that this had been happening three times a week for years, and that, in his opinion, it was time the woman found a new scriptwriter.

Sarah and Stephen had first met at an exhibition of Conceptual Art in a Church hall in Preston. She had been applying raspberry jam to the back of an unemployed Negro waiter, who sat patiently on a three-legged metal stool with his feet in a bath of cold coffee. Beside him there had been a label, which read, 'NEGRO WITH COFFEE AND JAM'.

Stephen had been ordered to visit the Exhibition by his Art Teacher in a last attempt to rid him of his formalist approach to painting.

He had said, 'It's a lot of nonsense really, isn't it?'

Sarah had replied, 'All student art is bad, and at least you can eat this.' Since there didn't seem to be much point in going out for coffee, they'd had it where they were.

They had continued to meet each other twice a week for five years. Then they had married. After a year of marriage, they had separated. Now Stephen visited Sarah on alternate Fridays.

Before letting the water out, Sarah sat on the side of the bath, leaned over, and removed the pubic hair she had shaved off while bathing. If left, it might block the drain. She wrapped the hair in toilet paper, and flushed it down the loo.

Once while they were lying in bed, Stephen had asked her why she went to so much trouble just for him. She had replied that it wasn't just for him, that it was also for herself, to prove to herself that she had not been so careless as to marry a person whom she would stop loving, even under difficult circumstances.

Sarah shook baby-powder over herself, and checked the areas around both her nipples, to make sure that no stray hair had grown there since Stephen's last visit. After making sure that her toenails were short, she began to pack all her toiletries into

51

a cardboard box. She exchanged the soap she had just used for a bar of Old Spice. All the towels in the bathroom were clean.

When her weekend case had been packed, she stood it in the hall, where Stephen would be sure to see it when he entered. Sarah lived in a self-contained flat on the top floor of a large house.

The box of toiletries, together with a bra and two pairs of knickers, were locked in a cupboard above the fitted wardrobe. All the clothes in the wardrobe were removed to the broom-cupboard, and were hung under a large sheet of brown paper. Anything that remained on the dressing-table would go into her handbag before she left the following morning.

Now there was half an hour before Stephen would phone from the station. He would sound shy and guilty. He always did. And she would try to disguise the excitement in her voice. She always did. She would be brisk and matter-of-fact. Then she would spend the ten minutes before he arrived worrying that she might have sounded cold.

In the bathroom, she checked once again that the towels were clean, and looked at herself in the mirror. What she saw was a face that had to be compensated for by a lot of movement. Recently she had discovered herself adopting expressions to match what the person who was talking to her had said. While doing this, she would allow her mind to wander into other paths. Since Sarah now worked with handicapped and autistic children, this face-pulling was affecting her work. The children had begun to take their problems to other teachers, where once they had always come to her.

She remembered the day she had married Stephen. She had pulled her face into a whole series of expressions that signified what she had thought she should be feeling. Modesty. Shyness. Pleasure. Apprehension. The apprehensive expression had been expressed to please her mother. The only real emotion Sarah could remember having felt was one of pity for Stephen. She had not married him because she pitied him: she pitied him because they were to be married. She remembered that she had kept pity off her face.

Her Busy Lizzie plant was wilting, and she gave it water before pouring herself a glass of Dubonnet. After the phone call she would clean her teeth. If Stephen smelled alcohol on her breath, he would make a mistaken assumption about why she was drinking it, and would ruin his weekend with worry.

Sarah sat on the settee with her feet up, and tried not to crease her dress, which was short and displayed the heaviness of her thighs. But there was no help for them: they had always been heavy. If she avoided quick movements, they didn't actually wobble. Usually she would wear trousers, but not for Stephen.

In her head she tried to prepare three jokes which she would tell him during dinner. She had heard one of the jokes on television, and seen the other two in children's comics at work, and had made a note of them. One of the jokes was a riddle, 'What wears yellow and black stripes and goes "Zub, zub, zub"?' to which the answer was, 'A bee flying backwards.' Stephen would like that.

Of course, if one considered it closely, wasps wore yellow and black stripes, not bees, but one couldn't alter the answer because bees buzzed (zubbed), not wasps. Sarah refused to consider it closely.

Stephen said, 'Hullo! You look well,' thinking that Sarah looked tired and nervous and very close to tears. Sarah said, 'Welcome home,' and kissed him on the side of his face. She smelled too strongly of baby-powder, and the words 'Welcome home' did not sound as she had planned them to sound. So she laughed, and stepped backwards into her weekend case. Stephen noticed the case, and placed his bag by the bedroom door.

Throughout dinner they confined themselves to safe topics of conversation. They had agreed long ago not to discuss Stephen's mother and Uncle Leonard, and the only other unsafe topic was marriage. Sarah asked Stephen what went 'Zub, zub' and Stephen, who knew the answer, pretended ignorance, and laughed when he was told. Usually they found that enough had happened during the preceding fortnight to sustain their conversation, and Stephen would have made notes, which he kept in his top pocket, and to which he sometimes referred, pretending they were memoranda of things he had to do during the following week.

Tonight they discussed the many textures of the *lasagne al forno* which Sarah had cooked, and the lack of flavour in the wine which Stephen had brought. Stephen knew that it was up to him to suggest going to bed, and since he also knew that they would both be more relaxed there, he suggested it as soon as they had finished their coffee.

Sarah cleaned her teeth again, undressed, and sponged away some of the surplus baby-powder, while Stephen lay in bed with the light off, and waited. As always, he worked her up to a climax with his hand, and she cried until they both fell asleep, Stephen curled up in Sarah's arms.

In the morning, Stephen accompanied Sarah to the railway station, and then returned to unpack his bag, walking around Woolworth's and Marks and Spencer's on his way, and looking through the windows of three coffee-bars. In a sense he was doing this merely to break the routine, for Stephen had spent sixty-four weekends in Blackpool, and trial and error had taught him that little could be gained from 'walking about' before lunch. The schoolgirls who spent their Saturdays working in shops were closely watched by the supervisors, and therefore unapproachable. Also walking about tired him for the evening.

There had been a time when he had spent Saturday mornings watching girls play netball at a school called St Katharine's. But he was unable to visit St Katharine's any more. He had spent six Saturday mornings pretending to sketch, and watching flexed bottoms jumping high into the air. He had seen small breasts pushing themselves forward and wobbling under white cotton blouses. He had seen tight knickers and loose knickers, and he had preferred seeing the tight knickers, and watching the small molehills at the front of the tight knickers, and imagining that the moles who lived there were longing to see the light.

On his last visit he had approached and introduced himself to the Physical Training Mistress in the hope of getting closer to the Changing Rooms. Up until then he had simply watched the girls file back into the school, and had seen steam and heard loud laughter coming from two small windows. Up until then he had imagined the Changing Room and Showers. The water running down over nipples which were getting harder and larger. The water running down over molehills, getting caught between molehill and thigh. Molehills being wiped, stroked, rubbed dry, studied, worried about, admired, played with. Molehills bending over, sitting down, laughing, being squeezed between crossed legs. Moles who liked it, moles who didn't.

54

Moles who watched other moles, and winked. Moles who covered themselves quickly, wishing they were fat snakes.

Stephen had said, 'Excuse me. I teach Art in Rossendale. Do you think I might see your Art Room?' The Physical Training Mistress had looked at his sketch pad and then at him, and said, 'I'm sorry, but have you any proof of that?' Stephen had shown her a letter addressed to him at the school, and she had said he might wander around while she went to the Staff Room to change. Stephen had ignored the Art Room, and found his way quickly to the Changing Rooms. He had been pulled there by an invisible rope and the excitement of danger. Standing in the doorway, he had watched the girls for three minutes, and for three minutes the girls had watched him. Some had been naked, and some had been partly dressed. None of them had spoken or laughed, and only two had turned their backs. Mostly they had been still, and they had stared. At the end of the three minutes, one girl had come forward and closed the door. Then there had been laughing from inside, and he had heard someone say, 'Who was that?'

Stephen had left the school without thanking the Physical Training Mistress. He could never go back.

From the radio Ella Fitzgerald sang, 'How strange the change from Major to Minor,' while Stephen unzipped his bag and laid the contents out on Sarah's bed. They included clean underwear, pale blue brushed denim jeans, a fawn cowboy jacket with studs and fringes, a pink shirt with a frill that was creased, and a tin of Vaseline. Sarah had once pressed him to unpack the bag in front of her, and he had laid out the contents just as he did now. When Sarah had seen the Vaseline she had wrapped her arms around his neck and kissed him, because she had felt such pity for him that she knew she must conceal it.

Stephen ironed his shirt, and then ate some cold *lasagne*, the texture of which had changed. Afterwards he sat in the bath, and washed his hair, rinsing it by kneeling under the tap. He removed a collection of fallen hair from around the plughole, wrapped it in toilet paper, and flushed it down the WC. He dried his hair with Sarah's hair-dryer, attempting to make it fall forward and cover his ears.

Deodorant was applied to his armpits, and the clean underwear he had brought with him was put on. Stephen added a clean handkerchief to the inside of the Y in his Y-fronts, and from the radio the Beatles sang, 'Happiness is a warm gun.'

Sarah was given a ticket with the words 'Candy Pink' written on it. She stood in a crowd, and watched the lids of twelve small paint tins light up, one after the other. The crowd stood for fifteen minutes, watching the lights and waiting for them to stop. They did not stop. Then the stallkeeper explained that the timeswitch had stuck: he would close his eyes so as to be fair, and stop the lights manually. This he did, and Sarah won a half-pint tin of Candy Pink paint. She had put it in her handbag, where it made a bulge.

It was over. It was necessary to move on to the next stand. Over. She wondered why her marriage should be 'over', and not 'finished' or 'ended'. But 'over' was the word her brain seemed to have chosen. Over.

She sat at a round table in a tent with blue and white stripes, and drank a glass of iced champagne for which she had paid thirty-eight pence. She held a copy of the Official Handbook and Programme of the Preston Guild Merchant, 1972. It had been edited by Frank Billinge with a cover design by Henry Johnson and photographs by Charles Dack. Some of the photographs were of Prestonians signing Scrolls of Friendship all over the world: these photographs had not been taken by Mr Dack. Sarah's mother had given her the Offical Handbook and Programme. The weekends which Stephen spent in Blackpool were spent by Sarah with her parents in Ormskirk, and Sarah's mother had said that it would be a pity to miss the Preston Guild, which was only held once every twenty years. The whole meaning of the Guild was friendship. People must forget the television and go out into the streets and rekindle human contact, said Alderman Fred Gray, the Right Worshipful the Guild Mayor; in his Introduction to the Handbook. So Sarah sat in a blue and white tent, decorated with a great many pot-plants and bearing a sign that read 'Champagne Comes To You From the Co-op', sipping iced Co-op champagne, totally alone in the tent, while from the entrance friendly Prestonians gawped at her, read the sign, and went away muttering, 'Seven shillings a glass!' And it was over. And as she sipped, a man from the

56

Co-op added a poster to the sign, letting the public know that there would be an auction of the left-over bottles when the day was done.

It was somewhere to sit. Except that when she sat, she thought: there was a conflict between the tiredness of her legs and the energy of her mind. She wished it were the other way round. If her thoughts could cover the last four years so quickly, and repeat the same moments so often, like a loop of tape or a record which has been left on auto-change and keeps playing itself over and over again until the plastic wears out, then all the days between the ones her brain had recorded must have been a waste of time.

'I've tried not to need anything else, but I find that I do.' Stephen had said that as though he had spent weeks studying every word. *I find I do.* I find it's over. I find a tin of paint, a glass of champagne from the Co-op, a free plate of curry from the packet-curry people. I find a photograph of the 1883 Preston North End Football Club, looking young and attractive as they pose, each with a hand on his hip, lying on their sides on a goatskin rug. They wear striped sweaters like the stripes of this tent, and I find that they remind me of fourteen-year-old girls. I find Morris Men and Clog Dancers performing in the square, and the newspaper says that Preston is to accept a thousand Asians, and I remember that I found in your pocket a pair of bloodstained knickers that could only have belonged to a child. And I find that I'm frightened of living alone.

Sarah rolled pennies on to a stall covered with numbers in squares, while the woman who kept it jangled coins and waited for her to lose. She watched a very tall girl, encouraged by friends, lean over a hoop-la stall and win a bottle of Emva Cream Sherry by placing the hoop over it. She saw the small child who was in charge of the stall weep when the girl and her friends had gone. She paid five pence to see the smallest man in the world, and found he was a skeleton. For the same five-penny piece she saw a lamb with eight legs, but it was dead. And as a surprise bonus she saw a dead and dusty peacock stretched out under glass.

Yates's Wine Lodge is to be found in a sidestreet in Fishergate. Sarah found it after she had walked a considerable distance round Avenham Park looking for one of the many prefabricated Ladies lavatories which the Handbook had told her would be constructed to relieve congestion.

The Wine Lodge has one very large room with unpolished floorboards, scrubbed almost white and smelling of lavatory cleaner. Behind the bar are six large barrels containing sweet South African wine and sherry, and six containing almost identical beverages, but from Australia.

Sarah sat at the far end of the long room, next to the Ladies (her reason for coming in), and drank half a pint of lager. She had not been able to kill time at the cinema, because neither of the two cinemas (which had once been one cinema) was showing a film until eight o'clock, and at that time the steps, the foyer and the outside of the cinema would be packed tight with people watching the torchlight procession.

She had killed a spider in the Ladies. It was a vicious act, since she did not fear them. If she had not read in the Handbook that Robert the Bruce had started the Preston Guild by burning down the city on one of his visits south, she would have left the spider to enjoy its web. Finding their city burned to the ground, the wise old City Fathers had gathered themselves together and decided to hold Preston's First Guild 'for the refreshment of the town'. Sarah found the logic hard to follow.

Ambrosia Sweet Wine had refreshed the old lady sitting at the next table so much that she had begun singing 'I'm a Lassie from Lancashire'. It was time to rekindle the warmth of human contact. One man stood holding the lapels of another, and shaking him backwards and forwards. The shaken man looked blearily at the ceiling, while the beer from the glass he was holding slopped down the trousers of the man doing the shaking.

I'm sorry, but you keep pushing my thoughts into a nutshell. They had both made lists of the reasons for and against declaring their marriage 'over'. This had been one of Stephen's. He was right. She had oversimplified everything he said.

A fat middle-aged woman sat alone at a table near the bar. Her hair had been dyed black, scooped up and piled high on her head. Her face was bloated, and there were dark brown stains beneath her eyes. It seemed that everyone who passed this woman bought her a glass of sweet white wine.

58

I've tried not to need anything else, but I find that I do. It was simple.

From time to time some old man, or some young man with a sunken face, would sit beside the fat woman, rest a hand on her thigh, and twiddle the fingers of that hand in the centre of her lap. Preston was rekindling human contact. The only movement the fat woman would make in response would be to raise one of the many glasses of sweet wine on her table, and sip from it. The men kept coming and the woman kept smiling, her eyes fixed on the barrels behind the bar. Proud Preston! The Handbook said that Preston took pride in a job well done for its own sake.

People were beginning to drift out into the street, and Sarah drifted with them. They had found sky-divers doing free falls above the fairground. They had found *Camelot* being performed by the Amateur Operatic in Avenham Park, and when the wind was in the right direction, some of them had found they could hear what was being sung. Some of them had found prefabricated portable loos. Now they were all anxious to find a place to stand from which they could see the whole of the torchlight procession. Some sat on the window-sills of banks. Others, more lucky, stood by the opened windows above shops, and continued drinking. People pushed and shoved, and children were held up on shoulders, spoiling the view for anyone behind them.

I'd like to come and visit you at weekends. I think we should try to remain friends. After all we've both lost contact with a lot of people.

Sarah felt cold, but she knew that the rekindling of human contact amongst the crowd would soon warm her up. Twice she was accidentally groped by a small child making its way forward to the barrier which bordered the pavement. Stephen would have loved all this. He would have wandered off into the night, and warmed his hands inside the woollen skirt of a drunken schoolgirl.

Beside Sarah a baby was crying, and the woman holding it seemed unable to decide what to do. Sarah held the baby while the woman rummaged inside her bag for its dummy. It was found covered in fluff, and placed inside the baby's mouth. The crying stopped. The pushing and shoving grew so agitated that over on Sarah's right a halfhearted fight broke out over

59

territory. Then the crowd on the opposite side of the road surged forward, moving the barrier with them into the road. Five policemen repositioned the barrier, and kept it in place with their backs, and the crowd pleaded with the policemen to move and stop blocking the view.

Perhaps, if she had refused to make her list, if she had said she did not wish to declare this marriage 'over'. Perhaps. Sarah, like the rest of the crowd, stared at the white lines in the middle of the road, and waited. Perhaps if she'd said she'd put up with anything, and try to understand. No, not understand. Being understood made Stephen nervous.

Autism: an extreme aloneness. Self-encapsulation in an isolated world.

When the first float arrived, it carried a group of Preston's Mentally Handicapped Children. The float was really a lorry belonging to a local cattlefood supplier. It had been decorated with pink and green tissue-paper tied in bows, and plastic flowers which lighted up had been wound round upright poles. Not all the flowers worked. In some the bulbs were dead, while others flickered on and off threatening to die soon.

A mongoloid girl in a cowboy hat clicked the trigger of a Woolworth's six-shooter. After each click, she stuck her thumb in the air, and winked at the crowd. When the parade started there had been caps in the gun, which made a bang, but these had all been used up in the first three streets. Another girl had been strapped to a totem pole. This girl wore a large feather headdress, and tapped the fingers of her right hand against her lips to indicate a war cry. But no sound came out.

Some of the children played real musical instruments, and some played makeshift ones. A tea-chest and a broom handle had been put together to make a double bass, and the boy who twanged it smiled and waved. Saucepan lids were banged together like cymbals, and a comb-and-paper was blown through. The boy doing the blowing dribbled a great deal, and had to keep changing the paper, tearing it from a Bronco Toilet Roll which he kept in his pocket.

Sitting at the back of the float was a boy with a very large head. His jaw stuck out, solid and square, and his cheekbones were so sharp and high that they almost hid his eyes. The boy had been put into a monkey jacket which was too tight, and a shiny top-hat had been placed on his head. The hat was too small, and the boy held it in place with his left hand. The hand was nearly as large as the hat. Patches of dark brown greasepaint had been daubed on the boy's face, and a drum had been placed between his knees. The drumstick hung loose and still in his right hand. He was staring at two clowns who walked along the street beside him, keeping pace with the float. The clowns wore enormous *papier mâché* heads. From time to time they would lower them, and run towards the crowd. Each time the clowns did this, the crowd would cheer, and the children standing in front of the barrier would scream, frightened and delighted. As Sarah watched, one of the clowns picked up a blonde-haired little girl from the barrier, and placed her on the float beside the boy with the large head. This was the only time Sarah saw the boy move, and what he did was turn away.

Preston was rekindling human contact. And Sarah cried.

The band played 'Another Opening, Another Show', and Sarah cried. The music thumped and vibrated at the right side of her head, and buzzed away into the distance on her left. The blonde-haired child had been taken off the float because she screamed. Sarah did not wish to see any more of the procession, but there was no alternative. When she closed her eyes, she felt giddy. The man behind her was smoking a pipe, and the smoke stung her eyes. The baby which was pressing against her shoulder had soiled its nappy. Her shoes had begun to hurt. And on top of all this, a man with a gap in his teeth was smiling at her.

'I don't know what I'll find to do with myself next Saturday night.'

Morris Men with fat stomachs, which they stuck out as they danced, pranced before her, arm in arm.

'They haven't got anything like this down south. If we had the weather, we could beat anywhere in England.'

Sarah continued to cry. She had seen the Morris Men in their white shirts and purple velvet breeches earlier on, and she had seen girls in long cloaks waiting for them. Some of the men had long hair, some had beards, and a few had both. Two of them were bald, and their beards were the longest of all. All the men wore beads and bells.

'I don't like that meaty smell you get in the tubes in London. Sweat, I suppose.'

The Jester wore a woman's straw hat covered in artificial flowers. He danced in and out between the men, polishing their rosettes with his wand, which seemed to be a cross between a bottle-washer and a feather duster. He also wore a kilt.

'To me Scotland's just the Lake District on a larger scale.' There was no way she could move. Her tears blurred the lights of the floats which followed, and made the coloured ones mix into shafts and rotate.

'I'm sorry. I thought you were crying because you were happy. But you're not, are you?'

'No. Will you please leave me alone.'

'Of course. Shall I send everyone home?' The man was embarrassed. It was only on special occasions like this that he became brave.

'If a burgess shall call a married woman "harlot", and she make outcry, and witnesses be present, then shall he clear himself by a single-handed oath. And if he be unable to make the oath, then he shall pay three shillings to she whom he dubbed "harlot", and shall take himself by the nose and say that he has lied, and thus there shall be concord between them.' There was the same procedure, the Handbook said, in the case of widows.

On the float which was now passing, two Young Farmers, one of either sex, sat upright in a four-poster bed beneath a placard which read, 'Make Hay While the Sun Shines'. Other Young Farmers, most of them male, hung from the side of the float: their function was not clear. Behind the Young Farmers came the Young Conservatives, and here the balance of the sexes was hard to determine, since many of the male Young Conservatives were in drag. They squirted the crowd with water in a conservative way from water-pistols and empty containers which had once held washing-up liquid. As a young man in bra and heavily padded knickers jumped off the float to direct a stream of soapy water into Sarah's face, she shouted, 'What will I find to do with myself next Saturday night?' Alarmed, and having no answer to this question, the young man retreated to the float, while Sarah continued to scream and began pushing at the woman with the baby and the man with the pipe. *What will I find? I've tried not to, but I find I do. What will I find?*

At first her screams were lost in the noise of the crowd, but because of the pushing and shoving and the fact that she was biting the back of her hand, people around Sarah began to be quiet. Suddenly she realized that she had enough room to sit down, and this she did. The man with the gap in his teeth took hold of the hand which Sarah held in her mouth, and pulled her to her feet. Then he began pushing his way through the crowd, and pulling Sarah behind him. When members of the crowd protested, he shouted, 'This lady's ill. Excuse us.' Sarah closed her eyes, and allowed herself to be pulled.

'The town has Europe's largest bus-station, from which Express Coaches run to most parts of the British Isles, and the M 6 Motorway is accessible within fifteen minutes at three points.'

The man said, 'You don't want to wait and see the Firework Display, do you?'

Sarah shook her head.

The man said, 'I've got a car in Lune Street. I can give you a lift.'

In the car, he gave her some brandy, and asked how her hand was. Sarah said, 'It's all right, thank you.'

'My name's Peter.'

Sarah heard a zip being unfastened.

'I live in a caravan at St Anne's. I'm a cable engineer. Please put your hand in here.'

A badly made-up girl stood at the front of the stage wearing hot-pants, a cowboy hat and knee-high wet-look boots. The boots were brown, and made the girl's legs look as though they had been dipped in treacle toffee. She held a microphone an inch away from her lips, and sang, 'How can we tell them this is not a puppy love?'

Six boys moved away from their position below the stage, and walked around the dance-floor in pairs, looking for girls dancing together, and splitting them up. Each boy wore a satin jacket, each in a different pastel colour, each too long for the boy who wore it, since the jackets had once belonged to the middle-aged members of a sedate dance-band. The young musicians who stood and played behind the singer wore their

63

own clothes and were not interested in uniformity. One wore a T-shirt, one a velvet suit, another what may have been plus-fours.

Stephen sat near the Kool–It Bar, drinking light and bitter from a beer-glass with a chip in it. Between sips, he sketched the face of the plump girl who sat opposite. The song ended, and a male vocalist asked the dancers if they were happy. Enough of them replied that they were for him to be able to begin a Reggae number. Small ultra–violet lights hung from the ceiling, and caused white articles of clothing to look blue, and blue to look yellow. The plump girl's short skirt was pink, but Stephen was only sketching her head and shoulders.

> *Little Miss Muffet sat on her tuffet,*
> *Her knickers all tattered and torn.*
> *It wasn't the spider which sat down beside her,*
> *But Little Boy Blue with his horn.*
> *Oh, yes!*

The plump girl giggled, and blew her nose. At the door it had been discovered that Stephen's membership card was out of date, and he had been asked to fill in a form stating his age and address. Stephen had lied about his age, and given Sarah's address.

It was all a matter of confidence, and Stephen's confidence had been built up during the sixty-four weekends he had spent in Blackpool. He would never now risk refusal by asking a girl to dance before having talked to her about his sketches, and before having placed his hand on some part of her body for a count of twenty while giving her the opportunity to move away. Confidence was not all Stephen had acquired over those many weekends: he had also acquired an instinct. And it was this instinct which had told him to start sketching this plump and plain girl.

The plump girl looked at Stephen, and Stephen looked at his drawing, shading each side of the girl's nose, which was broad. He was good now at picking girls who were on their own, and not those with boyfriends in the toilet or girlfriends queueing for hamburgers. He would start by sketching an area of the dance-floor, and then look to see who was watching him. There was always somebody. The regular dancers here now took him for granted. Over the earlier weekends it had been more difficult for him to distinguish between those girls who were simply vain and wanted their portraits drawn from those who were interested in him because he, like them, was alone.

This girl was alone. In all the sixty-four weekends he could not remember seeing a more alone-looking girl. She was also plain and plump, but because of the Illuminations, the dance was ill-attended, so Stephen's choice was not large.

She continued to watch him, and he picked out her eyelashes with a fine curving stroke of his pencil. The plump girl smiled. Stephen smiled back. There were always new faces here. Not that faces were as important as ages. This girl would be fifteen and a half, Stephen's instinct told him. Occasionally his instinct had let him down. Twice, when he had presented a girl with her portrait, she had offered to pay him, assuming that he did it for a living.

Only rarely nowadays would a girl stand up and walk away. Once he was sure she was watching him, he could get into conversation simply by asking the girl to sit still. Then the girl would giggle until he got up and approached her, making a pretence of wanting to look more closely at her eyes. It was essential, of course, that the portraits should flatter the sitter, but this never had been a problem for Stephen. His problem recently had been that all his drawings looked like the same girl. And that girl was Mary Whittaker.

The plump girl was nothing like Mary Whittaker. Mary was small and delicate: this girl was pudding-like. Mary was blonde: this girl had black frizzy hair and a centre parting. Stephen darkened the hair in his drawing with large energetic strokes, and the plump girl looked away. He realized that from where she was sitting it might seem as if she were being rubbed out, so, when she turned back, he smiled at her, since he did not want her to get up and move away. The plump girl crossed her legs, so that her knees looked like two large Swiss rolls, one on top of the other. Stephen got up, and moved to sit beside her. 'I was making your hair darker. What's your name?'

'Muriel.' Stephen scrawled 'Muriel' below the head and shoulders of his portrait before showing it to her. His instinct told him that a name helped the sitter to identify herself with his work. The plump girl's round pink cheeks became red as she looked at the drawing, and listened to Stephen pointing out her good points.

Stephen held the sketch over the plump girl's lap, his hands beneath it, and each hand touching a pink Swiss-roll knee. It was unusual for him to move so fast so soon, but the girl had hardly stopped watching him, and she had sat as still as anyone he had ever drawn, her eyes saying, 'I may be fat, but I'm also fifteen, and I know what you want.'

He chatted on about the drawing, dropping in questions. Important questions to find out where she lived, how she was getting home, what time she had to be there. Also the questions were to get her talking. The strategy at this point was to do one thing and talk about another. Stephen slid a hand on to the inside of the plump girl's left thigh. The plump girl closed both her thighs automatically, and Stephen's hand was squeezed.

After three minutes, he removed the hand, and placed his sketch-pad in the large pocket on the inside of his cowboy jacket. Stephen had stitched that pocket there himself in order to free both his hands for dancing.

As they danced, Stephen pressed his erection against the plump girl's molehill, and the molehill held firm and was occasionally pressed back. He slid his hands from her back to her buttocks, and the music stopped. Stephen bought the plump girl a gin and bitter lemon, and left her in charge of the sketch-pad while he visited the Gents. Leaving the pad was insurance against her having second thoughts and leaving him.

Stephen paid to enter a cubicle, and removed the handkerchief from inside his underpants. He placed the handkerchief in his pocket, and returned to his partner. As they left the Dance Hall, he pretended to remove an eyelash from her cheek, using the warm handkerchief. The plump girl asked what the handkerchief smelt of, and Stephen told her that it was a love potion.

Memories

Morris sat sucking a colourless piece of rubber, which he was prevented from swallowing by a pink plastic disc. The disc rubbed against his lips. His lips were sore, and the edge of the disc scraped the underside of his nose, which was chapped from constant running. At the back of the disc there was a pink ring, and a piece of wet string was tied to the ring. The string had once been white. Both the disc and the string irritated him, but he found the colourless rubber more satisfying than his thumb or the back of his hand.

From time to time he would be bounced on a knee. This he found less satisfying, since it sometimes made him sick, when the sore and chapped parts of his nose would be wiped with whatever was nearest to hand. (Once this had been a rag which had previously been used for wiping up spilled paraffin.) One of the reasons why bouncing might make him sick was laughter. Whoever did the bouncing clearly expected him to laugh, and since he was not one to disappoint, he would laugh, and having started, would be unable to stop, and be sick. Usually the person bouncing him would suggest that this sickness was Morris's own fault, and due to his having eaten something behind the person's back.

Altogether, bouncing was not what he liked best. Once he had indeed eaten something by mistake, and been sick. They had been lying on the floor under a table, each one individually wrapped in tissue paper. They had been small and black, rather like liquorice sweets, but they had proved bitter, and he had been obliged to swallow them quickly to get rid of the taste. It was said later that he should not have swallowed as many as eight, for they were not liquorice sweets, but Bile Beans.

67

He sat by the oven, watching his mother. The oven door was open, and the oven was on to warm the room: the little red light glowed to indicate that it had not yet reached the required temperature, in this case MAX, for it was a very cold day, and they had run out of coal. Morris's mother was peeling potatoes with a knife, the handle of which she had burned by leaving it for too long on the hot-plate. This morning, her hands were a very dark pink, and Morris noticed how white her knuckles were, and how they stuck out. A sticking-plaster hung from and would not stick to the finger he had kissed better when she had burned it in trying to set light to the oilcloth she had taken from his bedroom floor. The oilcloth had triangles on it of both pink and blue, because it had been bought just before Morris was born. He had watched her tearing it from underneath his bed, where its absence would not show. She had banged her head. Then the oilcloth had been damp, and would not catch fire: it was altogether unsatisfactory as fuel on a cold day. Morris's mother had sworn, and slammed the little doors that formed the front of the fire. He had been frightened, first because she was angry, and later that she might cry. He was ready to cry first. If he could judge the moment right, he would catch her just before she began. He would run to her, screaming, his arms outstretched, insist on being picked up into her arms, rub his face against hers, his cheeks hot and stinging with tears. The suddenness of his crying would either shock her into not crying (and she would shout at him for being soft) or she would let go and cry with him, except that now they would be gentle and comforting tears, and soon each would laugh at the other's red face, and she would wipe his nose on her apron, and they would plan what to do with the rest of the day.

But today his mother had not cried, or even got close to it. She had sworn, and slammed the doors of the fire, then seen his face about to crumple, pointed at him with her burnt finger, and said, 'And don't you start!' Just in time, Morris had stopped himself from starting. He had climbed slowly down from the chair in which he sat, and he had walked into the bedroom where the lino was now torn. His feet were bare, and the oilcloth which remained was cold, so he had climbed back into bed and hidden until his mother had come to find him and take him back into the warm kitchen.

Morris's mother turned the oven down to MID. They had been asked to keep a check on fuel consumption and count every lump of coal as they put it on the fire. Burning oilcloth did not have to be counted, since it could not be used in the War Effort, especially if it were damp. So she placed the torn oilcloth in the oven to dry out.

The heat from the oven played around Morris's face, and made his eyes itch. His mother leaned forward towards the oven. She had pulled her dress up above her knees, and he could see brown rings like rusty wire-netting, making patterns all the way up her calves and along the insides of her thighs. In the summer, so as to save clothing coupons, she had painted her legs yellow with a permanent dye from Woolworth's. Now it had worn away, and the brown rings, caused by sitting close to a fire without wearing stockings, showed clearly.

'Bite my nose off.'

'Not now. I'm busy.'

Morris pushed his hands between his own thighs, and placed one of his knees on top of the other. 'What are you thinking about?'

'That's my business. You're far too nosy.'

'Bite it off, then.'

'I will in a minute. Put these peelings in the dustbin.' Morris bent down between his mother's legs, and picked up the *Daily Mirror*, on which the peelings had been dropped. 'Don't throw the paper away. I haven't read it yet.' The dustbin stood beside the back-door step, so that it was possible to open the door and throw away rubbish without leaving the warmth of the kitchen. Except that both of Morris's hands were filled with the *Daily Mirror*.

Warmth went out of the kitchen with Morris. 'God! Shut the door quick.' His mother put her hands inside the oven, and Morris closed the door on the dustbin as quickly as he could, and came to stand beside her, placing one of his arms around her waist. Taking her hands out of the oven, she put one on each side of his face, and bit his nose off.

Sometimes, if it were not too cold, Morris and his mother would walk to the nearest shops. They might spend some of their sweet coupons on toffees, or they might buy tripe, which was not on the ration. Morris's mother would cover the tripe with salt and vinegar, and on the way home she would pull bits off the slimy white stuff and place the bits in Morris's mouth. Alternate and larger bits would go into her own mouth, and they would walk back slowly, Morris's mother laughing and holding the wet newspaper which contained the tripe well away from her overcoat. She said that people in Bolton ate tripe in the streets all the time: they were well-known for that. Morris had never been to Bolton, but it comforted him to imagine the streets of that place filled with tripe-eating people, bumping into each other as they ate, their fingers all smelling of vinegar.

If there had been a run on tripe, they would bring home parched peas, which were black and salty, and sold in paper bags twisted into the shape of an ice-cream cornet. These bags were difficult for Morris to hold, and so his mother would carry both bags, and inspect each parched pea before placing it in Morris's mouth.

Morris held his hand over his nose, and watched his mother pushing a loaf of bread around the top of the kitchen table. Morris's nose was cold and running, and consequently had not been bitten off for some time. The loaf was a National loaf. It was shaped like a bus, and grey like a bus, though a lighter grey than any bus Morris seen. 'Are you going to ride on my National bus?' Morris's mother said. Once upon a time bread had been white, although some people ate Hovis. Morris knelt on a chair at the table, and slammed his hand down on top of the bus as it passed.

'Is your journey really necessary?' Morris nodded his head. 'Where are you going?' Morris pointed to the other side of the table. 'Fares, please!' Morris's mother tickled him all over in order to find his fare. 'No fare! What's this?' She was tickling his dangler, and he rolled off the chair and under the table.

A tin of broken biscuits and a tin of dolly mixtures were kept on the floor under the table to distract Morris and his mother when they waited there during the air-raids. Morris's mother called the tins their Survival Kit, and Morris was in charge of the sweets, his mother the biscuits. Biscuits could be swapped for sweets, and five dolly mixtures were worth half a digestive. Some of the sweets looked like lipsticks, and with these Morris would decorate his mother's face. Sometimes they would have to sit under the table for hours, and Morris would fall asleep, and wake up in bed. When he asked why his father didn't come under the table, he was told that his father had to sit on the roof and look out for fires, and whenever there was a bang outside he was told that it was daddy getting comfortable.

It never seemed to Morris that under the table was a safe place to be. The table was large and heavy and, if a bomb did hit the house, the table alone would be enough to crush Morris to death. His mother explained that it was unlikely that a bomb would choose their house to hit, but that it might land on one down the road, and then there would be flying glass, and the table would prevent them from being cut, which was why it was always covered by a large chintz cloth which reached the floor. If there hadn't been a war, Morris's mother would have made a long evening dress out of the red chintz tablecloth, but as there was a war, evening dresses weren't needed. Sometimes Morris would get a pain in his head while sitting under the table. When this happened, he would lie down on the floor, and his mother would lift a corner of the chintz cloth, and waft it to let more air in.

Once he had been awakened by shouting, and had climbed out of bed and walked over the cold oilcloth to the window. His father was running down the garden, carrying a bucket of sand and wearing a tin hat, to put out a fire. In the morning Morris was told that the fire had been caused by an incendiary bomb, which a Gerry pilot had dropped from his plane in order to see where he was. It worried Morris that the Gerries should be so interested in knowing where he (Morris) was. He knew that the war was being fought for him: his mother had told him so. Everything the British Army did was in order that Morris should grow up free, and not have to work for the Gerries and eat black bread and German sausages. Morris had no great objection to German sausages which, as far as he knew, were just like English sausages, but not properly done up, so that bits of filling spilled out of both ends, but he did not even like grey bread, and black bread would taste like coke.

From the night the incendiary bomb dropped, Morris was never comfortable under the table, since now the Gerries knew where he was, and if they had seen him standing at the window, they would soon land in the field behind the house, and climb over the fence and find him, helplessly confined by red chintz—his father, being on the roof, would be unable to save him. Even the slightest noise outside, even his father getting comfortable, would frighten him, and he would scream, until his mother had locked all the doors and shut all the windows and comforted him with broken biscuits.

From then on also, Morris would dream. He would dream of Gerries looking in at all the windows. They were large, and made of iron. If he opened the window, he could push them over, but as soon as he shut it again, they bounced back. Sometimes he saw his father sitting on the roof and shivering, unable to get comfortable. Sometimes he sat on the settee while iron Gerries walked around the room. The iron Gerries laughed, and cut off bits of their iron hair, while Morris's father told them how Morris was bad, and deserved punishment. Morris would sit under the table with his mother, and beg her to let down the red chintz so that it would cover them and the Gerries would not see them, but always his mother refused, saying that with the cloth down they would get a headache and die.

When Morris was allowed to sleep between his mother and father in their bed, he did not dream about iron Gerries. But sometimes he dreamed that he was standing on tiptoe to reach the toilet, and then he would be wakened and told that he had wet the utility sheets again, and the underslip his mother wore in bed would be wet with warm pee, and sticking to her.

Morris liked breathing hard on the windows to steam them up, and then drawing pictures in the steam with his index finger. The windows were almost always cold, and he liked to feel the cold glass against his face. Sometimes he would pout his lips, and make an impression of them on the steamed-up glass. One of the neighbours always played an elaborate game with him whenever she caught him looking out of the window. First she would wave, then Morris would respond by sticking out his tongue and jumping down below the level of the sill to hide, then the neighbour would creep up the garden path to the window, and when Morris assumed that it was safe to stand up and look out again he would find the neighbour's face pressed hideously against the other side of the glass. The shock of seeing this female face, with its nose pressed upwards and the lips drawn back, exposing their pink insides and the network of tiny blue veins, would excite Morris so much that he would draw the curtains and keep them closed for the rest of the day.

Though it was easy to make an impression of his lips on the glass, his eyes were another matter. Every time he tried to press an eye against the glass, all that he made was a blur. He realized that the most he could hope to get was the impression of a closed eye, but he did not mind that: he would have settled for an eyelid and an eyebrow. But it was no good: his nose was always in the way, and his hair would make a great smudge above it. Of course Morris could draw an eye with his fingers, giving it lashes and an eyeball, just as he could draw lips as well as pouting them on to the steam. When Morris had drawn a face on the window, he would often pretend that it was the face of someone he knew, and he would kiss the lips over and over again, saying, 'How do you do? Pleased to meet you. Have a cup of tea.'

Sometimes he would take spit from his mouth with his fingers, and place it at the top of the window so that he could watch it roll down, melting the steam. It didn't always roll straight, and what he liked best was that it should roll through one of his drawings, and spoil it. If it went through the impression of his lips, it would cut them in half, and then roll on as if it now came from the lips themselves. Usually the spit was clear like rain, but, being thicker than rain, moved more slowly, and sometimes it contained tiny biscuit crumbs which would slide down with it.

Morris knew all there was to know about the window. He knew the cracks in the paintwork, and the putty which surrounded it and kept the glass in place. Some of the putty had been eaten by sparrows. A cold draught came into the room from around the edges of the window, and Morris liked to feel it with the tips of his fingers. If his mother complained of the draught, Morris would place his arms against the edges of the windows, and say that he was making the room warmer.

Morris's mother was reading a story about nuns in a prisoner-of-war camp. Sister Betty had been tied, buttocks down, to a table-top while the Japanese officers ate their evening meal around her, using her belly-button as a cruet. The story was in *Tit-Bits*, which had been brought home from the Works Canteen by Morris's father. It contained advertisements for Presbyterian Mixture tobacco, in the particular aroma of which (said Earl Baldwin, by way of recommendation) his thoughts had grown, and for Blatt's Union Cockroach Powder, Extermination Guaranteed, and for a toothpaste which alleviated pyorrhoea ('Four out of Five may be Victims').

She had given Morris five pieces of lined writing-paper torn from a pad, tearing each out with a sharp, decisive noise, so that Morris had decided to draw something very important. He made a pattern of dots on the first sheet, while he decided what to draw. 'Draw me a train, then,' his mother said, not lifting her eyes from the magazine. Morris thought about trains. On the first sheet of paper he drew a red engine with blue funnels and a green tender. In the tender sat a large lady with eyelashes that curled and blonde hair that frizzed.

'Is that me?' Morris admitted that it was. 'All right, draw a double-decker bus for Grandma.' Morris coloured the bus blue, because he had never seen a blue bus. The conductor hung by one arm from the rail at the back, and issued tickets which looked like carnival streamers. 'Where's Grandma?' Morris pointed to the driver's cab where a tiny figure in black sat controlling the large blue vehicle. The figure's hair was fixed back with hairpins which were larger than her head.

'What can I draw for daddy?' They both thought of and rejected a police car and an ambulance. They considered a tractor, a dumper and a crane with a lump on the end for knocking down homes. Finally Morris's mother, who was more interested in the Japanese captain who was slicing bread on Sister Betty's bosom, said, 'What your dad needs is an aeroplane. Do him a Spitfire.'

Again Morris began with a pattern of dots on the rough lined paper. He did not wish to give his father a Spitfire, nor a ship, nor a helicopter, nor a farm in Devon, which is what his father had always said he wanted. Morris did not know why, but he did not wish to give his father any of these things. The dots were forming themselves into something which might be a picture now, and Morris drew a line joining up the dots to see

74

what he had given his father. The drawing was of a woman. But it was not his mother.

Fudge

Stephen sat at his desk, and sharpened a pencil. He had never involved himself with any of the girls at his school. In fact he had always been extremely careful that nothing he did or said could be construed to indicate a sexual interest.

In one corner of the Art Room, two girls stepped backwards and forwards, and moved their arms up and down in time to the Reggae music. Bringing a record-player into the Art Room had been a mistake. Stephen had intended it to be used only at lunchtimes and then only by members of his own form. But the use of it had spread, and now even Religious Knowledge (which was given in the Art Room by a man with no will-power) was taught and learned to the accompaniment of Cat Stevens or The Jackson Five.

A mistake. There had been others. Before bringing in the record-player, Stephen had spent several free periods describing his dreams to a small group of his form who had seemed interested. In fact the dreams had not been his, but had been taken from a book on dreams, and mixed together: the intention had been to get the students talking, interpreting his dreams and describing their own, for Stephen had realized that his necessity to be careful with the girls might be misunderstood as cold indifference, and the exchange of dreams had been intended to stimulate free discussion between teacher and pupil leading to a situation of mutual respect and trust. It had not worked. Either Stephen's pupils did not dream, or they considered discussing such matters as a sign of weakness. Some had been willing to discuss Stephen's plagiarized weaknesses, and when finally he had spoken of a dream he had actually dreamed, they had interpreted it with such accuracy that he had felt the need to move on to something else.

He laid the register out on his desk, and looked at his children. Most were half-asleep, heads resting on hands, eyes either closed or gazing into the middle air. The few awake either talked or finished off homework. Stephen wished he knew what they talked about. Of girlfriends, boyfriends, spots, blackheads and Marc Bolan, of course, but there must be more in their lives than that. But whenever they caught him listening to their conversation, they would become silent and expect him to speak.

Stephen said, 'Register! Turn that record off.' One of the two dancing girls did as she was told; the other continued to dance without the aid of music. 'Sit down, Jane.' The second girl sat down next to Mary Whittaker. Mary rubbed her fingers over the scratch marks and pencil-drawings on the table in front of her. Stephen stopped himself from getting up to see what it was that Mary was rubbing out. The Art Room contained eight of these tables, and the one Mary shared with Jane and two other girls was the most drawn upon.

'Anderson!' Stephen always called boys on his register before the girls.

'Sir.'

Mary was a mouse.

'Arnold!'

'Sir.'

A mouse which seldom spoke.

'Barnes!'

'Away, sir.'

A mouse which sat with its head down, and scribbled away.

'Bewsey!'

'Sir.'

Mary's portion of the table was covered with doodles.

'Clark!'

'Sir.'

Doodles of flowers and trees and faces, all joined together like embroidery.

'Crossley!'

'Flu, sir.'

Stephen had studied the faces drawn in pencil. Had prevented a cleaner from wiping them away with Vim and a damp cloth. Had studied them every evening for the last five weeks in an attempt to guess what Mary thought.

'De Souza!'

'Yea.'

'DE SOUZA!'

'Sir.'

He had rubbed his fingers over them, as she was doing now, and sat where she was sitting.

'Edwards!'

'Sir.'

He had discovered new drawings, and remembered old ones.

'Gee!'

'Absent.'

'Thank you, Mills. Hawkins.'

'Sir.'

'I want a note about Friday, Hawkins.'

He knew, because he had been told, that Mary lived with her father, and her mother had died.

Hawkins came forward, and produced an envelope addressed to 'Sir'.

He knew, because he had seen him, that Mary's father walked around in a dirty old macintosh and scarf, and was said to spend all his time in the Reference Library.

'Jackson!'

'Sir.'

But then he was also said to have committed a bank raid, and to be living off the proceeds. Certainly Mary was well dressed for the child of a father with no job.

'Lamont!'

'Sir.'

Stephen thought, 'If only Mary would stay away for a week, or move to another school, I should be able to concentrate again.' But Mary never did stay away.

'Needs!'

An inaudible reply.

'*Needs*!'

Appeared to be saying something.

'NEEDS!'

'Yes, sir.'

'YOU'RE HERE, NEEDS?'

'Yes, sir.'

'THEN FOR GOD'S SAKE OR YOUR OWN, SPEAK UP.'

Stephen was no good at deciphering doodles: it was not a subject taught at Teachers' Training Colleges. So the neat flowers and trees remained as uninformative as the neat and silent Mary herself.

After Stephen had finished calling the register, he looked at Mary, and said, 'We've got four minutes before Prayers. Has anyone got something worrying them which they'd like to talk about?' There was a silence. The girl sitting beside Mary was applying make-up to the make-up she had slept in. 'No one?'

'Tell us what you dreamt about, sir.'

'No, I want to hear from you.'

Again there was a silence. It was Monday morning. This asking for confidences might have worked better towards the end of the week. Mondays were full of suspicion, and confidence had to be renewed after a weekend of freedom.

Stephen felt like provoking danger. Usually he would have controlled this feeling, but today he didn't care. 'What about you, Mary? You're always very quiet. Have you got something worrying you?'

Mary said, 'No, sir,' without looking up. Another silence, while Stephen listened to Mary's 'No, sir' as it swam in and out of the cavities inside his head. Then he said, 'Will you try looking at people when you speak, Mary?' And Mary looked at him.

If he had been clever, he would have chosen Friday for this. Friday would have been a better day. But he was not clever, and could find no word to break the silence. Nor could he take his eyes from Mary's eyes, and so they stared at each other.

After what must have been a full minute, a tall girl named Brenda came to his rescue by announcing that she had decided to work in a kibbutz, and did Sir think this was a good idea? Brenda had been reading *The National Geographic Magazine*, and had seen pictures of small children feeding their own chickens and Swiss secretaries picking grapefruit in Beersheba. The photograph most of all responsible for her decision had been of

79

an Israeli girl cleaning sand from her feet after having scrambled under barbed wire.

Stephen liked Brenda. He liked her positive attitude to life. She was a big girl, more self-assured than anyone in his class. Every week she replanned her future, and asked his advice. Of all the students, she was the only one who seemed positive she had a future, and would often make herself late for the next class by staying on to discuss her ambitions with Stephen. When he had asked the other members of his class what they would like to do on leaving school, he had received such answers as 'Nothing' and 'I don't know' and 'What choice do I have?' One undersized boy had answered, 'Police Cadets,' and a girl had wanted to drive a Moonrover round the moon. Only a boy named Eric had been as positive as Brenda. He had insisted that he was going to be a stonemason. Eric wore thick pebble glasses, and had to scrape his nose along a book in order to read it. Mary had answered, 'Work in a shop.'

It was safe talking to Brenda, for Brenda talked to everyone: talking to her could not be misunderstood. Brenda said, 'You can stay in the kibbutz until you're thirty-four or pregnant, and they say God is there.' Stephen answered, 'God can't be in Beersheba, Brenda. He's sitting in an office just down the corridor, and I'm about to turn him on.' Then he adjusted the volume control of the loudspeaker which stood in the corner of the room. He referred to Mr Heritage, the Headmaster, as 'God' only in the presence of his own form: taking the Lord's name in vain was safe wih them. It was no worse than the other names the Headmaster was called by his staff.

After Announcements from God, there would be an Act of Cooperative Worship, led by Granite Pad, the Senior Mistress, Dame Patricia Fairbrother. Having a Dame of the British Empire as Senior Mistress was an acute embarrassment to the Headmaster, even though it was well known that she had gained the honour by a clerical error, since it had been intended for a minor poetess of the same name, whose mother had given her all to the Red Cross. To alleviate his feelings of embarrassment the Headmaster frequently reminded the School in general and Dame Pat in particular of his own wide knowledge of poetry.

God warmed his voice up with a cough. Then the sound of rustling paper could be heard as He adjusted His script. God spoke sorrowfully of cigarettes. 'The number of boys caught smoking last week was eleven. This was a rise of thirty-three and a third per cent on the previous week, and four of the boys involved were old offenders. I shall say nothing of cancer, heart disease, bronchitis; I shall say simply that those who smoke shall clean the lavatories, and frankly I had rather the lavatories stayed as they have so frequently been. Dirty.' God ended by demanding a good week's work from everyone, and commanding that the entire school should stand and pray with Dame Patricia.

Stephen made his pupils stand. He had been caught out before when Dame Patricia, knowing that she would be late on the Monday, had pre-recorded her prayers, and arrived outside the windows of the Art Room just in time to see Stephen's pupils in the state of movement always brought on by a discussion of dreams while her recorded voice besought them to pray for an United Ireland and a speedy end to the war in Vietnam.

During today's prayers, which were for thalidomide babies, Mary Whittaker ran out of the Art Room, crying.

Arthur climbed down from the rocking-horse, and galloped backwards and forwards across the room. As he did this, he knocked three other children down. Sarah placed herself in a chair by the window, and waited. When she was sure that Arthur had his back to her, she called out his name in a loud firm voice. Arthur stopped galloping, lifted his head, screwed up his eyes, and looked towards the ceiling. Sarah called 'Arthur' again, but this time quietly and with affection. Arthur turned and ambled towards her, squinting out of the corners of his eyes and dribbling on to his pullover. When he reached her, he covered her face with kisses, and removed her hands from her lap in order to make room there for his large bottom. Sarah allowed herself to be hugged and kissed, for her hair to be smelled, and for her necklace to be played with.

I've read seven books by Tony Parker. How many have you read?

Not only was it cruel: it had been a lie. Little wonder it was 'over'. Stephen had learned a great deal from Sarah. She had developed his views on teaching and on children. She had developed his views on life. There had been dinner parties. Usually the guests had been her friends: Stephen didn't appear

81

to have any friends. There had been dinner parties, and there had been arguments. To him it had been more important to make one's guests feel at ease than to be merely logical in an argument. He would take what he had learned from her, put to it what he felt instinctively, and talk as though he had invented Child Psychology. Whereas she would back her views with references to books, and sometimes she had done this to deflate him. She had not read seven books by Tony Parker. She had read five.

Arthur began to spit into his hands, and rub them together. Sarah noticed that the tips of his thumbs were red raw from persistent biting, and that there were bite marks on his wrists, which she must cover before they became infected.

It was ludicrous. The arguments had been as important to her as the children they were about, and she had fought to win them, using every device she knew. Now there were no arguments in Sarah's life, just silence, except on alternate week-ends for one evening.

There had been silences then too, never before the guests had gone—Stephen was too polite for that—but almost always afterwards. She would pretend to read a magazine, and wish she could undo the damage, and Stephen would wander around 'doing things', feeling as unloved and uncertain as the children they had discussed. Finally he would break the silence, letting out his rage and disappointment that it was always she to whom the guests referred, always she to whom they listened intently while she gave what Stephen considered to be an over-long and indulgent reply to the question. And he would speak about that point at which the evening had 'gone wrong', and Sarah would say, 'Yes, but I only put you down because you were being slipshod with Melanie Klein.'

Now it was left to her to break all silences.

'What shall we play at, Arthur?' Arthur made a noise that sounded like 'How!' and stared at her from the corners of his eyes like a large cat. He was holding the finger on which she wore her wedding-ring in a tight grip, and attempting to bend the finger backwards. 'No, you can't have that. It's stuck on. Shall we paint a rainbow?' Arthur jumped to his feet, and nodded violently. Sarah moved to the sink at the other side of the classroom, where two girls were drinking the red water in which they had washed their paintbrushes.

'I shouldn't do that if I were you,' she said.

Mary Whittaker's father turned the pages of *The Alice B. Toklas Cook Book*, and started to read the recipe for Bird's-Nest Pudding in an attempt to keep himself awake. Bird's-Nest Pudding is not made with birds' nests, but with apples, and served with sweetened heavy cream: it is a pudding we should not neglect, Miss Toklas has written. Mary Whittaker's father had been waiting in the Reference Library since it had opened at nine a.m. It was now one fifteen.

The recipe was followed by an account of a visit Miss Toklas had made with Gertrude Stein to Scott Fitzgerald in Baltimore. He had offered them 'an endless variety' of canapés, to remind them of Paris. At one twenty-five, the man for whom Mary's father was waiting came into the Reference Library, and approached the shelves marked, 'ENGLISH DRAMA'. Mary's father removed a brown envelope containing twelve one-pound notes from his inside pocket, and slipped it between the recipes for Bird's-Nest Pudding and Oysters Rockefeller, a dish which has made more friends for the United States than anything Miss Toklas knew, and reminded her of her own friends, Thornton Wilder, Bobsie Goodspeed and Miss Ella Hockaday. The man for whom Mary's father had been waiting also took a brown envelope from an inside pocket, and placed it between the pages of a book he had taken from the shelf before him. Then he returned the book to that shelf, provided himself instead with *The Oxford Dictionary of The Theatre*, and moved away from the shelf to a table, where he pretended to read it.

Mary Whittaker's father left his own seat, carrying *The Alice B. Toklas Cook Book*, and went to 'ENGLISH DRAMA'. He removed from the shelves a copy of *Ludus Coventriae or The Plaie Called Corpus Christie*, which is published by the Early English Text Society. He opened it at *The Harrowing of Hell*, which is after the Crucifixion, but before the Resurrection.

> *Ffayre ffrendys now be Ze wunne.*
> *on zow shyneth pe sothfast sunne.*

Mary Whittaker's father took the other man's brown envelope

83

from between the pages, closed the *Ludus Coventriae*, and put it back in 'ENGLISH DRAMA'. When he decided that he was satisfied with the weight of the envelope, he moved across the Library to 'GAMES AND PASTIMES' and returned *The Alice B. Toklas Cook Book* to 'COOKERY'. Then he left the Reference Library, to go home for lunch.

Mary opened the door to Stephen, who noticed a mixing-bowl and various ingredients on the kitchen table. He said, 'Can I taste your cake-mixture?' but Mary replied, 'It's not ready. It's fudge.' She covered the mixing-bowl with a tea-towel, and began washing up breakfast crockery. Stephen took another tea-towel and began to dry.

He stood beside her at the sink, and dried the crockery as she washed it. He was not required to teach Art immediately after lunch on Mondays, nor was it his day for Dinner Duty, and if anyone were to comment on his absence he would say that he had been shopping for his mother. There was no need to rush. He said, 'I'm here because I'm worried about you.' Mary was not wearing an apron, and as she filled a milk bottle with soapy water and shook it, some of the water splashed out, and made the front of her dress wet.

Stephen said, 'Times have changed since I was at school. No one ever followed me home to see why I was upset.' A silence. 'They haven't changed enough, though. Only four years ago, a schoolmistress was fined for beating a girl on the backs of her legs with a wire clothes-brush.'

Mary's method of cleaning forks was to grab them with a dishcloth and hold them under hot water. She said, 'Why?'

'Why did she hit the girl, or why was she fined?'

'Why did she do it?'

'The girl hadn't done any work, and the mistress wanted to give her a shock. Why did *you* run away?'

Mary stopped washing up, held the sides of the yellow plastic bowl, and stared at the cold tap. She said, 'Dad will be home for his dinner in a minute. If you go now, I'll come back to school this afternoon.'

For a moment, Stephen imagined everything draining away from him—his bravery at having looked up Mary's address in the files, the perverse satisfaction he had felt as he had walked through the streets looking for the right house, the excitement at doing something adventurous, daring, unguarded, of grasping the opportunity and not missing it, and now the relief of finding he could hold a conversation with the person who had been obsessing his thoughts for so long. Would all these feelings disappear, and would he have to go back to being careful?

He placed a hand on the back of Mary's neck, and said, 'How do you manage for money, if your father's not working?' Mary started to cry. Stephen had asked the question so as to prolong the interview, and because he had felt that a question of this sort would distract Mary's attention from the hand on the back of her neck. The fact that she was now crying again seemed to indicate that money was what worried her.

She continued to cry, and Stephen moved his hand, stroking the short golden hairs on the back of her neck. She stopped crying abruptly, and said, 'We live off mum's insurance. She died.' Stephen said, 'I know,' and kissed Mary's hair.

As he lifted his head, his instinct told him that at this moment he could touch Mary anywhere he wanted to, and she would not move. He had touched her, he had kissed her, and now she would know some of what he thought.

Stephen looked at the small body, with its pale arms and tiny hands. He looked at the hand Mary was holding in front of her eyes, and noticed that it was shaking. He said, 'I'm sorry. I shan't ask you any more questions. See you this afternoon. Bring some fudge to school.'

Grandma

The Train-Ride

The first train-ride Morris ever took was with his Grandma. As they walked up the long straight road to the station, he knew that he should be excited, but somehow his Grandma's excitement overshadowed his, and later he found that he had been so caught up in watching her enjoy herself that he had missed most of the sights she had been talking about for days and telling him to look out for.

The station was hardly more than a level crossing, but some trains did stop there. Trains stopped at Platform One at twelve minutes past the hour, and went on to Bedford. But that was only on every third hour. And from Platform One, trains left for Bletchley and Beyond at twelve minutes to the hour, also every third hour. At least, they went to Bletchley every third hour. Not many of them went Beyond.

Not many people seemed to know what there was beyond Bletchley, but Morris's Grandma did. She knew that beyond Bletchley there was London, and it was to London that she always threatened to go if things got on top of her.

Nothing was going to get on top of her today, however, for today Morris was taking his first trip by train, and she was taking him. Just for the ride.

When they arrived at the level crossing, Mr Consodine, whose job it was to open and close the gates by day, tried to explain to Grandma that they were early. Grandma always did arrive half an hour early for any train or bus, because you could never tell with them, but on this occasion she had misread the timetable, which was in small print, impossible to read.

Grandma did not believe that she was early, but she allowed Mr Consodine to issue her with two tickets, one adult and child day-return, and to persuade her to wait in the Waiting Room.

There were in fact two Waiting Rooms, one on each of the two platforms. One was open, like a bus-shelter, and the other was a real Waiting Room, but shrunk, a small wooden box with windows, painted inside with brownish cream paint and furnished with hard wooden benches, a tiny fireplace, and a view of the Old Coach House, Bletchley. Morris kneeled on the bench-seat and gazed out at the creosoted sleepers which supported the railway line, and Grandma paced backwards and forwards between the door and the fireplace, telling Morris that the train was nearly an hour late, until at last a bell rang somewhere and Mr Consodine came into the Waiting Room and asked them to 'stand by' as he was just about to open the gate. When Grandma heard this, her irritability disappeared completely, and, as Mr Consodine began to push and pull at four stiff-looking handles, she grabbed Morris a little too tightly and pointed him towards the signals, just in time for him to see them clank into the welcome position for the train from Beyond Bletchley.

Now Mr Consodine, who had changed the signals, and sold them their tickets, and opened the gate, ran out of his office with a set of three highly polished wooden steps, and placed them in front of Grandma, who ascended the steps, and boarded the train. Morris followed. And Mr Consodine, who had done so much already, loaded goods into the Goods Van, and took a whistle from his pocket, and blew it. Morris noted that the goods consisted of a basket containing a vicious-looking cat, and two bicycle wheels with a total of five spokes missing.

'Backs or Fronts?' Grandma said. She giggled, and the question was clearly important. Morris thought that perhaps this was another form of 'Heads or Tails', one which he had not come across before, but he did not know why they should be playing it now. So he said, 'You choose.'

'I want to face the engine, don't you?'

Morris said, 'Yes,' so they sat side by side, facing the way the train now began to go. There was no question of who should have the seat nearest the window. Grandma had it.

Along the side of the railway line, there was a track used by brick lorries and also by some of the brickmakers, who would cycle along it as a way of getting from one brickfield to another without the inconvenience of passing through three villages. The railway line also passed through the middle of the brick-works itself, and since the train had to stop at the level crossing, it was possible to sit in it and watch men removing baked bricks from the kiln.

All the men wore something on their heads—a flat cap, a beret, or a handkerchief tied at the four corners with a large knot. A large black man wore a straw boater. Some men were naked to the waist; others wore vests which were grey with brickdust. This grey brickdust covered all the men. Their hair was grey with it, and their eyelashes were so pale that it seemed to Morris that they had none. Their faces were mottled—grey where the dust had stuck and pink where sweat had washed it downwards to the neck or chest. The black man, in particular, looked very odd.

The bricks themselves were orange or red. It seemed unfair to Morris that the dust they gave off should be grey. He tried to imagine the black man with orange and red dust trickling down his face. But perhaps the black man liked being grey, if only in patches.

Suddenly the black man looked towards Morris, and started waving. Morris turned away, and saw that Grandma was waving back.

'That's Willy. Wave, Morris.' Morris waved. Willy had lodged with Grandma for a fortnight. At the end of that fort-night, Grandad George had got drunk, raised himself up to his full five feet four inches, and thrown West Indian Willy out. Although Willy was a big man, he was very placid, and later that night Grandma had found him sitting by the rhubarb at the bottom of the garden. A blanket had been taken to him, and he had spent the rest of the night in the outside lavatory.

As the train pulled away from the level crossing, Morris saw lorries being loaded, and men running along by the side of the train, their barrows piled high with newly baked bricks. The men doing the loading had tied strips of rubber to the palms of their hands so as to avoid being burned. From one side of the train, Morris and his Grandma could see the tall chimneys of the brickworks stretching up into the sky, and on the other there was a large lake. Grandma explained that this was where the clay came from to make the bricks. The clay was dug out, and then rain came along, and filled the hole with water. The name of the hole was the Knot Hole. Morris could see wild ducks floating across the water in twos and threes, and Grandma said that heron and guinea-fowl lived round the Knot Hole also, and there were lots of other birds whose names she could not remember.

Trucks like those a train pulls moved slowly along the banks of the Knot Hole, but no train seemed to pull them, and all the trucks were numbered, but not in the right order. These trucks carried clay. The full ones moved towards the brickworks, and the empty ones came away from it. At one point, they had to cross the real railway line, and to do this they moved along a rail which was supported by stilts. Morris asked his Grandma what pulled them. Grandma said they pulled each other.

The journey from the station to Bedford took forty-five minutes, and once they had left the brickworks, apart from the occasional, 'Look at that,' or, 'Horses! Look!' or, 'Cows, Morris!' almost every minute was taken up by Grandma's singing, 'Where shall we stop? Where shall we stop?' to the rhythm made by the wheels. On the rare occasions when the train did stop she sang, 'When shall we start?'

Only as the train approached Bedford did Grandma stop singing, and concentrate on tearing their day-return tickets in half. They left the train, and Morris watched the cat in the basket and the bicycle wheels being unloaded, and heard the guard tell the porter that the bicycle wheels stayed but the cat wanted Platform Three for the fast train to Halifax. Then Grandma took Morris's hand and guided him across the foot-bridge to the platform on the opposite side, where they settled down to wait for the next train back. Grandma didn't like Bedford.

Grandma's Lodgers
Although Grandma's house was small, and she was not sup-posed to keep lodgers, she did from time to time 'take them

in', either because they had nowhere else to go, or because she had got behind with the bills.

West Indian Willy's fortnight with Grandma was over before Morris had grown acquainted with any of Grandma's lodgers. The first he knew well was Old Fred, who opened the level-crossing gate at night-time, and consequently did not enjoy the responsibility enjoyed by Mr Consodine of issuing and collecting tickets, changing signals, loading cats and setting up wooden steps. Old Fred had once worked for the Brick Company, and then he had lived in a tin hut with bachelor Poles. Now that he had been retired to less demanding employment, he had lost this accommodation, and Grandma took him in.

Old Fred and Grandma were friends, as well as his being her lodger, and if anyone had a bad word to say about Old Fred, Grandma wouldn't hear it. He himself spoke only rarely, but when he did it meant something. One reason he spoke so little was that he voted Labour, while Grandad George was a very blue Conservative.

When Morris knew him, Old Fred was sixty, and smelt of tobacco, which he kept in a tin. The tin had the picture of a spaniel dog on the lid, and Morris thought that perhaps Old Fred talked to the spaniel when he was alone in his room. What Old Fred liked most was picking winkles out of their shells. He was by no means averse to eating the winkle once it was out, but it was the act of picking around with the pin and seeing the winkle impaled on the end of it which gave him real pleasure. His other chief pleasure was white pepper, which he would sprinkle on almost all his food, and certainly on custard. Custard, he maintained, was nothing without it.

His head was almost completely bald, and he waxed his moustache so that it stuck out at each side in two points. The middle of the moustache overlapped his mouth, so that when he ate, some of what he ate collected there, and he had to wipe it away. This he did methodically, for he was a clean man, and used to doing for himself. First the fingers of his left hand would wipe the moustache from the centre, giving it a little twist as it reached the point. This would happen during a meal, when Old Fred felt that a sufficiently large deposit had collected. After wiping the left side, he would continue eating for a short while, and then repeat the procedure on the right. This would happen several times during a meal. Morris thought that in anyone else such special care for a moustache which looked silly anyway would be irritating and put down to eccentricity, but Old Fred had so few pleasures. However, he did wonder why Old Fred was never to be seen licking the moustache, since food was scarce, and the portions Grandma dished up were not large. The moustache had been stained ginger, either by nicotine or white pepper.

Old Fred died while he was opening the gate of the level crossing to let through the 9.48 to Bletchley and Beyond. Grandma cried on and off for two weeks. Fortunately there had been a motorist waiting to drive his car across, and he had seen Old Fred's lamp fall. So Old Fred had been pulled clear, and not disfigured by the 9.48.

For a long time after that, Grandma shunned the idea of lodgers, and made an all-out effort to keep her accounts straight. But after a while, a young man who was part relation and by no means silent arrived on the doorstep. He explained that he was the nephew of Grandma's sister's husband, and had hitch-hiked from Rugby. He was on the look-out for work, and could he stay for a month or two?

This young man did not have a moustache, though he did try for a while to grow one, but gave up, saying that it was standing in the way of his getting a job. His name was Pollack, and from time to time he received letters, on the envelopes of which this name had been mis-spelt. He himself was not put out by this, but it caused Grandma and the postman some embarrassment, particularly the postman, who was a Methodist lay-preacher and well known for his rendering of 'Dare to be a Daniel. Dare to stand alone. Dare to pass a public house, and take your money home.' 'I assume this one's for you,' the postman would say to Grandma, trying to cover with his thumb the B that should have been a P, and Grandma would take the letter without looking at it, and make some comment about the weather or the Methodists' annual trip to Wickstead Park.

Andrew Pollack got out of bed every morning an hour earlier than he needed to, in order to run a mile. If Morris were about he might be taken along, but this was not often, and Morris was always allowed to walk back slowly and feel a sense of

91

failure. Andrew maintained that running kept him fit and ready for work, if any should be offered, though to Morris he seemed thinner than necessary, and it later turned out that Andrew had T.B.

Another of Andrew's rituals was the cleaning of shoes. It began with wiping the shoes with a damp cloth, to remove all traces of soil or dust. Next, with the stiffest brush that could be found, the polish would be applied, not only to the uppers but also to the soles. Andrew explained that this was very important, because, often when being interviewed for a job, he would cross one leg over the other to give off an air of casual confidence, and if the soles of his shoes were polished they looked new. And if not new, at least tidy.

Since polish was to be applied to the soles, it was of course necessary to put down newspaper before starting. The other important part of the ritual was that polish must always be left on the shoes for at least a day: it was a waste of polish to take it off sooner, Andrew said. The ideal, therefore, was to have two pairs of shoes, and wear them on alternate days, allowing the polish to soak in and nourish the leather of the pair not being worn. Either that, or one arranged interviews on alternate days, and wore plimsolls when not being interviewed. In fact Andrew was only able to arrange three interviews for himself in the whole of the four months he lodged with Grandma, but he put polish on his shoes one day and wiped it off the next, just in case. Taking the polish off was done with a soft brush and a fluffy rag. Each was used alternately. Five times each. Ending with the fluffy rag.

At the end of the four months, Andrew hitch-hiked back to Rugby, and Morris lapsed from the shoe-cleaning ritual.

Reggie was a Pole. He was fair, and very good-looking. Norma was from somewhere near London. She was a bus conductress, and extremely ugly. She had a large head, large mouth, and large brown teeth. Her hair was black, and already going grey, and she scraped it back, and presented it in the form of a roll, which circled her head like something between a halo and a black pudding. The pudding was kept in its place by large combs which were brown like her teeth.

Norma's breasts were also large, and they hung like swollen

92

pendulums, and shook when she giggled. Norma giggled often: she did have a sense of humour; it was her redeeming feature. It was necessary to have a sense of humour if one lodged with Grandma, as Norma did. Grandma insisted on it.

It was not clear how Norma had met Reggie. Some said, at a Social. The Brickmakers' Club held Social Evenings every other Thursday. Thursday was payday for most of the people who used the Club. Others said that Norma had met Reggie simply by walking down the road, for the Refugee Camp where Reggie lived was no more than five hundred yards from Grandma's house. Some ungenerous people said that the close proximity of the Refugee Camp had been the very reason Norma had come to live with Grandma in the first place.

All the refugees were sex-starved. The Poles, the Czechs, and later the Italians. Particularly the Italians. Once Morris and his cousin Vera had found some money at the side of the road, halfway between Grandma's house and the Camp. Four sixpenny pieces and two half crowns, lying on a grass bank below a tall hedge. Vera had spotted and grabbed both the half crowns and one of the sixpences, and on the way home she had given him the sixpence to make their riches more equal, and explained with gestures and giggles how she assumed the money to have got there.

Despite Norma's appearance, Reggie had married her, and they shared her small room at Grandma's. Luckily Reggie was a short Pole, much shorter than Norma. From the day of their wedding, they were never seen together but what they were holding hands.

The Brickmakers' Club supplied two kinds of chairs for the comfort of its members. One kind was of wood, the other of wicker, the wicker chairs being lower than the wood. So Reggie always sat on a high wooden chair and Norma on a low wicker one, and this suited Norma well, since her bottom would always overlap a wooden chair. Also the wooden chairs were folding, and it was easy for one to fold while Norma was sitting on it, whereas the wicker chairs were rounded like baskets, and large baskets at that, and apart from the creaking and spitting sound of dry wicker under pressure, which Norma was able to ignore after the second rum-and-blackcurrant, she enjoyed the feeling of support around her.

Sometimes when Norma and Reggie entered the Club, they would find that all the wooden chairs were occupied. Then Reggie would fly into a rage, shouting and swearing in Polish at the people who were already sitting down, blaming them both for the occupation of his country and the situation in which he found himself—i.e. not only a refugee, but chairless. Norma would move away from him, embarrassed by this show of temperament, but Reggie would be unable to stop once he had started, but would go on working himself up, railing against the world for ganging up on him and casting him among people who neither loved nor understood him. Towards the end, as he spoke of being alone, he would come to tears, and his fellow Poles in the Club would mumble to one another, and console themselves by reminding each other that Reggie had once had a nervous breakdown, and they had not.

After Reggie had exhausted his outrage and tears, and only guilt and sadness were left in him, he would go and sit by himself on a high stool at the bar. And Norma would collect her coat and walk to Grandma's home, and if the fire in the grate were still alight she would heat some curling tongs and wave her hair.

Grandma's Worms

When Morris asked his mother what the strange lady was doing in the living-room, his mother said, 'Laying Grandma out.'

They had told him that she was dead. His mother and father had sat on either side of his bed, and his father had said, 'Grandma passed away quietly last night.' Morris's mother had added to make it clearer, 'She's dead now, Morris.'

He had known what his mother meant. Grandma hadn't been Grandma for some time, so it was only what had been expected. For some time now, Grandma had just been a body lying in a bed. The bed had been brought from Grandma's house, and set up in Morris's mother's living-room. The presence of the body in the bed in the living-room had meant that they could not go to the pictures, or for a walk to pick holly for Christmas. And Morris had been sent with notes to get the shopping. Twice he had lost the money, and once he had dropped four eggs. The butcher's was worst. Morris had burst into tears in front of four women at the butcher's, because the butcher had said, 'I suppose your mother wants me to book it?' and Morris had nodded with a nod so small that it had not satisfied the butcher (who liked his pound of flesh) and he had said, 'Well, does she? Or are you hiding the money in your shoe?' Then the four women had laughed, and Morris had said, 'Mum says will you please book it till Friday?' and the butcher had slapped the sheep's head down into Morris's hands with such force that he nearly dropped it in the sawdust, and the butcher had said, 'Tell your mother my books are full. I've no more pages to write on, and unless she pays me something, I can't afford to buy another one.' And then the butcher himself had laughed, and Morris had cried, and Morris's mother had said that they would never again patronize that butcher, but since he was the only butcher there was in the village, finally the bill was paid, and the butcher promised never again to make jokes in front of Morris.

During the weeks that Grandma had just been a body lying in a bed, Morris had wandered into the room from time to time, and stood beside the bed looking down at her. Occasionally he had held her small dry hand, and occasionally she had smiled at him. But by that time she had taken to smiling at the window, the curtains, the sideboard, the ceiling, and just about everything in range of her smile. She had smiled at everything, and called everything 'George'. She had smiled at Morris, and called him 'George', and Morris had started to say, 'I'm Morris, Grandma,' but before he had finished the sentence, Grandma's gaze had wandered towards the window, and she had said, 'Didn't you like Skegness?'

Grandad George had died two years before, but the death had been in hospital, the funeral from Grandma's house, and Morris had been only four years old, and had not known Grandad George very well. He had known him better after his death as a photograph in Grandma's house. This photograph was of Grandad George in army uniform of the 1914 War, and a peaked cap. Long after it had first been taken, it had been returned to the photographer to be colour-tinted. Consequently Grandad George's cheeks were much pinker than they had been in life, and what could be seen of his hair under the peaked cap was the brightest of bright yellows. Grandad George's eyes had been blue, and people had remarked on their clear brightness. Grandma had transmitted this information to the man who was to do the colouring, and he had followed her instruction with an enthusiasm which gave the picture a slightly unnerving quality: to give the photograph more than a glance could disturb the glancer for several hours afterwards.

Morris's mother had brought the picture from Grandma's house to her own living-room, and nailed it to the door which faced the bed in which Grandma lay. But Grandma seemed to prefer Grandad George to walk about the room, and she conversed with him while he was on the move.

'What does "being laid out" mean?' Morris asked his mother, who had turned the oven on, and was washing her hands.

'Being got ready for your coffin. Having your face washed and your hair combed. Come here! Your nose needs wiping. It will happen to you some day.' Morris's mother wiped his nose with the bottom corner of her apron.

'Will I talk to people who aren't there?'

'Depends if you were in love with them.'

'Did Grandma love Grandad George?'

'Only for three weeks. Until he ran away to Skegness. And don't ask, "Why Skegness?" because I don't know.'

Later that day Grandma's coffin arrived. It was made of walnut, and looked much too nice to be buried in the ground.

'Can't we keep it on the sideboard? Or put it under the window for sitting on?'

'No, Grandma wouldn't like that.'

'Would she rather be put in the ground with all those worms?'

'Much rather.'

'Grandma didn't like worms.'

'Then they'll know it, and keep away from her. Worms are very sensitive to that sort of thing.'

'Can I kiss her before they put the lid on?'

'Not when she's just had her face washed. You can blow her a kiss from the window when they put her in the car.'

The road outside the Rose and Crown was flooded when the car came. The water came nearly as high as the running board, and for a while it looked as if Grandma were to be buried at sea. Morris watched from the window, from which, while Grandma still lay in the bed, he had moved back the curtain so that Grandma might talk to Grandad George. He had stood beside her bed, holding her hand. He had wished he could get

96

into bed with her, but he had been told he mustn't, and suddenly Grandma had said, 'Look, Morris, he's come back. Didn't you like Skegness, George? It's all right; you can come in. I don't love you any more. Do you mind?' At that point, Grandma had paused for a reply. Morris had not heard a reply, but Grandma must have done so, for she went on, 'That's all right, then, isn't it? Come in. You can stay. As long as you don't touch me.'

Morris had stood holding Grandma's hand, and listening to her calling the curtains 'George'. Sooner or later everyone in the house had listened to her give this speech, for any time anyone came close enough to her bed for her to realize that she was not alone, she would tell them that George had come back from Skegness, and ask him didn't he like it, and explain to him that he could stay, but that he must never touch her. In fact, Grandad George must have touched her many times after his return from Skegness, for she had given birth to nine children, and all of them had been his. But right to the end, Grandma had insisted that she felt no love for him once he had left the house for his visit to Skegness. Nobody had ever found out why he had gone there. Or why, having gone, he had only stayed there three weeks.

Morris watched the large black car with many windows sail through the floods outside the Rose and Crown. Grandma was going to the worms. But maybe the walnut box would keep them out. He did not believe that worms were sensitive to whether or not they were liked, or why did they allow birds to get so close? Why did they not stay underground where there were only coffins and the roots of vegetables to avoid? Perhaps when Grandma was really reunited with Grandad George, he would protect her from the worms.

Now the car with its flowers, his mother and father, and the walnut box were all gone: he could see them no more. The large pool of water outside the Rose and Crown had settled back into stillness and into reflecting the front of the pub and its sign. That sign reminded Morris that he was supposed to be trimming up for Christmas. The lady from next door had been asked to look after him, and she was doing this by making him a paste of flour and water with which to stick together strips of

97

paper he had cut from several women's magazines in order to make paper chains.

His Grandma had died on the nineteenth of December; she had not waited for Christmas. When Morris had asked to be allowed to go to the funeral, his mother had told him that he was too young, and funerals were depressing: she would tell him all about it at some later date, and this would make up for his missing a ride in the big black car. She had explained that, although economies would have to be made to pay for the funeral, and therefore they would not be bothering with a Christmas tree, yet she intended to celebrate Christmas as Grandma had always done, and so she expected Morris to have the house trimmed up by the time they returned.

Grandma herself had always liked trimming up. Only two years earlier, the Fire Brigade had been called because Grandma had insisted on tying birthday-cake candles to the Christmas tree, and lighting them. The tree was one which she had tried to save from the previous year, by planting it in the garden. It had not done well, and when the candles were lit it had flared up like a pile of kindling wood. Grandma had complained that the floorboards in her bedroom smouldered for three days.

All the covers of all the copies of *Woman's Weekly* which Morris had been able to find were blue, and every one of them showed a picture of a lady wearing some garment which could be made by simply turning to page twenty-three. The other pages in the magazine were not coloured at all, except for the occasional knitting-pattern, but this was a rare find. Morris spread paint from his paintbox over the pages which contained only letterpress, and so used up all his red, and his green, and the yellow was so pale that it hardly showed, and certainly did not cover the bold print. So while the lady from next door was in the kitchen making them each a cup of cocoa, Morris took down the colour-tinted photograph of Grandad George, and cut it into neat slices with which to make chains. The lady from next door noticed that Morris seemed to have found something coloured to work with, but since she had never known Grandad George she assumed it to be a picture from one of the magazines.

No one noticed the absence of the picture from the back of the door, or the brightly tinted coils of Grandad George hanging from the corner nearest the fireplace to the light socket of the overhead lamp in the centre of the room. No one, that is, until on Christmas Day after Christmas Dinner, Morris's mother sat back in her chair, looked up, and caught a glimpse of a very blue eye looking back at her. It was not the eye of someone wearing a knitting-pattern: it was the eye of someone she knew. For years that eye and its companion had looked out at the world as if it were saying, 'Bugger off, you lot!' Now the eye was saying, 'Will somebody help me down?'

'I like your paper-chains, Morris. They're very unusual.'

Drama

There wasn't any money, but it did happen to be Thursday, which was a payday. Morris's mother had known money would be needed, but she had assumed, as often she did, that God would look after His own. Now it was Thursday. God was looking after His own, but she was not among them.

Morris's mother was to appear as The Manageress in a performance by the Biggleswade Amateur Comedy Club of *A Lightly Boiled Egg* by Gertrude Jennings. She had first created the role of the sadistic tea-shop manageress five months before at the Church Hall, and the play had been so successful that the Biggleswade Amateur Comedy Club had been asked to repeat it at Cranfield Working and Social Club, ten miles away.

Unfortunately Morris's mother had sold her black dress to a neighbour, and the neighbour had cut it down to fit herself. Also the woman who had supplied the crockery had moved away. And as for the three-tiered cake-stand which was so important to the plot—well, the fact was that nobody had been able to find the three-tiered cake-stand: it was assumed that some over-enthusiastic lover of the drama had decided to keep it as a memento.

Morris's mother had promised to supply all these things. When the hired bus arrived at six thirty p.m. to carry the Biggleswade Comedy Club to Cranfield, she was expected to be ready, wearing her black dress and carrying her props. Luckily it was Thursday, the day Morris's father got paid.

Morris might have been at school, but his mother liked the company. His father was painting an aerodrome. He sat in one of those little troughs by the side of the hangar, and was pulled up and down by pulleys. It was like bridges: once you had finished, you started again. The work was not exhausting, and its chief drawback was the amount of lead contained in the paint, which seemed to give Morris's father indigestion.

The aerodrome was sixteen miles away, nine miles into Hitchen, and seven on. Morris's father would be paid at twelve thirty, but he did not finish work until five thirty. He had rejected the idea that he should leave work and come home the moment he had received his pay packet. He had already done this on three consecutive Thursdays, and his employers had suggested that it was not a practice in his or their best interests.

Morris was sent on a tour of the neighbours to ask if any of them wanted shopping done in town. Only Mrs Richards required anything: she required a pair of knitting needles, Size Nine. The money she gave Morris provided him and his mother with the fare to Hitchen. One and a half, single. The rest of the way must be walked. Morris's family never troubled with return tickets in those days or any other.

They had been walking since ten thirty, except that for the last twenty minutes they had been standing under this tree. The rain was so thick and heavy, and the sky so dark that Morris had become frightened. Both he and his mother were soaked to the skin. They were still three miles away from the aerodrome, and at one thirty his father would climb back into his trough, and be pulled up the side of the hangar. Morris's mother said, 'I wonder why cars don't use this road.'

Three times Morris had seen a man and a woman appear from behind the curtains of the nearest house. Now the woman opened her front door, and beckoned. Morris and his mother ran to the house. The woman said, 'I wasn't sure if you were waiting to be picked up.' She backed away from them and their wet clothes.

'No, we've just got off the bus,' Morris's mother lied. Morris could tell time, and saw by the clock on the mantel that it was now five minutes to one. The woman said, 'It's not the sort of day to go walking,' and began to unbutton Morris's wet jacket, and take it off. The shirt beneath the jacket was just as wet. She stared at it as if she had never seen a wet shirt before. Then she looked directly at Morris's mother, and said, 'The poor thing's soaked through.'

'We'd been standing under your tree twenty minutes.' Morris's mother had seen the faces at the window too. 'Twenty-five,' corrected the woman. 'It's not our tree.'

'You can't be too careful.' These words came from the man. The man stood by the door to the kitchen. He rested one bedroom-slippered foot on top of the other. It seemed to Morris that the man stood like this in order to be able to come or go at a moment's notice. The woman said, 'Fetch a towel,' and the man went.

Morris's jacket had been placed on the arm of a chair close to the fire. The jacket was already too small for him: soon it would be smaller. The wet shirt had been unbuttoned and taken from him, and the woman was just about to sneak her fingers inside the waistband of his trousers to bring them down, when Morris shouted, 'Mum!' Morris's mother said, 'I'm sorry. He doesn't like being interfered with. Have you got the towel?' The woman's husband had returned with a towel, which he now passed to Morris's mother, who placed it round Morris's waist, and removed his trousers from beneath its protection. Morris wriggled while this was done. His mother said, 'You can keep this on till I get back. Pretend you're an Indian Chief and this is your camp fire.'

The woman had risen to her feet, and was backing away slowly. She said, 'You're not going?' Morris's mother said, 'You won't mind if I leave Morris here while I go on an errand?' After a long silence, the man asked where she intended to go in the rain. His wife seemed unable to speak.

'The aerodrome. My husband paints it.'

'What, Rackley?' Morris's mother nodded and smiled. She had always maintained of a smile that it worked wonders, and of wonders that they never ceased. But today they had ceased.

The woman said, 'I'm sorry. No. What would happen if you didn't come back?'

'You'd ring the police, I hope.'

'I mean about the boy.'

'If I wanted to get rid of Morris, would I walk five miles through pouring rain to do it?'

'I thought you'd just got off a bus.' Morris took a step towards his camp fire.

'We had. In Hitchen.'

'You've walked? From Hitchen?' Morris stood close to the woman, holding his sarong in both hands. The woman became disturbed by his piercing stare.

'Does he always look at people like that?'

'Only if he likes them.'

Finally it was settled. The woman's husband would get his car out and drive Morris's mother to the aerodrome. Thereafter he would return with her, thus making sure she collected Morris. Morris's mother made a mental note that the man might be persuaded to go further, and return them both to Hitchen. She hoped that the man was a fast driver in spite of his appearance: there were only twelve minutes before Morris's father would be drawn up the side of the hangar.

When the car had left, the woman asked Morris if he liked cocoa, and he allowed his head to nod up and down, indicating that he did.

When the woman returned from the kitchen with toast and cocoa, it seemed to Morris that the toast had been covered with a thick black substance. He decided not to have any.

'Don't you like Bovril?' Morris did not know what Bovril was, but, feeling confident in his decision, shook his head. 'Look, I'll scrape it off for you.' The woman passed him a piece of toast with most of the Bovril, and certainly all the butter, scraped off. Morris found that he was hungry after all.

'Why did you come all this way just to see your father? Won't you be seeing him tonight?' Surprisingly the traces of black stuff tasted like gravy, which Morris was known to like. 'You must have started out early this morning. Where was it you came from?' It was safe to let go of the towel now that he was sitting down. He was not going to tell the woman anything: he had seen her three times at the window, watching him and his mother get wet. The rain had come down so suddenly, 'in sheets' his mother had said. He had been afraid, was still afraid. The rain made a noise on the roof: the force of it frightened him. It was rain from an unhappy sky, and brought darkness even in the middle of the day. This woman had watched him from her window. Three times. He was not going to tell her anything. He would not speak of his father, or his father's wages, or what they must buy from those wages, namely a short black dress, twelve cups and saucers and a three-tiered cake-stand. He would not speak of any of these things to the woman, but he would be as nice as it was possible to be without speaking, for if the woman took to him she might offer his mother some of the toast which was left over: she had made six slices, and only eaten half a slice herself. His mother would be hungry when she came back, and would want to stop in Hitchen for tea and cream cakes, but if they did she would miss the Comedy Club bus. Morris looked at the remaining four and a half slices of toast. If his mother ate three of them, she would not want cream cakes in Hitchen.

'More toast?' Morris accepted another slice of scraped toast. There seemed to be no way of explaining that he would now prefer it with the Bovril left on.

'I expect you're fond of your mother, aren't you?' Morris did not understand the question. Was this woman asking him to tell her that he was not fond of his mother? He stopped chewing toast, in order to show that he was giving the question proper consideration. 'She seems very nice, your mother. I bet you like her. I expect you're very close.' The woman was waiting for an answer. Clearly she wanted him to shake his head. Why couldn't he?

At last he said, 'The toast's good,' and had broken his silence, and given in. The woman took him into the kitchen to make him more cocoa, and he stood in the door as her husband had done, one foot on top of the other, holding up his towel. The kitchen table was covered with yellow oilcloth which shone. 'Do you have any brothers and sisters?' Morris shook his head, and said, 'Do you have any children?' being sure that he already knew the answer, but wanting to see the woman turn away. She turned away.

'I don't know what to call you.'

'Morris.'

'That's the name of our car.'

'My father says they're very reliable.'

The woman made cocoa for herself as well as Morris. They sat at the kitchen table, and Morris made patterns in the gloss of the yellow oilcloth as they talked. Morris told the woman about his mother's performance as the tea-shop manageress in *A Lightly Boiled Egg*, and about the three-tiered cake-stand and the cups and saucers, and how his mother had also agreed to

104

find something which would resemble smoked kipper when seen by the audience. The woman gave Morris a three-tiered cake-stand in chrome, and said she never used it.

The woman's husband did drive Morris and his mother back into Hitchen, and pointed out a shop where cheap crockery could be bought. The purchase of a black dress took up the rest of the time before the departure of the bus at ten past five. They did not need to take time for tea, since Morris's mother had eaten the rest of the toast.

The clouds parted. The sun appeared. Morris and his mother sat together on the top deck of the bus, and she told him how his father had been found standing in the middle of the road in front of the aerodrome. He said that he had been standing there for an hour and a half, and complained that the rain had prevented him from smoking a cigarette. Also, said Morris's mother, his indigestion was playing him up again.

That night Morris's mother played the sadistic manageress with even more gusto than she had displayed five months before in the church hall. Such applause had never been heard before at the Cranfield Working and Social Club, and this time nothing was stolen, not even the mashed banana which so resembled smoked kipper from the front. Next day Morris's father paid a visit to the hospital in Bedford, because the nurse at the aerodrome had arranged that he should be looked at for his indigestion. And a week later he received a letter, instructing him to return to the hospital, taking with him a pair of pyjamas and his personal toiletries. Also he was not to eat anything fried. Apparently Morris's father's indigestion was caused by three duodenal ulcers.

On the morning that he received this letter, Morris's father vomited blood.

This was the summer that Morris won Third Prize in the Fancy Dress, though his father was not there to see it. Morris's father did not die of his ulcers—at least, not then—but he recovered only slowly from his operation, and languished in the Bedford Hospital, visited twice a week by his wife.

The Fancy Dress Parade was to end on the lawn of a house at which John Bunyan had once preached. The lawn was large and sloping. Therefore it drained well and was firm underfoot.

The Parade would begin outside the village Post Office, and would proceed through the village in order to remind everyone that there was a Fete in aid of the Playing Field. The Parade would begin at three thirty, and judgement would be given on the sloping lawn at four o'clock.

Morris had been dressed in a single sheet. Cocoa had been made into a thick paste by adding two teaspoons of water, and this paste had been rubbed over his arms, legs and face. Some of the paste had got on to the sheet, and rubbing the marks had only made them larger, so Morris's mother had covered them with Meltonian Shoe-Cream. Then she had placed a corner of the sheet on top of his head, and secured it with an elastic garter so that it represented a burnous.

Sandals were needed. It was agreed that those Morris wore to school would not be open enough. But Morris's mother had some sandals, which were gold in colour, and had a slight heel. Morris was not convinced that golden sandals with heels were appropriate to his character of an Arabian Sheikh, but Morris's mother pointed out that the gold would add a touch of richness, and as for the height of the heels, if it was noticed at all (which she was sure it would not be), it would only be as a brilliant piece of subtlety, suggesting that the Arabian Sheikh was not only wealthy but vain as well, wishing to be thought taller than his natural height. So Morris wore the sandals.

It was a hot day. The Parade started twenty minutes late, the time taken by a battle of wills between a fairy who refused to carry her wand at any reasonable angle, and the fairy's mother who would not allow the procession to start while her daughter's wand still trailed in the dust, saying 'I'd have given the silver paper to the Blind Dogs, if I'd known you were going to play me up.' Morris stood quite still for these twenty minutes plus the five before them which his mother had insisted were necessary to get himself into the part. While Morris got himself into the part, two boys, one a pirate, the other Dick Turpin, giggled at Morris's gold sandals, and asked him if he was supposed to be a choc ice. The cocoa paste which had dried on Morris made his face feel tight, and his arms and legs itch. Also it was being washed off him by rivulets of sweat, which ran from somewhere beneath the elastic garter on top of his head, rolling slowly down following the contours of his face, and dropping gently off the end of his chin, spotting the brilliantly white sheet with brown. Other beads of sweat ran down his back and between his buttocks, making the cleft itch. He remembered the workmen covered with brickdust, and wondered whether they felt like this every day.

Four little girls had arrived dressed as Crinoline Ladies, so that they knew, and their mothers knew, before the Parade began that none of them would win the prize for originality. The mother of one of them had gone to considerable trouble to make a high wig out of cotton wool, and to stitch a wooden hoop inside her daughter's crinoline dress so as to make it stand out, whereas the other three Crinoline Ladies merely wore long dresses, and one of them wore a poke bonnet. This mother was heard to remark that, if she had not been so closely questioned in the Village Shop as to why she needed so much cotton wool, they might have seen more variety in the choice of costumes.

Four weeping Crinoline Ladies, a mutinous fairy, an Arabian Sheikh, a pirate, Dick Turpin, and other children fancifully attired, followed at a little distance by their mothers, paraded from the Post Office up the village street, behind the garage and across a small field towards the lawn of the house at which John Bunyan had once preached. In the field rides were being sold on Prudence, a donkey, to the more carefree children who had not been entered for the Fancy Dress. For the whole afternoon of the Fete, Prudence suffered for her usually carefree existence by constant exercise. Exercise made Prudence's bowels move, and the children enjoyed this almost as much as they enjoyed riding her, especially since, as Prudence left more and more deposits in the field, the straight line of the penny ride became more and more pronounced an arc, so that by the end of the afternoon, the small field resembled a midden, and the penny ride had doubled in value. To ride Prudence, children had to be under the age of thirteen, and it must have seemed to her that free school milk had produced some of the heaviest twelve-year-olds in village history. As the Parade entered Prudence's field, the mothers of the contestants came forward in a body, holding their children tight and steering them away from the donkey's liberal offerings.

Waiting nervously in a canvas square on the sloping lawn was the adjudicator, and to him the Parade displayed itself, while

107

from all over the lawn those who had been guessing the weight of a cake, pinning the tail on a donkey who was not Prudence, dropping pennies into a bath of water in the hope that one of them might cover a half-crown, buying lucky programmes (which could not all be lucky) and hunting buried treasure hidden under that part of the lawn which was due for cultivation came to stand behind him and to encourage the contestants with applause. Morris was by now parti-coloured and in an agony of self-control brought on by the need to scratch his bum, but he did not scratch, and was awarded Third Prize. First Prize for originality was awarded to a plump girl, who wore Cherry Blossom Boot Polish on her face, a turban on her head, a candy-striped dress with a white apron, and carried a placard reading 'Persil Washes Whiter'. A Geisha Girl was second. She had walked as if her feet were bandaged, gaining laughs from the spectators, and frustrating the characteristic lollop of the Hunchback of Notre Dame, who was just behind her in the Parade, and was given a prize for patience.

Morris was allowed to spend some of his prize in riding Prudence. His costume forced him to ride her side-saddle, and as he sat, holding tight to the reins and feeling the muscles of her back ripple slowly beneath him, she stopped and moved her bowels once more to the renewed delight of the watching children. One or two of the grown-ups who watched him remarked that he looked like Jesus Christ entering Jerusalem on an ass, and that, if Morris had ridden Prudence in the Parade, he could not have escaped winning First Prize. Morris's mother was the first to make this observation, and she did so close to the local photographer, who was intended to overhear her, and did, and dutifully took a picture of Morris on Prudence. This picture was printed a week later under the heading, 'Boy Makes Life-Like Christ on Donkey, and Comes In Third.'

Morris would have been prepared to give all his prize money to his mother, for she had only recently told him that with his dad in hospital it was going to be hard to make ends meet. He did not realize then what 'ends' were, and how they were going to meet.

(*'Morris, it says here that you Interfered with Angela Richards, and that you were found in the act of Interfering. . . Do you know how babies are born, Morris?. . . Does he know how babies are born, Mrs Cowley?'*

'I don't think so, madam.')

This was still a good time for Morris. He did not object to his father being in hospital, because that gave him interest and importance, and anyway Morris preferred to have his mother to himself. Sometimes, when the money would run to two bus-fares, he would be taken to visit his father in Bedford Hospital.

Morris's father was in a bed at the far end of the ward, and Morris would stare down the long line of beds until he spotted his father, sitting upright with his hair neatly parted and his face very white. He wore grey striped pyjamas, which the hospital had lent him, and his eyes seemed smaller and very bright as they looked at Morris.

Morris would sit in silence and watch the other patients while his father and mother talked. They talked of money—about the rent, about Morris's school dinners, about debts. They talked about debts a lot, and Morris would sit in silence, and watch an old man in a neighbouring bed coughing and spitting into a stainless steel bowl. The old man seemed to be without visitors, and his spit was dark, and each time he would cover the bowl with a white cloth after spitting. Then, a moment later, he would remove the cloth, and spit again. Morris wondered why it was necessary to cover the bowl, since covering it seemed to cause the man to cough again. While his father and mother talked of debts, Morris made the moments pass by counting the number of times the old man covered and uncovered the bowl.

At the end of visiting-time, a nurse would come into the ward, and ring a handbell. Then Morris's father would grab Morris's head between his hands and kiss him on the side of the face. Morris could not remember this happening before, and was embarrassed that it should happen now. After the first time it happened, he would sit beside his father, his head turned away from the small bright darting eyes, as he counted the number of times the old man spat into the bowl, and dreaded the moment when the nurse would ring the handbell. Although his mother had frequently kissed him, Morris found it hard to

109

re-create any of those moments, but for a very long time afterwards he remembered the closeness of his father's face to his.

Drowning

While Morris's father was in hospital, Morris's mother received a letter informing her that the family had been allotted a council prefab. They had been on the Housing List for so long that they had given up any hope of ever moving from the old and damp house in which they now lived.

Morris stood among the brick foundations and drains, and watched half of what was to be his new home arrive from Rugby on a lorry. The other half would arrive the following day. The drains and brick foundations and roads had been waiting for over a year because the factory where Morris's new home had been built had been on strike for better working conditions. The estate was to consist of seventy prefabs (a hundred and forty halves), and the roads were so narrow that the long lorries bringing the new homes had to drive on to the pavements in order to pass each other. Consequently some of the pavements were already cracked.

On the following day, Morris watched Number Twenty-Seven Montpelier Avenue being fitted together with large screws. The tin walls had been treated to give the effect of white pebbledash, and the doors and windowsills had been painted Sherwood Green to resemble wood. One of the other children who were watching the assembly with Morris stopped wrenching a snail-like latch from a creosoted gate, and used a penny to scratch a large N on the front wall of the new home. The noise set Morris's teeth on edge.

Morris's mother borrowed a large handcart from a member of the Comedy Club, and with this the move was made from the old home to the new. Empty or full, the cart needed two people to control it, and several journeys were necessary to transport the beds, the wardrobe, the dining-table, the chairs and the oilcloth, which was lifted from the floors of the old house and rolled. Even the small pieces of oilcloth which had torn while being lifted were put into a cardboard box and taken as fuel.

Since Morris was playing truant from school in order to assist in the move, and each journey he made between the shafts of the handcart took him past the school gate, his mother found him a large felt hat with a floppy brim, which he wore with the brim pulled down. Consequently he could see little more than his own feet, so that from time to time (and often when they were directly in front of the school), his mother, who pushed the cart from behind, would find it necessary to shout, 'Morris!' and Morris would swerve violently, missing by inches a line of people queueing for a bus, or some patient horse standing with its head in a nosebag and only its eyes watching the approaching collision.

Two weeks after Morris and his mother had completed the move into their new prefab, and the floorboards around the old oilcloth had been stained Dark Oak, an ambulance stopped outside, and Morris's father walked up the garden path, wrapped in a large grey blanket.

Morris opened the door to his father, and showed him where the main bedroom was. Morris's mother was not at home to welcome her husband, because she was delivering milk in order to pay off a debt to the milkman. Every morning she worked, she was given two free pints, and five shillings were deducted from the long-standing debt. And so every morning the milk-man left twelve large crates on the footpath outside the house, and knocked on the door to make sure that Morris's mother was up, and every morning she would fill two small handcrates from the twelve large ones, and walk around the prefab estate delivering milk to the newly-arrived estate-dwellers. Morris's part in the work was to watch the twelve crates of milk from behind the curtains, and make sure that nobody collected milk that hadn't been ordered.

This job now passed to Morris's father. Morris was sent back to school, and his parent's bed was moved to a place by the window, from which his father could guard the crates without having to get up. In fact the only times his father did get out of bed during the next few weeks were when it was necessary to visit the new bathroom, or for half an hour during the evening. He explained to Morris that the half hour was important because it stopped his legs from becoming too weak, and also prevented bedsores. While he was out of bed he would sit down to tea with his wife and son, and tell them about the routine in hospital, a topic in which he had succeeded in becoming an expert. Morris's father covered every detail of life in his particular hospital ward several times during those important half hours, and never grew tired of describing it.

She would not explain again. She would not stand at the door, being watched by neighbours, while the Rent Man shook his head, and walked away. Or argue. If the Rent Man argued with her in front of neighbours, she would cry. And if she invited him in, and then explained, and he discovered that he had stepped inside for nothing (since there was nothing she could give him but an explanation), then he would have more time to point out the terms of their tenancy, and she would cry.

Morris's father watched his wife pouring tea, and speculated on the amount of milk she would leave him to feed his ulcers. His job was simple. It was to stay in bed with the door locked. He was in no condition to argue with anyone, or even explain, least of all over six weeks' rent. The fact that they had only lived in the prefab seven weeks was beside the point. He was ill, and should have special consideration. In five or six weeks' time, when he would be fit enough to find a light part-time job, he would make it his business to see that the rent was paid before anything else. They would then pay it regularly, with a little on top to cover the arrears.

Five slices of bread had been borrowed by Morris from Mrs Richards, and as he listened, he spread margarine on to them carefully. His mother had bought a sliced loaf from the man who brought groceries round the estate in a van (well, she had not paid for it: he had written it down in his book), and when she had unwrapped it, the top slice had been covered in green mould, and his mother had closed the wrapper again quickly, and placed the whole loaf on the living-room fire, since she could not very well complain when there was money owing.

The fireplace itself was only fractionally bigger than the loaf, and two small doors were attached to the front of it to 'draw' the fire. In the doors were tiny windows of what looked like glass but was not, and through them Morris now watched the whole sliced loaf refusing even to burn.

That night Morris's mother lay beside Morris's father in the double bed, and tried not to think. When she thought, she became frightened. When she was a child this kind of fear had always brought an attack of asthma.

Her husband slept on his right side, facing the wall which she and Morris had stippled pink and green. In her mind there was a list of people to whom she owed money, and beside each name was the amount owed. Both the names and the amounts were too blurred to be read clearly, and she had no other record, save a few bills, of what she owed. She knew that the list started with the most recent debt, but with whose name and what sum the list ended (if it did end) she could not remember. She had always intended to keep a book in which these names and sums would be written, but the thought had depressed her, and anyway it would be unfair to do so now, when the list would be incomplete. Morris's mother tried to count the blurred figures, hoping that they would turn into sheep and give her some rest, but they refused to do this, and, in fear of arriving at some kind of total, she stopped counting.

Everything had been needed: it was not that she was wasteful. Perhaps she could have waited for some of the things, as her mother would have done, saving pennies and threepenny pieces in a biscuit barrel, and then making a special trip into town to buy what had been waited for so long. She herself had occasionally been entrusted by her mother with the purchase of some special item. She had walked with her brothers, to save the fare, and being the eldest, she had been in charge. Her brothers had carried back any heavy item, and if they fought, as they almost always did, she had reported them to her mother and they had been caned. She had not enjoyed their punishment, but every time she had watched them wrestling on the ground, it had brought on an attack of her asthma, and only when they had been caned and had come to her, showing their red hands, only then would she feel sorry for them, and her asthma would start to go away.

Morris's father pulled at the bedclothes in his sleep, and uncovered his wife. Through the gap in the thin cotton curtains she could see the moon. That was it: the moonlight was keeping her awake. She had restrained herself from ordering curtain-material out of the Littlewood's Home Shopping Catalogue, because thick curtains were not as important as pans to cook with and a rug for in front of the fire. The fear came back as she remembered sending off the Littlewood's Order Form. Why should she feel guilty about buying ordinary things like pots and pans, a new clock for the mantel and flannelette sheets for the bed?

Morris's father rolled on to his stomach, and broke wind. The more she thought about it, the more Morris's mother realized how little she enjoyed life. She had not been cast in the Comedy Club's current production, and without that to think about, her mind was free to worry or to fear as now it did. There was nothing to look forward to. She remembered that, even as a child, that had frightened her. Suddenly and without reason it would come to her that nothing was worthwhile, everything pointless, even praise, even love, even being held by her mother. It all ended. And then what?

Grey hair was beginning to show on both sides of her head, and unless she could find the money for a good strong corset she would look fat within the year. At least there would be no more children. Morris was more than enough. If it were not for Morris, she could leave, might have left already, before the appearance of grey hair and a tyre of flesh around her hips, before she had acquired scars on the sides of her legs—which now itched. She had not yet discovered a way of carrying two milk crates without their scraping the sides of her calves, and probably there was no way, since the milkman himself had advised her not to wear stockings.

There was no way either by which she could ever pay back the money she owed. Would she have to lie awake frightened every night? She had grown out of her attacks of asthma. Even when her mother died, and she had expected the loss to make her ill, she had only felt hungry. Her husband had ulcers, and spent all day in bed. They were all expecting her to solve their

115

problems, and she could not do it. Surely a wife can expect to be taken care of? Ulcers were an excuse. He had never intended to work hard and keep her in the way she had been brought up. Already the moonlight had turned to dawn. In another hour the milk crates would be delivered. Morris's mother contemplated the unfairness of having to choose one man with whom to throw in her lot, and the difficulties that arise when one realizes that one has chosen badly. For she had chosen badly. And there had been choice.

Morris's father curled up, and placed his knees against his wife's hip-bone. At the age of twenty-one, he had seemed so promising. He had started so well, yet already he had finished, and lay all day in a bed full of crumbs reading *Film Fun* and *Tit-Bits*. She had not expected the excitement of those first six months to last, but nothing had replaced it, and for the twelve and a half years which had followed, she had been making do, living with a man who never surprised her, a man who now used making love as a way of getting to sleep, who expected her to keep them straight, and allowed himself to be bossed about.

Well, the perforated ulcers had been a surprise, but not a pleasant one.

If only, on the day she had first met him, she had not been feeling old, and he had not looked so young, like a small dog which has lost his owner, but sniffs at every new pair of legs with hope. She might have chosen someone who would have kept her, someone with imagination, someone to argue with.

Morris's father never argued. He said it gave him indigestion.

At seven thirty, the sound of twelve milk crates arriving at the front gate could be heard through the thin curtains. The milkman was stacking them, as he always stacked them, in piles of four. Morris's father rolled on to his back, and started snoring. Morris's mother tiptoed to the front door, opened it, and waved to the milkman to let him know that he needn't knock. Morris had already been woken by the milk crates, and was rehearsing an excuse to the teacher about the lateness of last week's dinner money when his mother came into his bedroom, placed a finger to her mouth, and began taking his clothes out of a cupboard and packing them into a carrier-bag.

116

By ten minutes to eight they had left the prefab, and were crossing the waste ground that led to the churchyard. After that they would take the footpath to the main road, and then she would decide. The Rent Man started work at eight thirty, as all council employees did: that was well known. He did not usually visit the prefab estate until the afternoon, but she did not wish to bump into him on his way round the village.

She had brought very few clothes of her own, since none of the clothes she had were in a condition to sell. Instead her luggage consisted of three bottles of milk, the carved biscuit barrel of chrome and wood which her mother had used as a piggy-bank, and the most valuable object she possessed, a brass ornament made by her father out of three cartridges cases and two Gurkha knives. The base of this ornament was of solid brass, and the blades of the two knives were crossed, so that it was uncomfortable to carry, but it would, she hoped, provide their train fare somewhere. If she decided that they were going anywhere.

On the road to Millbrook Station there was a large house, set back among some trees. Morris's mother stopped by the gate, and told Morris to look after the carrier-bags. First she wiped her face with a handkerchief, then she polished the brass ornament and the biscuit barrel. Then she left Morris, and walked up the long drive towards the house.

Forty-five minutes later she returned, and showed Morris two pound notes. At almost the same moment, Morris's father was awakened by someone knocking at the front door. Assuming it to be the Rent Man, he did what he had planned to do, and remained absolutely still. After a while the knocking stopped, and footsteps could be heard, then the sound of milk bottles being removed from one of the twelve crates. Morris's father peeked from behind the curtain, and saw a neighbour, who had come to inquire after the milk, now helping herself. Throughout the day others came to collect milk. Some of them knocked first and some didn't, but every time there was a knock Morris's father remained absolutely still.

In the Waiting Room at Millbrook Station, there is writing on the wall, and during the course of the day Morris's mother read it all. She and Morris drank the three bottles of milk, and shared four caramels which she had found in the lining of her

117

coat. She had the fare to take them both as far as Bletchley, and at least a little way Beyond. They could spend the night on Bletchley station, and tomorrow she would find a job. The train ride would be comfortable, and would give her time to think, though indeed she had thought, thought all day. While Morris had walked up and down the platform, watching the trains which arrived, and went on, and which they did not catch, she had sat in the Waiting Room, going over in her mind the fors and the againsts of leaving home or going back to it. If they went back, she would have to face the Rent Man next week, and the week after. There would be no end.

Five years ago she would not have hesitated: she would have jumped on a train. There had been that holiday in Southport. They had gone without any money, and had waited for Morris's father to wire some to the General Post Office. Both she and Morris had enjoyed themselves. Only Grandma had not.

Morris sat on the wooden bench beside her, and placed his head in her lap. Soon it would be dark. They must get on the next train. The porter had closed the Booking Office and gone home: she would pay the fare on the train or at the other end: Morris was too big now to be wrapped in an overcoat and passed off as an infant. It was silly to be frightened. One never got anywhere with fear.

A bell rang somewhere, and the Night Watchman lit a red lamp, and left his box to open the gates of the level crossing. With both gates open, he stopped in the middle of the railway line, and put down the lamp to fasten his shoelace. Morris's mother remembered Old Fred, Grandma's lodger, whose heart had attacked him while he was opening the gates for the 9.48. She looked at the Night Watchman, and then at the red lamp. She remembered Old Fred, and she no longer felt frightened, for she had thought of a way to pay back what she owed.

She said to Morris, 'We'll go home now.'

Mr Bunker always stood in front of the Sunday School congregation, and led them in prayer. He never actually said, 'Let us pray,' but he would simply stand, close his eyes, clasp his hands together and wait until one by one the children noticed him, nudged each other, and, knowing that it was time to pray, copied him. Not that they could have mistaken the voice he used for prayers for the one he used for selling groceries from a van.

When Mr Bunker sensed that everyone else's eyes were shut, he would open his own. He did not understand why, but this was his favourite moment of the whole week.

He looked at the Under-Fives in the front row. He saw sixteen tiny pink hands pressed together, and eight tiny mouths praising God, all of them nourished at some time on cereals and baby foods from his own van. He looked at the second row, at the growing limbs, and serious expectant faces, and saw that his work was good. In the third row, he saw the slim legs of young girls gently rubbing together, and his heart rejoiced. He saw the muscular legs of young lads, strengthened by cycling holidays, and he saw Morris scratching the front of his trousers. He said, 'Thank you, children. You may open your eyes now. See you all next week, and learn your text.'

Morris opened his text book, and looked at the new stamp. It was green, and had a picture of a crocus opening. The text had been printed across the petals, and read, 'Suffer Little Children To Come Unto Me'.

He didn't need to learn it: he already knew it. They had given him an easy one because they knew that he had almost filled his book, and that he would have to pay them sixpence before he could get a new one. Morris didn't like Sunday School. Shutting his eyes and praying embarrassed him. He always imagined that everyone else's eyes opened when he shut his, and were staring straight at him.

Morris left the chapel with the other children of the prefab estate who were returning for their Sunday dinners. Next to the estate was a patch of waste ground, where the bulldozers had created more space than was necessary for the number of prefabs actually built. Part of this area was low-lying, and had filled with water to form a pond. The estate bordered the churchyard, and was divided from it by a fence, but where the pond had formed the fence had rotted away, and left the pond half sacred and half civilian, with an equal ease of access from either side. The pond was nowhere more than four feet deep, and as large as a back garden.

Now a crowd of people had gathered beside the pond. They had formed a circle, and were looking at something on the ground. Morris and the other children moved instinctively towards where the crowd was, but the mothers of several children were waiting, and came forward, gathered up their children, and took them a roundabout way home so as to avoid the circle of people.

Morris could see his own mother among the crowd, so he went on towards her, and into the circle. No one stopped him. Everyone was too busy watching a man pump water from the little boy who was lying on the ground.

Morris knew the boy. They were the same age, both eight years old. His name was Graham Stanley, and he was the only child of a middle-aged couple who lived on the estate. Now he lay on his stomach, his face to one side, while a man pumped water out of his lungs, and the middle-aged couple stood by, holding each other and crying.

The man was kneeling astride the boy. He learned forwards and then back, his arms straight, his hands pressed down on the boy's back. Each time he leaned forward, his large thumbs pressed hard against the boy's ribs. When he had done this for a while, he lifted the limp arms and stretched them back above the boy's head. Dark green water spurted from Graham's mouth, and Morris noticed that patches of skin around the mouth and below the eyes were the palest of pale blue. The eyes themselves were tight shut, and the boy's lips were dark and wet from the green water. A strand of dark brown weed rested on the left side of the boy's lower lip.

Next time the man applied pressure the boy seemed to retch, and waterweed, and sick came spurting from his mouth. At no point did he open his eyes. Somebody asked the man if he were tired yet, and the man replied, 'I'm all right.' The bells of the church began to ring, and worshippers began to emerge on their way home to lunch. Some of them gazed across the gravestones towards the crowd at the other side of the pond, but not one of them came over to see what the matter was.

Sixteen minutes later the ambulance arrived, and the driver pronounced the boy dead. But as they drove Graham away, they kept the bell ringing and the light on top of the ambulance flashing. Just in case.

Morris's mother said, 'This is Mr Henderson.' Morris looked at the man who had pumped weed and sick out of Graham.

'He came all the way from Yorkshire to see your Grandma's grave. We were just clipping her turf when we spotted little Graham in the water. Mr Henderson used to lodge with your Grandma. Now he's going to stay with us.'

The man bent down to shake Morris by the hand, and Morris noticed that his clothes were wet. Also the man's hand smelled of Graham's sick.

The church bell went on ringing for another hour. Someone was practising. And a week later, Graham Stanley was brought home, and buried in the churchyard close to the pond.

Mice

Stephen's mother and Uncle Leonard sat close together holding hands in the corner of the Snug Bar. Uncle Leonard wore a clean bow-tie, and Stephen's mother had curled her own hair and had then brushed it so vigorously that the hair bushed out at the sides of her face in frizzy waves. Lipstick had been applied to her lips, and she was wearing the pale blue dress she kept for Church Socials.

As Stephen entered, he saw his mother try to remove her hand from inside Uncle Leonard's. He also noticed that Uncle Leonard held firmly to that hand. With his free hand, Uncle Leonard lifted an empty glass from the table in front of him, and having lifted it, stared into it. Stephen said, 'You'd like that filling, I expect.' His mother refused the offer of another drink, and fumbled in her bag, using the only hand available. Finally she found what she was feeling for, which was a powder compact given to her by Stephen. Uncle Leonard let go of the hand he was holding in order to allow Stephen's mother to use the compact, and as Stephen moved away to the bar, he heard Uncle Leonard whisper, 'There's no gain without pain.'

He had arrived home to find a note on the kitchen table, telling him that his mother and Uncle Leonard had decided to take a coach ride to the Trough of Bowland, but that they would meet him in the Traders' Arms at about eight. Now he sat, and faced them. Uncle Leonard said, 'We've got an announcement to make.' Stephen looked at his mother, and she wiped the nose she had just powdered, at which Uncle Leonard reassured her by placing one hand on her knee and using the other to raise the fresh pint of bitter to his lips.

Stephen looked at the fat hand on his mother's knee, and

imagined the hot sweat seeping through the crimplene. 'I feel a lot for your mother.' Uncle Leonard had drunk at least a quarter of his pint in one swallow. When the hand was removed, it would leave a damp stain on Stephen's mother's dress. 'I'm very fond of her, as you know,' Uncle Leonard said.

Stephen forced himself to look away from his mother's knee. On a shelf behind the bar, the shade of a small table lamp turned round and round, depicting a man running after a pint of Guinness, and in the bricked-up hearth beside them the electric fire squeaked, as if mice were trapped inside it.

'I wish we could have worked things out differently, and had your blessing.' A small wheel in the fire rotated behind a red light bulb, reflecting an imitation flame: the squeaking must come from that. Holes had been made in the imitation coal of the fire by cigarette stubs.

'But your mother is very lonely, Stephen, and I'm—'

'Very broke.' Stephen had not meant this comment to be heard, but Uncle Leonard placed his now nearly empty glass on the table, and looked sadly at Stephen's mother. After a moment's pause he said, 'Children and chicken will always be picking.'

Beside the electric fire was a very old suitcase, held together by a thick leather strap. Uncle Leonard's initials had been painted on the lid in white paint. Perhaps the mice were in there. Stephen looked at his mother, and said, 'You realize he'll be tired of you inside three weeks?' His mother looked away. 'Well, do you?' Uncle Leonard, who had become preoccupied with what was once more an empty glass, said, 'Now look here, Stephen,' and Stephen said, 'No, you look. And take your hand off her knee.'

Stephen and his mother were not regular drinkers at the Traders' Arms, and they had by now attracted the attention of the people who were. Uncle Leonard removed his hand, and wiped it and the other on a grey handkerchief. As all other conversation in the bar had stopped, Stephen lowered his voice and said, 'All right. What are you going to live on?' Uncle Leonard said, 'Pardon,' and Stephen's mother began to cry, saying, 'I'll live on what I've always lived on. Charity from my own son.' Written on a slate behind the bar were the words, 'If you need glasses, see an optician. Don't take ours.'

'You'd better give me a list of the bus and railway stations you'll be sleeping on, so that I can wire money to the nearest Post Office when you're desperate. Because if you're taking to the road—a woman of fifty-eight and a man of—what is it—fifty-two?—you'll need something. Yes, you'd better do it now, while you're still young, though I'd have chosen the summer myself. And where's your suitcase, mother? Or are you just taking a haversack?' Uncle Leonard and Stephen's mother exchanged looks. 'Don't tell me you found a cottage in the Trough of Bowland?'

Uncle Leonard said, 'I'm coming to live with you, Stephen.' Even the mice were silent.

Uncle Leonard said, 'Your mother's asked me to. She didn't ask before because of your father's will. But there's something we've only just realized: I don't know why we never considered it before. If I come to live with you, the only person you can take to court is your own mother.'

'Yes.'

'And she's prepared to risk that, Stephen, because as I've explained to her, a teacher can't afford that kind of publicity.' Stephen watched Uncle Leonard grasp and squeeze his mother's knee. 'Obviously it'll take a week or two for you to get used to the idea. There's bound to be an atmosphere to start with.'

'You asked him?' Stephen stared at his mother.

'I don't like being left alone at weekends. You don't know what it feels like to be fifty.'

Stephen repeated the question. 'You asked him?'

'It was Leonard's idea, but. . .'

'But you agreed?'

'Yes.'

Stephen stood up. One of the regulars had lost interest in their conversation, and had started playing the fruit machine. It had been designed to attract the eyes of gamblers, and to this end, globules of coloured oil were constantly in movement, joining together and breaking apart again. Always the small globules returned to the largest, and always on contact the newly formed large globule broke into tiny bits and scattered like rabbits at the sound of rifle fire.

Stephen said, 'You realize that if dad's solicitors find out, we could lose the house altogether?'

'I rang from the station, but you weren't in.' Stephen stood outside Sarah's door, holding his weekend bag.

'I went for a walk. Has there been an accident?'

'What?'

'Is something wrong? You were here last weekend. Come in.'

Stephen put his bag down in the hall. He said, 'I didn't think you'd mind.'

'You knew I wouldn't. I don't. You're welcome any time.'

'If you're expecting anyone else, I'll go.'

Sarah started to laugh. Stephen picked up his bag again, and she took it out of his hands and put it back on the floor. She said, 'You know bloody well no one else comes here.' As Sarah laughed, she also cried, and since both of these activities caused her eyes to water, she moved around the flat searching for a handkerchief. Stephen followed. She said, 'I was just about to apologize. I was going to apologize, and explain why I can't go to Ormskirk tomorrow.' The water in her eyes made it difficult for her to concentrate on finding a hankie, so she decided to stop looking, and let the tears come. She said, 'Dear husband, I hope you'll forgive me for not being able to leave you to your little girls tomorrow, but—'

Stephen slapped Sarah across the face, and she stopped crying. She said, 'I've promised to take Arthur to the Zoo.'

'We can both take him. Uncle Leonard's moved in. I came to ask if I could spend all my weekends here. There'd be no need for you to go to Ormskirk more than once a fortnight.'

Sarah looked at him for a long time. Then she returned to the hall, picked up his bag, brought it into the living-room and unpacked it, throwing the contents down on the carpet at Stephen's feet. The bag was found to contain a pair of pyjamas, some clean underwear, a painting on thick hardboard, wrapped in brown paper, a toothbrush and a razor. Sarah said, 'I'm sorry.'

'Just as well to be sure, I suppose.'

'What's the painting?'

'It's Korky the Cat, standing on a roof. Would you mind keeping it here? I don't want Uncle Leonard seeing it.'

'Why not keep it in your room? Surely he won't go in there.'

'You never know. He might start wandering around. He doesn't work much.'

Sarah unwrapped the brown paper and looked at Korky captured in mid-scream. She said, 'Where shall we hang it?'

'I thought you'd just keep it wrapped up for a while. Somewhere out of the way.'

'But it's very good. It should be seen.'

Stephen picked his pyjamas off the floor, and folded them up. He said, 'Well, don't decide yet. Wait a bit, and think about it.' He picked up his underwear, toothbrush and razor, and moved to the door. 'You might find Korky a bit difficult to live with.'

Throughout most of the afternoon Stephen carried Arthur around the Zoo, and Arthur used the lapels of Stephen's jacket sometimes to wipe his nose on, sometimes to wipe his mouth, and sometimes to try to get his head under in order to hide from the great apes, the gorilla, the orang-utan, the chimpanzee and even the Barbary Sheep.

Only when they reached the Free Flight Bird Hall did he consent to stand on his own two feet. Then he stood, squinting at the canaries and love-birds out of the corners of his eyes.

Stephen sat on a bench beside Sarah, and asked her if she thought Arthur had enjoyed himself. She said, 'You've been very good. He's taken a shine to you. If I'd known you were going to be here, I'd have brought all the children.' Stephen shuddered, and Sarah laughed. 'Now you know how lucky you are with your lot. No runny noses. No wetting the floor, and then trying to lick it up. No tempers and biting.'

Stephen said, 'I had one run out on me the other day.'

'Where did she run to?'

'How did you know it was a she?'

'Boys usually stay and fight.'

'It wasn't a fight. She just went. Ran home. Domestic problems, I think.'

Arthur was wandering away, and Sarah got up, brought him back, and placed him in front of the parrots. Then she said, 'Didn't you ask about them?'

'She's a funny girl. Very quiet. Doodles a lot. She walks with

126

a slight shuffle.' He was silent for a moment, and then he said, 'She's so pale, you want to—'

'Feed her?' But Sarah took Stephen's hand, and held it, when she said this. Twelve doves took to the air, making a noise like canvas cracking in the wind. Arthur staggered backwards, and landed on his bottom in a pool of melted icecream. Stephen said, 'Yes.'

On the tram to Thornton Clevelys, which was where he lived, Arthur sat on Stephen's knee. Sarah asked Stephen which animal he had most enjoyed looking at, and Stephen said, 'The one in the hamburgers we had for lunch.' The conductor of the tram looked at the shape of Arthur's head, and refused to charge him a fare. He said, 'I think it's worst for you parents, you know.'

Sarah looked out of the window of the tram to her left, and watched the sea and the long grass on the dunes that merged with the sea-shore. There was a strong wind, and all the grass seemed to be blowing one way towards the sea which came rolling in towards the grass. But however strong the wind, and however high the tide, there would always be space between. The grass would never reach the sea. She said, 'What was the name of that girl?'

'What girl?'

'The one who ran home.'

'Mary.'

'Tell me more about her.'

'There's nothing else to tell really. She's just a spotty kid. I feel sorry for her.'

'Spotty?'

'Well, she's got a couple of those white-headed spots on her chin.' Sarah appeared to be thinking about those white-headed spots. 'Mind you, I'm not surprised. She goes home at lunchtime to give her father his dinner, but the only sign of cooking I saw was chocolate fudge.'

Sarah said, 'You followed her home, then?'

'There's a boy of yours sitting cross-legged on the floor outside the headmaster's study. He refuses to move.'

Stephen looked up.

'Well he doesn't actually refuse. He just won't speak. I've

instructed two of the bigger boys to lift him up and carry him away.'

Stephen said, 'Where to?'

'The cloakroom of course. Unless you'd like him in here.' Stephen's class, who were supposed to be working on designs for a new prefect's badge, began to giggle.

In the cloakroom, Stephen found Eric, the prospective stone-mason, sitting cross-legged on a bench and studying his finger-nails. Stephen said, 'What are you doing, Eric?' There was a long pause before Eric replied, 'Sitting.'

'Yes, I can see that, but why here?'

Eric continued to study his fingernails, and make an indescrib-able noise by flicking his tongue against his teeth.

'Eric, look at me when I'm speaking.'

Eric repeated the word 'look' slowly. Then he repeated the word 'speaking', and made it seem like a question. He decided that he liked the first word better, and said, 'Look, look,' several times, all the while staring at Stephen through his pebble glasses.

Stephen said, 'Look, Eric, I want to know—' and Eric said, 'Look, Eric, look, look, look, look.' Stephen turned to one of the boys who had carried Eric to the cloakroom and told him to ask Dame Patricia to phone the School Doctor and find out what his Surgery Hours were. Meanwhile Eric had returned to examining his hands and was whispering the word, 'Chip, chip, chip, chip, chip.'

Stephen knelt down, and shook Eric by the shoulders. Eric's head lolled about, and his glasses slipped down to the end of his nose. Stephen stopped shaking, and pushed the glasses back up to the mark they had made on Eric's face. Then he asked the remaining bigger boy if Eric had seemed all right earlier in the day.

'I don't know, sir. He's not in my class, sir.'

Stephen said, 'No, of course not: he's in mine. It was a silly question anyway. The trouble with Eric is that it's never easy to tell.'

Eric took the word 'trouble', and repeated it over and over like the others. As he did this, he lay down along the bench, took his glasses off, and closed his eyes. Stephen took the pebble glasses from Eric's dangling hand, and placed them in his own top pocket. Then he picked a pair of football shorts from the peg above Eric's head, immersed them in the water on the floor of the Showers, and began slapping Eric around the face with the wet shorts, after which he pulled him to his feet, and set him in motion.

After nine slaps and three trips round the cloakroom, Eric said, 'Those shorts are needed for Games, sir. Last period. Have I been asleep?'

'I wouldn't know, Eric: I really wouldn't. How do you feel?' Eric confessed that he did feel a little sick, and went into a cubicle to be so while Stephen waited outside. When Eric finally emerged, he was searching his pockets, and mumbling that he would have noticed if they'd dropped into the bowl.

Stephen gave Eric the pebble glasses, and said, 'What was it you took?' Eric thought for a long time, and then said, 'I don't know, sir. But I did have a penicillin tablet this morning, and they often affect me in a funny way.'

He also added that he had been thinking, and that what he had been thinking about was that stonemasons have to wear goggles against the dust, which might prove difficult and cumbersome on top of his own. Consequently he had decided that a job as a market gardener would probably be just as rewarding.

Uncle Leonard had said that there might be an atmosphere, and there was. Stephen found it unbearable. His mother began to wait hand and foot on what she called 'her two men'. She became preoccupied with 'being fair' and showing no favouritism. This drove Stephen from the house.

Before Uncle Leonard's arrival, most of their evenings had been spent in watching those television programmes his mother wished to see. Now she declined to speak of her preference, and insisted that Stephen and Uncle Leonard took it in turns to plan the evening's viewing.

He could not leave the house completely. It would be too expensive to pay the rent on a flat somewhere else and yet continue to keep his mother and her 'lodger'. Also the house was his, and his instinct told him that once he left, he would find it very difficult to regain possession.

So he would leave the house in the morning without breakfast, and return in time for bed. His mother had discovered an interest in the cleanliness of his shirts and underwear, and would leave him notes on the kitchen table concerning this subject. Snack suppers would also be left out, but more, Stephen believed, to impress Uncle Leonard than to satisfy any hunger in himself. He never ate the snack suppers.

The first evening on which Stephen left the house in order to wander about the streets and eventually into the Traders' Arms was one during which his mother was reading aloud items from the obituary columns of the local paper. She announced suddenly that she did not wish ham to be served at her funeral, and Uncle Leonard replied, 'That's right. I've no time for Race Relations.' Stephen took his coat, and went into the night, and eventually into the Traders', where he sat listening to the squeaking of the mice inside the electric fire.

On the next evening he went straight from school to a nearby park, where he watched five small children playing on a wooden horse. Even the horse squeaked, as it bobbed up and down and was pushed back and forwards. At nine o'clock he went into the Commercial Hotel, where he listened to the portable Disco, and lost seventy pence on the fruit machine. In the Gents there was a wall-dispenser for the sale of rubber protectives, and since Stephen was in a mood to put money into anything, he bought a packet of five Samoa Protectives 'in South Sea Colours for an Erotic Experience'.

On the third of these evenings, he sat in the park again. This time he had brought a book, *Puberty Rites the Whole World Over*. The book told him that in parts of Southern Brazil pubescent girls are sewn into hammocks and suspended from the ceiling for three or four months. From time to time, the hammocks are beaten, to discourage the evil that is in them. In other parts of Brazil, the people are less brutal, for there they merely tear out the girls' hair.

On the fourth evening, Stephen sat in the same park, but on a different bench. Beside him were several triangular rose beds. Stephen counted them: there were eight. One dozen rose bushes had been planted in each bed, and were now blooming. There was not a regular number of blooms on each bush, and little point in counting them, since it was easy to lose count, and count the same bloom several times. Yesterday all the roses had been pink, but there had been heavy rain during the night, and now they were grey and battered. On the grass near the bench

130

long-dead pussy-willow-like things lay about in tangled rusty-coloured patterns, so that the grass looked like a carpet he had once prevented his mother from buying.

People passed quickly through the park, taking short cuts home, but the bench on which he sat was hidden from the two main thoroughfares, and no one passed near enough to disturb his thoughts.

His thoughts were about crying. Suddenly. Without reason. He had been buying a birthday card for Sarah at lunchtime when he had felt the urge to weep, bitten hard on his lower lip, heard himself make little choking sounds, and felt tears, uncontrollable tears, running down the front of his face. An old lady had offered him a lace handkerchief. She had pointed to the bereavement cards, and so as not to look foolish he had bought one. And then the stamp on the envelope to Sarah had been crooked, with the Queen's head looking downwards instead of across the address.

There was a square of crazy paving under the bench. Life was unbearable. He could get by if he controlled himself, but those tears had been out of his control. Who knew when and where they might happen again?

It was almost seven o'clock. There were another three and a half hours to kill. His mother and Uncle Leonard went to bed at ten o'clock, so ten thirty was a safe time to return home. Tonight he would listen to the mice at the Traders' Arms. At least they were quieter than the portable Disco and the boys playing Babyfoot at the Commercial Hotel.

As he rose from his bench, Stephen saw Mary Whittaker come into the park. She crossed a stretch of mown grass, and sat down on a bench near the aviary. She was carrying a brown carrier-bag. Stephen moved to the other end of his bench, from which he could watch her, and sat down again.

At five past seven, a young man with long blond hair sat beside Mary, and was given something from inside the bag. Stephen could not see what had been given.

At fourteen minutes past seven, three young men approached Mary, and stood talking to her for two minutes. To Stephen it seemed longer. When they had gone, Mary sat with her head back, looking at the sky.

At twenty minutes past seven, Stephen himself decided that

he would go over to Mary's bench. When he was about ten yards away from her, Mary turned round sharply, and said, 'Hello, sir.' Then she started to walk away. Stephen quickened his step, and caught Mary's right hand, which was holding the carrier-bag. At that moment, a man who was standing on the pavement by the park gate whistled. Mary said, 'I'm sorry, sir. I've got to go. Dad's waiting.' Stephen was reluctant to let go of Mary's hand, for the tiny fingers seemed cool and dry, and his own hand had begun to sweat. Mary said, 'Sorry,' again, and wrenched her hand out of his, leaving him holding the brown carrier, except for its string handles which were still clenched in Mary's fist.

He watched her run aross the grass towards the gate. When she realized that she had lost the bag, she glanced round towards him, and threw the string handles to the ground. At the gate she joined her father. Or at least it was someone who could have been her father, for he looked old enough.

Stephen found four large cubes of chocolate fudge in the carrier bag, which he wrapped carefully in his clean but tear-stained handkerchief, to be eaten at some later time.

High

Sarah and Stephen collected Arthur from his home in Thornton Clevelys, and brought him back to Blackpool on the tram. They were to look after him until seven p.m., when his mother would return from visiting her husband who was in prison.

It was Saturday, and Sarah's thirty-fifth birthday. Stephen had wanted to make it special, and had bought her flowers as well as a nightdress of yellow satin. The commitment to look after Arthur had been made a month earlier, which was the last time Arthur's mother had visited the prison. Sarah explained that, with any luck, Arthur might spend the afternoon asleep, but that the morning had to be filled. Although she had lived in Blackpool for many years, she had never been inside the Tower. But she had been told that, once one had paid the entrance fee, there were enough free amusements inside to fill a whole day.

Next door to the Tower was a shop which sold nothing but rock and sweets. Blackpool Rock had been made into many shapes for sale at this shop—shaving brushes, babies' dummies and bottles, kipper fillets, all coloured realistically, and all wrapped in cellophane to be given as presents. There were bags of sweets, speckled and grey to look like pebbles from the beach, and there were large flat lollipops on sticks, with round cat faces, to be licked until the cat's face disappeared or the brittle toffee fell to the ground, and broke.

Arthur pointed at a cat lollipop, drew in breath loudly, and sucked his lips. Sarah said, 'I don't think we'll get him into the Tower unless he has one.' Stephen thought of his jacket, and the damage a cat lolly might do to it. He felt in his pocket, and brought out his handkerchief, which still contained the four pieces of chocolate fudge he had found in Mary's carrier bag. Holding the handkerchief close to Arthur's face, he unfolded it slowly, and said, 'Look what I've got for you.' Arthur lashed out instantly with his whole arm, and the four pieces of fudge fell on to the pavement. Then, while Stephen dodged in and out of the passers-by to retrieve the fudge, Sarah carried Arthur inside the shop and bought him a cat lolly.

Stephen wiped the fudge carefully on his handkerchief to remove dirt and germs, and placed one piece of it in his mouth. As Sarah came out of the shop, he offered a piece to her, but she shook her head. Stephen said, 'A little piece of dirt won't harm.'

'If that fudge was a present from Mary, I think you should eat it all, and not give it away.'

Stephen decided that the sooner he got rid of the remaining three pieces, the sooner Sarah would forget about Mary and how he had followed her home. He had better eat them. If he threw them away, Sarah would comment, and anyway it was good fudge and should not be wasted. Stephen hated waste.

Outside the Tower there was a notice to tell them that if they had come on Sunday, Ernest Broadbent would be In Concert on his Wurlitzer, but that today, and every day, and twice a day, Uncle Edgar would entertain the children with fun, magic and free gifts. So Stephen paid sixty-four pence for himself and Sarah and fifteen pence for Arthur to enter the Tower and meet Uncle Edgar in the Ocean Room.

Uncle Edgar was a small, very fat man in his early sixties. He had entertained children with his fun, magic and free gifts for many years, and knew the formula of his act so well that all interest and spontaneity had disappeared from his voice. Instead of talking to the children, he whined at them, and sometimes in too loud a voice, for although he had been performing for many years, he had only recently been presented with a throat-mike. Since it was secured near his Adam's apple by a piece of cord, he found the throat-mike distracting. On the pier he had used his own vocal apparatus to project the act along the many rows of deck chairs, and often he had fought the wind with his consonants. Later he had been issued with a stand-microphone, but he did not object to that: he could get away from it. Now he felt throttled, and indeed he *was* throttled from time to time, whenever he accidentally trod on the flex which protruded from his trouser turn-ups, and ran along the floor to a plug at the back of the stage.

What kept Uncle Edgar in work was the skill with which he chose children from the audience to go up and help him on stage. First the choosing itself took time, because he explained that, in order to be chosen, the children must sit up nicely. During this time Uncle Edgar assessed the children, and chose only those on whom he could rely to amuse the adults among the audience.

The atmosphere in the Ocean Room was informal, for in the evenings it was used as a bar. Stephen and Sarah sat in black plastic armchairs, set at a round table. Arthur sat on Stephen's knee, and toyed with his cat lolly instead of licking it, rubbing the lolly over his hair and poking at the cat's eyes with a finger. Uncle Edgar did not choose Arthur, and Arthur ignored Uncle Edgar. Stephen turned his head away from Sarah, and placed the second piece of chocolate fudge in his mouth.

Uncle Edgar whined, 'Are you a boy or a girl, my dear?' and the child under assessment explained that he was a boy. Uncle Edgar whined, 'Oh, what a pity! We've got enough of those,' and did not choose the child.

The chosen six stood in a straight ('*Straight!*') line along the front of the stage, with the tallest at one end and a very small child at the other. The very small child had been specially chosen, for the act would revolve around him.

'What's your name?'

The child whispered that it was Jim.

'Jim? That's a nice name. How old are you, Jim?'

The child shook its head.

'Don't you know, Jim?'

The child shook its head.

'He doesn't know. Give him a big clap. Are you three, Jim?'

The child nodded.

'Are you married?'

The child shook its head.

'Do you like girls, Jim?'

The child nodded.

'Well, that's all right. He likes girls. Give him a big clap.'

The chosen six played Musical Hats, and Uncle Ronnie at the

organ watched carefully to make sure that three-year-old Jim ended up the winner.

'I'm going to make you all winners today. Give them all a big clap.'

All the hats had been too large for Jim, who now stood centre-stage, struggling to get from below an enormous floppy sombrero.

'You stand back there, sausage. What's the matter? Can't you see?' The sombrero shook from side to side. 'You know, when I was three, I was your age. Here you are, poppet. Don't fall off the stage. Give him a big clap.'

Each of the chosen six was given a brooch, on which they were instructed to write their own names and 'To Mum With Love'. They were made to promise that they would help with the washing-up, and then each was given a pencil with 'Blackpool' written along the side.

'Hands up those who don't want a badge of Blackpool Tower.' No hands were raised. All received a badge of Blackpool Tower. A Punch and Judy box was pushed on to the stage, and Uncle Edgar announced that he was going behind the box to see if Mr Punch was asleep. Sarah took Arthur on to her own knee, and said, 'This might frighten him.'

Mr Punch dropped the baby instead of rocking it, and was hit on the head with a large stick by Joey the Clown. Arthur began to scream, and had to be carried out. As this was being done, it was discovered that Mr Punch, who had been lying motionlesss for some time after having been hit on the head, was not dead after all, and Stephen heard Uncle Edgar (speaking as Joey) say, 'You'll never die, Mr Punch.'

When they reached the Ballroom, Arthur stopped screaming. Written in letters of gold above the stage were the words, 'Bid Me Discourse, and I Will Enchant Thine Ear,' and in the centre of the Ballroom was another notice with the words, 'Keep Off the Floor'. Sarah and Stephen took Arthur on to the Zoo.

Having visited a larger Zoo a week earlier, they walked through the one in the Tower rather quickly, passing Micky the Mandril, Tony the Puma and Jacky the Spotted Hyena. Stephen stopped to look at the lavender finches, and noticed that the bird who seemed to be lowest in the pecking order had been, and was being, pecked heavily. It perched on the centre of the rail with its head on one side, while the birds on either side jabbed at its featherless and raw neck. Stephen wondered how the bird managed to remain so still and only very occasionally flinched.

As Sarah and Arthur had walked on and were out of sight, Stephen placed the third piece of fudge in his mouth. He rejoined them in the Apollo Playground, where fortunes were told over the phone. A recorded voice warned Stephen not to concern himself so much with money, and to hold at least two Premium Bonds. His lucky number was red, and his lucky colour was red too. The voice then said, 'The next person to listen to my voice will hear something surprising about happiness.' Sarah said she could hardly wait, and the voice told her that happiness was just around the corner. Her lucky number was actually a number (one), and her colour was a colour (yellow).

Next to the Apollo Playground was The Launching Pad, from which people were launched to the top of the five-hundred-foot Tower. The Pad was a kind of balcony suspended over the Cafeteria, from which two elderly lifts ascended. In spite of the fortune-teller's warning, Stephen was reluctant to pay another forty-three pence (sixteen pence each for adults, eleven pence for the child) for the three of them to take off, but Sarah pointed out that they were unlikely ever to come here again, and that Blackpool might seem more pleasant when viewed from a distance. As for Stephen's concern for Arthur, Sarah was convinced that he would be unaware of any danger. Violence performed with a large stick was something he had experienced: his father had often used a stick on Arthur, thinking it to be a suitable cure for backwardness. But a difference in height, Sarah felt sure, would not upset him, and if it did, then she would have discovered something about 'him, which would be useful, and they would come down again quickly.

Sharing the stately and somewhat shaky rocket to the top of the Tower were two young boys. Each carried a yellow gas-filled balloon, on which was written, 'W. H. Smith Sells Many More Things Than Books'. As they ascended, one boy said, 'Look at the Big Wheel. Isn't it small?' and the other added, 'Where's Bolton?'

The crisscross pattern of chocolate-coloured girders fell away below Stephen, and was replaced from above with a new, identical pattern. Arthur was being talked to by an attendant who was travelling to take up his duties at the top of the Tower. 'It's windy up there. You mind you don't get blown off.' As the attendant spoke, he placed a hand on Stephen's shoulder, and leaned forward pressing his face close to Arthur's. He was wearing a khaki raincoat over his uniform, and he smelled of stale pee.

Below was the glass roof of the Zoo, and shadows could be seen, moving about or standing to stare at Jacky, the Spotted Hyena. Stephen remembered Jacky stretched out on the floor of his cage, basking in the warmth from the artificial heating system, and he began to smile. He remembered the unflinching lavender finch, with its blood-red neck stretched out to be pecked, and the smile stretched upwards into a grin. Down there Uncle Edgar would have started his second dispensation of fun, magic and free gifts. Already a very small child would be struggling to get from below a large floppy hat. Stephen's grin turned into a quiet giggle.

One of the two boys said, 'The Empire State Building in France is three times bigger than this,' and Stephen's quiet giggle became a loud giggle. Everyone in the lift stopped talking. Stephen found this funny, and began to laugh. Sarah nudged him, and Stephen laughed even louder, and found he couldn't stop. The attendant's teeth reminded him of broken biscuits. Still laughing, Stephen pointed to them, and said, 'When my teeth are like that, I shall be your age.'

The attendant turned away from Stephen, and addressed himself to the people at the other side of the lift. 'Some people don't like heights. This is not what I call really high, though. I reckon it's really high when you get among the clouds.' Then he turned back to reassure Arthur, and leaning close said, 'Don't worry, lad. Nowt can go wrong up here.'

The roof of the Fun Palace had been made out of empty egg cartons. The crisscross pattern of moving girders suddenly remained still, and Stephen discovered that his vision had changed, so that each girder became more distinct, yet he could no longer see as much of the pattern at one moment as he had before, and that, in order to take the whole pattern in, he had to move his head. He stopped laughing, and asked, 'Why have

138

we stopped?' Sarah lifted Arthur out of Stephen's arms. Then, as it seemed to Stephen, she put him back in them, lifted him out, and put him back again. As she made the identical reaching out gesture for the third time, Stephen said, 'It all takes time.'

At the top they found a Souvenir Shop, where they could have bought a leather holder for a pension book or a doll in Welsh national dress. There was a postbox for the posting of letters or saucy postcards. And there were a great many signs, all warning of the dangers of throwing even the smallest of objects over the side.

Sarah insisted on carrying Arthur herself, and the attendant followed them, walking behind, but attempting to maintain conversation. 'There's never very much to do up here. I brush up, and if people ask me a question, I tell them where it is.' Names and dates had been scratched on almost every area of flat surface.

Stephen leaned on the iron grille which reached the level of his chest. Above the grille, vertical bars curved outwards, so as not to obscure the view, but preventing anyone except the thinnest of athletes from squeezing through and throwing themselves over.

'You could throw yourself down from the landing above this one, but unless there was a very strong wind, you'd only end up on those spikes.'

Sarah let Arthur down, and watched him move forward to the grille and peer out of the corners of his eyes. The building site below and the piles of rusty iron rods looked like a table on which breakfast cereal had been laid for four people, and cars on the roof of a multi-storey car-park were like the spaced-out parts of a mosaic. On the beach, a yellow dumper lifted sand from one place and carried it to another, so as to fill in pools of water left by the tide. In these pools, Stephen saw lights flashing on and off, and as the wind caught the surface of the pools, more lights flashed, and moved across the pools in formation like dancers. Stephen felt his hips swaying from side to side involuntarily.

'The Tower moves slightly when there's a wind, you know. Not that anyone notices it.' Holiday-makers crawled like flies along the Promenade. The flies either chased their shadows, or pulled them along behind, and seagulls with motionless wings

139

hovered over the flies, and followed them along the Golden Mile.

'What was once Central Station is now Tudor Bingo. Down there, can you see? The sign saying "Platform Seven" gives it away.' Stephen leaned out further over the grille, and felt both the Tower and himself sway from side to side. The attendant came and stood beside him. A lorry carrying squares of vivid green turf made a right turn. Then it made the same right turn over and over again, just as Arthur had moved over and over again from his arms to Sarah's, until Stephen mumbled, 'It all takes time,' and looked away.

Donkeys on the beach were being made to run, and the ringing of the bells round their necks drifted upwards. A grey dog ran across the sand towards a white dog, and sniffed its arse. From five hundred feet away, Stephen heard the dog sniff, saw its nose wrinkle, and smelled what it smelled. The two dogs ran round in circles, playing tag, and taking turns at being 'it', and the circles drifted upwards.

The attendant said, 'I didn't like the height when I first came up here. Do you know how I got used to it? I ignored it.' Sarah asked the attendant what he did in the winter, and he replied, 'I don't work in the winter unless I can get a job. Your husband's sweating, have you noticed?'

On the landing above them, Indians in grey suits and sandals took photographs of each other, posed against the sky. Stephen heard a woman's voice telling him that he was shivering, and saying that they had better go down.

The water in the guttering of the Palatine Hotel was like tears, and Stephen began to cry. Sarah moved away to collect Arthur, who was following a small girl with very red hair. He needed his handkerchief to wipe his eyes, but there was a piece of chocolate fudge in it, so he ate the fudge first. The attendant turned away, and reached out through the rails to catch the string of a pink balloon from W. H. Smith. He said, 'Gets you in the eyes when it's windy like this, and you're exposed.' Then he saw the writing on the balloon. 'Bloody advertising!'

Stephen saw litter being blown along the streets, and flies chasing it. The Tower was bending over, leaning towards the ground, and he was being pulled from the Tower towards the litter and the flies. A line of cars at the traffic lights had become one long car, and the signs in the road reached up and pulled at him, and the woman who was with him pulled at his fingers, and the attendant pulled, so that the woman and the attendant each had one of his hands and were unprising it, finger by finger, from the iron grille, and the attendant even banged his fist down on top of Stephen's hand to loosen his grip. And so he loosened his grip, and went with the woman, Sarah, to the lift, and sat down on the floor and wept, while the woman held a small child in her arms, and kissed it.

A taxi had been brought to the rear entrance of the Tower, and Sarah sat in the front seat with Arthur on her knee, while Stephen lay across the back, and cried. From time to time Arthur tried to turn on Sarah's lap to watch Stephen cry, and his bottom lip trembled.

When they arrived at her flat, Sarah asked the driver to watch Stephen, rushed up the stairs with Arthur, and locked him in the bedroom. When she returned to help Stephen, he was lying on the floor of the taxi, and the driver helped her pull him out and carry him upstairs. This done, the driver refused payment, saying that a man at the Tower had settled with him, and he drove away.

'What have you taken?'

He was sitting on the edge of the settee, watching the room move round him. He held up his right arm to stop it, but the effort tired him, and any movement had to be repeated three times. His arms and body were too heavy for his legs to support. They shook. In a moment, he would lie on the floor again.

Someone was asking a question. He must answer. His mouth dropped open to speak, but his tongue was too large: it moved slowly behind his teeth, making noises but no words. Stephen tried hard to form the word 'Nothing', but the word had no consonants and seemed to take forever to say.

'You're either having a nervous breakdown or a bad trip, and I need to know which.' His mouth was dry, and his skin felt cold. He tried again to explain that he didn't know what was wrong, but the noises he made were only noises. He pulled himself up and, using the furniture as support, crossed to the window to open it.

Sarah followed him, and closed the window again. Standing

141

behind him, she felt in all his pockets, removed the contents, and placed them on the table. Keys. Money. A wallet with membership cards. No pills. No cigarette papers. Nothing to explain Stephen's behaviour except his handkerchief, stained with chocolate fudge. And fudge was the only thing Stephen had eaten which she had not shared. She said, 'I think Mary may have given you the wrong sort of present. I'll have to get rid of Arthur. The lady downstairs will look after him if she's in. Promise me you won't open the window.'

When the words had travelled the distance between them to reach him, and he had sorted them out, Stephen nodded his head. The urge to open the window had passed anyway. It was merely an action.

While Sarah took Arthur downstairs, Stephen staggered around the flat looking for somewhere to hide. The moment he sat down, he felt the need to move again.

He went into the bedroom, sat on Sarah's bed, took his shoes and socks off, and made himself into a ball. He had grit all over him and the feet he liked so much were beginning to peel. They were red raw, with gaping crevices between the toes. The crevices grew wider. His feet were enormous. Now they began to itch.

Stephen leaned forward, and placed a finger into one of the cracks between his toes. It was warm and wet. Smooth jellyfish clung to the side of the crack, and twined themselves round his index finger. Stephen climbed inside the crack, and slid down over millions of jellyfish. As he descended, some of the jellyfish became dislodged from the walls, and the maggots they had covered scurried away to hide under other jellyfish. The heat became stronger, and the fish bigger, softer and more slimy. The force of his body sent him through the big jellyfish, breaking them into pieces which formed again into small fish, and floated upwards to take their places at the opening of the crack.

Someone was wrapping a blanket around him, and first he clung to this person who was trying to warm him, then pushed her away. His heart was thumping at the inside of his chest, making his whole body shake, so that soon it would rupture his rib-cage, burst out and splatter on the floor. Stephen wished it would. He wished it would end. Sarah said, 'There's no one in downstairs. We'll have to keep Arthur here.'

142

Arthur stood by the bedroom door, watching Stephen out of the corners of his eyes. He was licking what remained of the cat lolly, and staring at Stephen, who was crying again.

Crying and shaking all over, his mouth stretched outwards and downwards like a thick rubber band. It had started with fear at the top of his stomach, and the fear was still there, fear in a tight knot, butterflies fighting to get out of a confined space, tearing each other and him.

'Fear is anger, Stephen. Be angry. Let it out.'

Each row of tufts on the candlewick bedspread was a high wall topped with broken milk bottles. He was lying along one of the walls, and the muscles of his stomach ached from being held tight. If he moved, the broken milk bottles would open the wounds in his back, and the candlewick bedspread would be stained.

Someone was trying to put fingers into his mouth. He ground his teeth tightly together, and felt the teeth crumble like broken biscuits.

'I want to give you something.'

A woman was wetting his lips with water which she took from a glass with her fingers.

'Let me in, Stephen. I want to help you.'

The fingers on the woman's hand plucked at the rubber band that formed his lips, and stroked the perished cracks. Long fingernails scratched at the broken biscuits in his mouth. '*Help me!*' Stephen screamed, and like Arthur (who had burst into tears) he rolled his eyes, and bit on the fingers that were in his mouth. Crumbs of broken biscuit fell, covering his chest and legs entirely, and all that reached him from the outside world was a terrifyingly calm small voice that wept, 'I'm trying to, love. I really am.'

The small voice said that time would pass, and he would get better. Two white tablets were placed in his hand to prove to him that time was passing, and he clenched at them with such force that the powder had to be licked from his palm. 'Valium', the voice said. 'It will help.' Water was brought to him in a small glass many times, and each time took time, so that time passed, and he would know it passed, and the water was drunk from the small glass in small sips, each action causing time to pass. But often the level of the water in the glass remained the same, however many sips he took, proving to Stephen that no time had passed at all.

'You will get better.'

For a moment the butterflies stopped fighting to get out of his abdomen, but he remained tense, waiting for the next attack. Before the butterflies moved in, there had always been a hollow there. The bedclothes were cold. They were cold and wet.

'I'm looking at my watch, Stephen, and counting the minutes. Two have passed since you licked your hand.' Had he licked a hand? Whose? Who would be generous enough to allow it? Didn't they realize what licking hands might lead to? Fingers might be dug into plasticine, into clay, into nylon blouses. Stale pee might be smelt, and molehills jumped on. Flattening them down, plasticine, clay, molehills, into neatness and order. *'That's all right: he likes little girls. Give him a big clap.'*

'That's another minute gone.'

Morris had had the dirty mind. Stephen had cleaned it for him. Pulled the chain and closed the door.

'The wardrobe is pink, Stephen. And the curtains blue.'

The only feeling he could attach to the fear was the feeling of nothingness. Of being nothing, and coming from nothing. His mother had been something, but 'having been' wasn't the same as 'being', and all that remained was the need to cry.

Four fingers were being held up close to his face. 'Four minutes have passed since you licked your hand. Every minute that goes by, you're getting better. Arthur's finished his lolly. I've left him in the living-room. He'll be all right there.' Sarah put her watch on the bedside-table, and lay beside Stephen on the bed.

The wardrobe was pink, and the curtains blue, and Arthur was licking the whiskers off a cat which could no longer scream. Stephen closed his eyes, and saw pictures that frightened him. They were simple coloured shapes, but they wouldn't stay still. He released his breath in a long deep sigh. The butterflies returned, and Stephen opened his mouth wide so that they might find a way out, and not rupture his chest.

The people who walked along the concrete paths below never looked up, never heard the scream. The grey slates beneath his feet were wet and slippery. If he turned, or tried to sit, he would rip the hardboard, and might tear himself. Red paint ran out of the sky and into his ears. As it trickled along the folds of his ears, it felt cold and sticky. His fingers dug into the thick cat fur on his body, trying to untangle it, and find the skin from which it grew, but there was no skin, and lumps of matted fur came away in his hands. In its place grew more and thicker fur. It was oily, and smelled of linseed, and it stained his hands black. The muscles round his mouth ached from screaming, but the paint there had dried, and would flake if he rested. Down below he saw a boy he recognized. He tried to turn the scream into a name without closing his mouth. The name was 'Morris'. He shouted it, 'Morris!' But when the boy turned round to answer his name, he had no features, just a round pink blob, with the marks of brush-strokes curling upwards, and ending at the neck.

And time, as he had been promised, did pass.

When the trip was over, and Sarah lay beside Stephen on the pink candlewick bed-cover in the dusk, Sarah said, 'You've been living in a box for thirty-three years. It's about time you burst out.'

Doves

At six twenty-five in the morning, Stephen woke, and climbed out of bed. Sarah, whose rest had been less interrupted, was slower to follow him.

Arthur's mother had arrived to collect him at seven thirty the evening before, and had been allowed no further in than the doorway. 'I'm sorry; I can't offer you a cup of tea: I'm in the middle of a domestic crisis.' The fear that Stephen might at any moment wake up and scream had made Sarah cold, efficient, and more than usually middle-class. The expression on the face of Arthur's mother had changed very quickly from pleasure and relief at seeing Arthur to the one she wore when confronted by the prison authorities.

Having closed the door on Arthur and his mother, Sarah had leaned her back against it, and contemplated the first day of her thirty-sixth year. Only one good moment could be salvaged from the general disaster, and that was the moment when Arthur had refused the chocolate fudge and had preferred a cat lolly. She had then changed into her yellow satin birthday present, and gone back to lie again beside Stephen.

Now she found him in the living-room, searching through the drawers and cupboards.

'What are you looking for?'

'The picture I asked you to keep for me. Where is it?'

Sarah brought the picture of Korky from the top of the wardrobe where she had been storing it. Stephen looked at Korky on the roof for a moment, and then began to bend the hardboard.

'Helping Mary to get off drugs might do more good than tearing a perfectly good picture.'

'It won't tear. I'm bending it.'

'Do you want to know what happened to you?' Stephen had succeeded in folding the picture in half, and now bent it back the other way, so that parts of Korky's face and fur fell on the carpet. He said, 'I assumed it was some sort of a breakdown. I was frightened. You know better, do you?'

'I'll make some coffee.'

Stephen picked up bits of flaked paint, looked at a green eye and part of a right ear, rubbed the flakes between his fingers, and crumbled them into powder. And said to himself, 'I don't want any more of that.'

He found a waste-bin in the kitchen, and dropped the piece of bent hardboard and the flakes of paint into it. Sarah said, 'Even now it doesn't seem to want to be torn,' and handed him a mug of coffee. Stephen took the mug, but kept hold of Sarah's hand, and said, 'I'm sorry. I nearly died.' Sarah held Stephen's hand to the side of her face, and said, 'It's important you know what really happened.'

Stephen let go of Sarah's hand. He took his coffee into the living-room, and stood gazing out of the window. Sarah followed, and sat on the settee.

'When you got really bad, I rang Michael. I tried to describe how you were behaving, and he told me to give you Valium, and try to talk you down. I did my best.' Sarah sipped at her coffee, and some of it dripped, making small brown rings on the yellow satin nightdress. 'The fudge Mary gave you probably contained acid, or a very large dose of hash. It had to be in the fudge. It was the only thing you ate which we didn't.' Stephen opened the window, and smelled the sea. 'Surely you could tell by the way she behaved when she gave it to you, that something was wrong?'

Stephen shook his head.

'You really thought it was just fudge?'

Stephen nodded. (He liked little girls. Give him a big clap.)

'Hash is very expensive. I'm surprised she can afford to give it away on that scale if she's only fifteen.'

Stephen remembered the white paper bags, and the young men who had paid for them. He said, 'She didn't give it to me. I wasn't meant to have it. It was a mistake.'

147

'And if Arthur had eaten it? Would that have been a mistake?' Rain hit the window, and began to roll down it.

'Michael says you may get recurring forms of the trip. Milder but nevertheless worrying.' Stephen drew a picture in the steam his breath had made on the window.

'Mary won't go to prison: she's under age. But the real pusher should. It's ten years, I think. She's bound to be expelled.' As he pressed his face against the glass, the spit from his mouth rolled down through the drawing.

'She'll be put into care, of course. And watched. So she should be. If it's acid now, it could be heroin by the time she leaves school. And think of all the twelve-year-olds she may be turning on. She should be watched.'

Stephen said, 'I'm sorry about your birthday. We must try to do something different next year.'

He sat on a bench in the park, his arms folded tightly across his chest, his eyes fixed on the toe-caps of his shoes. Mary had to be helped.

He had placed a newspaper on the bench before sitting down, because rain had left the bench damp, but the *Guardian* was not a newspaper thick enough to prevent the cold from striking through his trousrs. It was no use worrying about piles. Piles he had already.

Two gardeners with besoms swept up dead leaves and toffee-papers. A third gardener, whose job it was to push the wheeel-barrow, stood instead behind a girl on a swing and pushed her as high as she wanted to go. Mary had to be helped.

A cramp formed in the muscles behind his knees, and Stephen left the *Guardian* lying on the bench, and walked towards the bandstand. Old wooden doors had been nailed together and boarded up where once the bandsmen would have sat to play. Prickly bushes and chestnut palings surrounded the bandstand, and at one point barbed wire had been added to the barricade. The prickly bushes had been there for a long time. Perhaps they had been planted for the protection of the bandsmen.

In one corner Stephen discovered a small gap in the chestnut paling and a narrow path through the prickly bushes. So it seemed that there was a way into the bandstand. Presumably it would be used by tramps and courting couples.

148

He continued his search for a dry bench, and found one near the Aviary. The Aviary had been partitioned into two parts. Doves were housed on the left, budgerigars on the right. No lavender finches. Stephen closed his eyes, and tried to concentrate on the problem of how Mary was to be helped.

Someone had approached the bench, and was standing behind him. Stephen opened his eyes, and waited for the someone to speak.

'They're not doing it now.'

The someone was not Mary. Stephen said, 'Not doing what?' without looking round.

'The budgies have made a hole in the wire-netting, so that they can get into the pigeons' side, and steal their food. Look! There it is.'

The someone was an elderly lady, and she was pointing to a place at the bottom of the wire separating the birds, where the ground had been scratched away, and there was a hole just large enough for a small bird to walk under the wire.

'You should see the budgies walking through that hole, one behind the other in a line. And then being chased back by the pigeons. It's very funny.'

'Yes, it must be.'

'I always come at this time. I sit where you're sitting.' Stephen moved along the bench, so that the old lady could sit where he had been sitting, and she placed herself down where he had warmed the seat. 'They're not doing it today,' she said. 'I wonder why not. Taken a day off work? It's all right for some.'

Stephen rose to his feet, and said, 'It's my holidays.'

'Go on! You'd say anything except your prayers, and them you'd whistle.'

Stephen moved away to find another seat. He had lied: it was not his holidays. This was the second day he had spent in the Park. He had telephoned the school to explain that he was ill, and Dame Patricia had wished him a speedy recovery, and reminded him that, if he intended to be absent for more than three days, the school would require a medical certificate.

Mary had to be helped. She had to be stopped from selling drugs, and if she were also taking them herself she had to be stopped from doing that. Both were important. And it was also important that she should be stopped in the right way. '*Nobody*

149

was ever helped by punishment.' Those were Sarah's words, and he had often heard her use them, though not in this case.

He found another seat, sat, and took a small notebook from his pocket. He had bought it that morning. It was always wise, when trying to come to an important decision, to write down a list of possible alternatives. So he wrote the word 'ALTERNI-TIVES' on one page, and on the facing page he wrote the words 'REASONS AGAINST'.

This was the list. Art was the subject taught by Stephen, not English, and his spelling was insecure.

I. Inform police. They willfind pusher, prosekute, etc.

Police question Mary, Juvenile Court, put her under care of Welfare.
A fifteen-year-old criminal.

II. Inform Headmaster.

Hell of a stink. Wind and water. Do all worst things. i.e. Scare to death. Only tell police himself anyway. Expell her.

III. Talk to her myself. Keep it quite. Get her promise to stop trafficking in drugs, fudge, etc. No *punishment*, or blackmail. Common sence, consern, friendship, etc.

Stephen closed the notebook. Two separate lists, one made by each of them on thick drawing-paper, had ended his marriage. Until he had started making his list, he had been prepared to try to make the best of a bad mistake, but both his list and Sarah's had been long, and the discussions about them had made matters worse. There would be no discussion this time. Mary had to be helped. And he must do it himself. There was no alternative.

'What's in the fudge you sell, Mary?'
Mary drew in her lower lip, gently bit into it, and released

the lip again slowly. The lip was wet now, and darker, round and full. She was pouting. He was looking at her, and the pout was a conscious attempt to draw on his sympathy.

Stephen reached out, and stopped Mary from twisting her identity bracelet. It consisted of a round disc on a heavy chain. The chain accentuated the narrowness of Mary's wrists.

'I have to talk to you about the fudge, Mary.' She allowed the wrist to be held, and stared at the fingers which gripped it. Stephen felt a slow determined pulse throbbing inside Mary's wrist. He said, 'Do you ever eat the fudge?'

Mary's eyes moved from his fingers and stared right at him. Underneath the eyes were pale blue patches of skin, dotted with freckles. There were freckles too on the eyelids, above the straw-coloured lashes. Mary lowered her pale eyebrows. Her expression was one of incomprehension, and Stephen thought she had not understood the question. He was unable to bear the look of worry which filled her eyes and twisted the corners of her mouth, and he looked away. Her fingernails were tiny. Stubs of nail, in the shape of half-moons. The fingers were pink, and chapped, and looked sore. Mary said, 'I have to eat a bit of it to make sure it's all right.'

Stephen slid his hand from her wrist, and brushing his palm over hers, placed his own warm damp fingers between her dry chapped ones.

'What happens to you when you eat it?' As Stephen asked this, he squeezed Mary's hand to reassure her. Mary turned her head, and looked from right to left, making sure that no one was close to them. As she looked towards the Aviary, she shook her head, and a young man with a beard turned in his tracks and walked away.

'Was that a customer?'

'I should be home be now.'

Stephen held tight to Mary's hand, and Mary made no move to go. They sat where they were in silence for another three minutes, when she leaned forward, and brushed a piece of grass from her left shoe. The shoes were in two shades of brown, with a high unnatural gloss, and broad heels. As Mary leaned forward, her chest touched the back of Stephen's hand. When she had finished brushing away the grass, and had studied her shoes for a moment, she said, 'I ought to go.'

'Did you know there was fudge in the carrier-bag you left with me last week?' Slowly Mary shook her head. The pale eyebrows were lowered again, and the bottom lip bitten and then rolled forwards towards him. This time he was closer, and could see the inside of the lip. It was paler, and more shiny than the outside.

Stephen turned his body in towards her, and placed his free hand over the identity bracelet. 'I'm sorry, but you see, I'm not the only person who knows about it.' He had lowered his voice to a whisper. 'There were four pieces left in the carrier-bag, and I offered them to a small child.' His face was so close to hers. If he blew gently, she would feel it. 'The child ate the pieces of fudge, and was very. . . ' He stopped, and waited for a reaction. Mary blinked, and he felt her fingers tighten around his. 'Someone else was there when all this happened. I had to explain where I'd got the fudge. The someone wanted to go to the police. Right away.' Mary's eyes gazed at him. Stephen leaned in closer, pressing his shoulder against hers, and staring at the small cleft in her chin. 'Finally I managed to persuade them to wait a week.' Her lower lip was fuller, more rounded, and very dark now. 'But I had to promise to find out where the fudge came from, what was in it, and how much you got for selling it.'

Mary's grip tightened on his fingers, and she pressed her knees together. Stephen said, 'I suppose we shouldn't talk about it here?' Mary shook her head. 'I've found somewhere a bit more private. It's not very comfortable, but at least we shan't be seen.' Stephen kept hold of Mary's hand as he rose to his feet. Mary remained seated. She said, 'Does it have to be tonight, sir?'

Stephen stopped. It was the 'sir' that stopped him. He could get Mary's promise to stop selling the stuff, walk back to the Traders' Arms, listen to the mice, and go home to eat the supper left out by his mother. He let go of the hand he was holding, and looked down at the pale almost white eyebrows, the small freckled nose and the knees pressed tightly together. He had shown concern, common sense, compassion, friendship. Now Mary would give him her solemn promise to stop, and everyone would have behaved well. He said, 'A small boy was made very ill. He had what you'd call a bad trip: it's not certain he'll

152

ever recover properly. I think we need to work something out quickly, before someone goes to the police.'

Mary rose to her feet, and walked slowly beside him to the bandstand. As she walked, she glanced over her shoulder from time to time to make sure that nobody followed.

Stephen found the opening he had spotted earlier, and they picked their way through the barbed wire and prickly bushes.

The inside of the bandstand smelled of damp, and parts of the floorboards were rotten, and crumbled as Stephen and Mary trod on them. Scrawled on the walls were messages. These messages were about Wally, and said that Wally was great, and Wally was a sex-bomb.

'I think if we sit down here, nobody will see us through the window.'

It was not a window: it was a hole, which had been made by the removal of three planks of wood. Stephen looked out through the hole, and listened for any sound which might indicate that they had been followed. Mary sat on the floor, and curled her legs under her. Stephen sat beside her, and took hold of her hand.

He was shaking, and he worried that she might notice it. He said, 'I didn't want to alarm you, but you do see how serious it is, don't you?' Mary nodded. He placed an arm around her shoulder, and said, 'Don't worry. I'm sure we can work something out.'

'I can't tell you who gave me the stuff.' Mary crumbled a piece of rotten wood between her fingers, and looked at the dust she had made. Stephen stroked the shoulders of her cardigan, saying, 'Never mind. Tell me what you can.'

Mary hesitated. She had found a small stone, and with it she was scratching out a doodle on the floorboards. Stephen stretched his legs out in front of him, and, leaning back, he attempted to pull Mary back with him. But Mary resisted his pressure, and remained sitting upright.

He was acting too quickly, making too many unprepared moves. He had an erection, and it showed clearly as it pushed against the inside of his trousers. Mary would be frightened, not only of him, but also of the police. She needed time. Reassurance. He must wait.

Mary said, 'It'll be dark soon. Nobody comes to the park

153

after dark.' Stephen said, 'Don't be frightened. You're not on your own.' Then he took Mary's hand again, and placed it over his erection.

Mary drew in breath sharply, and pulled the hand quickly away. Stephen leaned his head against hers, and whispered, 'Was it hash or LSD?'

'Only hash. I didn't know you could have a bad trip with hash.'

Now his mouth was close to her ear. Stephen said, 'He ate four pieces very quickly, and then tried to throw himself out of the window.' His lips moved over and round the small pink lobe. 'It'll be all right, I promise you.' He kissed the lobe, and ran his tongue between the delicate pink folds of her ear. 'Try to relax. I don't like seeing you all tensed up.'

Mary allowed herself to be lowered into a lying position, and Stephen placed an arm under her head to support it.

When he had looked at her lying below him, her eyes tightly closed and one bare leg crossed over the other, when he had studied her hands, the chapped fingers holding his hand tighter than ever now, both hands gripping and squeezing until his one hand and her two were all three red and warm, when he had examined the hem of her dress, that hem at which she had pulled every thirty seconds since they had entered the bandstand and smoothed tightly round her thighs before lying down, when he had done all this, he leaned his head forward, and pressed his top lip on the darker, softer, more rounded lower lip below him.

He kissed the outside of her lips. He pressed his tongue into the tiny dry mouth. He felt with his tongue along the even teeth, and circled the small smooth tongue that was hers. He moved his lips over the freckles on the closed eyelids, and drew a fine brush-stroke with his tongue along the cleft in Mary's chin.

Mary held her breath, and released it only when, his face away from hers, Stephen said, 'What do *you* feel like when you've eaten the fudge?'

Patches of dark pink appeared on Mary's neck. She turned her head to one side, and screwed up her eyes even tighter. After a long silence she said, 'If you try to do it, please don't hurt me.'

154

The dark pink patches spoilt the picture. They had spread from her throat to the side of her neck, and as Stephen placed his fingers under the collar of her dress, and undid the first button, he saw more of them on her shoulders.

'I promise you it won't hurt.' The tiny mounds which surrounded each nipple were also mottled with pink and freckles. Stephen licked the breasts, and touched the nipples, moving them up and down, and pressing them gently between his thumb and forefinger. His fingers shook.

'I promise you.' The dress had buttons to the waist. 'I love you.' Stephen undid the remaining buttons slowly, rolling his tongue round each of Mary's nipples, and sucking it as he did so. When all the buttons had been undone, he slid his hand down inside the dress. Mary held her breath, and Stephen lifted his hand away from her body until she began breathing again. Then he lowered his hand, and stroked her stomach.

Mary clenched and unclenched her fists, as Stephen lifted the hem of her dress, and placed his head in her lap. Moving his head slowly from side to side, he rubbed his face against the front of her knickers. Next to the band of elastic there were three small holes, and Stephen poked his tongue through each hole in turn. Mary's legs remained crossed.

He slid his fingers under the elastic, and the tips touched pubic hair. The hair was soft, and had been slightly moistened by sweat. Stephen stroked the hair, brushing it back and upwards towards her navel. Mary's legs remained crossed.

When Stephen pressed his tongue into the pubic hair between Mary's thighs, Mary's hands jerked up, and covered her mouth. Stephen now placed the tip of his longest finger into the cleft, but Mary squeezed her thighs together, and prevented the finger from going any deeper.

'I promise you it won't hurt.' Stephen pushed his mouth and tongue into the cleft where his finger had been, and used his hands to try to uncross Mary's legs. Then he raised one hand, and taking her left nipple between his thumb and index finger, he squeezed it hard.

Mary's legs parted slightly, and Stephen slipped his left hand between them. His longest finger found the opening, and the tip was eased into it gently, and began to move round and round. After four minutes, Mary uncrossed her legs.

155

Stephen used his hands to hold Mary open, and with his tongue he found her clitoris. As he sucked it, Mary moaned. He rolled his tongue around it, and Mary's head moved from side to side. He made his tongue hard and flicked it backwards and forwards, and Mary spread her legs wide and touched her breasts.

The fingers of Stephen's left hand groped in his pocket for the pot of Vaseline, placed the pot on the floor beside Mary, and then undid his trousers, and pulled them down. His right hand continued to hold Mary open. While he applied Vaseline to his penis, Mary tensed herself. Stephen placed his tongue inside her again, and then removed it, and inserted two fingers.

Stephen wiped his mouth on his sleeve, lay on top of Mary, and placed his lips against hers. While his left hand held her open, his right guided the tip of his penis towards the opening.

With the tip once inside, he rested, and said, 'It won't hurt. I'll go very slowly. Please trust me, and try to relax.' Mary opened her eyes. She said, 'When I'm high, I can think more clearly. My mind used to go too fast, and I got confused.'

Stephen moved his penis in another quarter of an inch. 'Once it's inside, your body will relax, and accept it.' Mary placed a hand on either side of his face, and said, 'I don't get much for selling it.'

Stephen moved in half an inch. He said, 'The moment you feel uncomfortable, tell me. It's always difficult the first time.' Mary lifted her hips to meet the next half inch. She said, 'I really didn't know you could be ill from taking it. Will the little boy be all right, do you think?'

Stephen withdrew himself half an inch, and then thrust in an inch. He said, 'I think he'll be all right after a while.' He could feel that she was wet and open. He kissed the veins which stood out on her thin wrists, and plunged again. He was diving deeper and deeper into the small body which lay below him. He could feel the tiny bones. Stephen said, 'As long as you stop making fudge right away, I don't think the police will find out. Am I hurting you now?' Mary shook her head. A fieldmouse ran from its cover beneath a stack of iron chairs, and darted for the far corner of the bandstand. Mary neither saw nor heard it. She smiled for the first time, and said, 'Don't bite me when you come. My dad'll see it.'

156

Stephen stopped plunging, and watched Mary underneath him. She continued to move her hips, lifting herself on to him and pulling back. The pink blotches had gone from her head and shoulders, and she lay with her hands above her head, looking at him and smiling.

Slowly he started to move again. Mary reached up, and grabbed him round the neck, kissed him on the mouth, and bit his ear. She said, 'Don't you give me a baby.' Stephen said, 'Don't worry. I'll come out quickly when I get close.'

And came.

Pigs

At six thirty a.m. one Sunday morning, an American jeep pulled up outside the Cowleys' prefab, and the driver honked his horn. Morris's father dressed quickly, and went out to the jeep, only to return a few minutes later to ask Morris if he would like to pull sugar beet. Morris now slept on a camp bed in his parents' room, since Mr Henderson, their lodger, had been given Morris's room. Since liking did not really seem to enter into his father's question, he climbed off the camp bed, and dressed himself, joined his father in the back of the jeep, and they were driven off by their new employer.

Mr Henderson had heard Morris's father's question and now heard the jeep drive away. He got out of his bed, removed the underpants and singlet in which he usually slept, and stood naked on the cold oilcloth until he had counted up to fifty. When he had reached fifty, he opened the door of his bedroom, crossed the hall, and entered the room in which Morris's mother was pretending to be asleep.

Mr Henderson had been lodging with Morris and his parents for three weeks.

The jeep carrying Morris and his father was driven very fast. It was old, and from time to time, as it turned a corner, it gave them both a mild electric shock. The driver wore khaki shorts and a khaki shirt. He was a gentleman farmer.

The name of the gentleman farmer was Mr Spark, but he looked to Morris so like Winston Churchill that Morris expected him to drive along holding two fingers in the air. But Mr Spark used both his hands to steer the jeep, and Morris noticed that two of his fingers were, in fact, missing.

'Soon be there.' Mr Spark changed into a lower gear and

158

accelerated in order to cross a major road without the inconvenience of stopping, and Morris and his father received another shock. Not only did Mr Spark look like Winston Churchill: he spoke like him as well. During the three years he had spent in a Japanese prisoner-of-war camp, Mr Spark had perfected a way of talking out of the corner of his mouth, and this slowed down his speech and accentuated the gentlemanliness of his accent.

The field from which sugar beet was to be pulled was large and flat, so that the wind had easy access to it. Rain began to fall. The beet themselves reminded Morris of very large turnips, and they seemed to have been planted in cold hard modelling clay.

Between the rows of beet, deep trenches had been made by tractor wheels, and these were full of yellow water. As Morris pulled at the long rough leaves, the leaves broke, and he staggered backwards, sometimes landing on his bottom in one of the trenches of yellow water, and sometimes managing to retain his balance, but standing up to his knees in the water, his once-black plimsolls squelching as he attempted to climb out.

He would need the plimsolls next day for school. He removed them. He also removed his socks, and laid both socks and plimsolls on top of some beet he intended to leave unpulled.

As his bare feet slipped about in the mud and became numb with cold, he remembered the nylon stockings Mr Henderson had given his mother, and he thought of his mother and Mr Henderson still warm, at home, in bed.

He had been working for an hour and a half, and had only managed to pull (or to dig out with his fingernails) fourteen large roots of beet. Morris did not know that he had only been working for an hour and a half: to him it seemed much longer. And the fourteen roots of beet which he had laid neatly side by side at the corner of the field seemed a lot to him, considering the amount of time it had taken him to pull each one.

His jacket was wet through, and smelled of soap, having been sponged with a soapy flannel every day before school. Since Mr Henderson's arrival, he had attended school regularly. His mother no longer seemed to need his company, and his father was available to run errands and to help in preparing meals for Mr Henderson. Morris disliked going to school, even though now his dinner money was always given to him for payment on the correct day.

He turned himself round, and began working with his back to the wind and rain. Now when he fell, he would fall on the beet yet to be pulled, and break their leaves, but most of the leaves broke as he pulled them in any case, and at least this way he could see more clearly what he was doing, because the rain would no longer get in his eyes.

At eleven thirty Morris's father left the pig-sty he had been mucking out, and crossed the fields towards Morris, bearing a mug of cocoa. By the time he reached Morris, the cocoa was cold. He complained of the mud and water that Morris had collected about himself, and asked Morris why he had removed his socks and plimsolls, adding that he hoped they were not the plimsolls Morris wore to school. He counted out loud the number of beet that Morris had pulled and laid in a neat row, and said it was lucky that he had bartered with the gentleman farmer, and persuaded him not to put Morris on piecework, because the wage would not in that case have covered the damage Morris had already done to his clothes. He had explained to the gentleman farmer that Morris was new to farm work, and the weather unfavourable for pulling. Consequently he had managed, he announced with some pride, to secure for Morris a wage of one shilling and sixpence an hour.

Morris sipped the cold cocoa. His father had handed the mug to him with a hand stained with pig-shit. The mug smelled sweet and sickly, and Morris remembered the floor of the pig-sty his father had shown him on their arrival at the farm. Morris's father said, 'Drink up. It's not hot. I've got to get back. We're lucky to be working here. Mr Spark is a gentleman farmer: that means we'll be taking some eggs home.'

Morris closed his eyes, and drained the contents of the mug in three large gulps. Then he began to pull beet again, and pulled it until one o'clock.

During the six hours from seven a.m to one p.m., during which Morris pulled beet, he had pulled altogether one hundred and two roots, and they all lay in a neat row at the corner of the field. Morris was paid nine shillings, and Mr Spark told Morris's father that it was the most expensive beet he had ever grown. Then he gave them six cracked eggs, and drove them home.

A month later the local paper was to carry an announcement of the death of Mr Spark, who had been found hanging by a rope from a beam in one of his barns. By this time Morris's father had worked only four Sunday mornings for the gentleman farmer, and now the farm was to be auctioned.

All the curtains were still drawn, when Morris and his father returned home. Morris removed his muddy plimsolls, and left them on the back-door step. His father did the same with his muddy boots.

Morris was told to put the kettle on, and his father walked through the living-room and entered the bedroom. Morris, who was worried by the fact that his mother was not yet up, filled the kettle quickly, and then followed his father.

His father met him outside the bedroom door. He held the door closed behind him, and said to Morris, 'Don't go in there.'

Morris walked back to the kitchen, and waited for the kettle to boil. His father sat on a chair in the living-room and without drawing the curtains back, he lifted the corner of one of them, and looked out.

When the tea had been given enough time to brew, Morris poured a cup for his father, and took it to him. His father remained looking out of the window, his head hidden behind the curtain. Morris stood with the cup in his hand, and after a very long time, he said, 'Here's your tea, dad.' Morris's father signalled with his hand that the tea should be left on the table, and Morris put down the tea and went back to the kitchen to look at the meat which had been bought for Sunday dinner. It was a leg of pork, and since the time was by now five minutes to two, Morris turned on the oven to 300 degrees, and began to peel potatoes.

When he had finished peeling his fifth potato, Morris went back into the living-room to ask his father if he would like another cup of tea. He had brewed a whole pot full, and only one cup had been drunk. In fact, as Morris now saw, his father's cup of tea had not been drunk, and remained where he had left it, untouched. His father was no longer in the living-room, and someone was running the water for a bath. Morris picked up the cup, and went into the hall. The door of what was now Mr Henderson's room was half open, and Morris went to the door, knocked on it, and waited. Nobody answered, so he looked round the door and saw that Mr Henderson wasn't there. So

Morris placed the cup of tea down on the chair beside Mr Henderson's bed, and left the room.

As he emerged from Mr Henderson's room, his mother came out of her own bedroom and closed the door behind her. She said, 'Have you put the meat in yet?' Morris shook his head, but explained that he had turned the oven on. Morris's mother said, 'Good.' Then Morris asked his mother if she was all right, and after looking at him for a long time, his mother replied, 'Yes. I just had a lie in.'

Later Morris sat on the back-door step and scraped the mud off his school plimsolls, while his mother sang to herself as she moved about in the kitchen, getting dinner ready. When he had scraped off all the mud, he intended to do what Anthony Pollack would have done, to fill the plimsolls with old newspaper and place them in front of the fire to dry out. The fire wasn't alight, but the ashes would still be warm from the night before.

As he stood outside the door, with his hand on the doorknob, Morris could hear his parents arguing. They were arguing about money and about Mr Henderson.

His father was arguing quietly, and Morris could not hear what he said. But Morris's mother, who was standing closer to the back door, argued in a loud voice, and could be heard clearly.

She was saying that if Mr Henderson were thrown out, then she would go also. They could not afford to ask Mr Henderson to leave, she said. Twenty-five shillings and six cracked eggs did not make up what Morris's mother considered a proper weekly wage. It was not even enough, she said, to keep Morris's father in the fish he needed for his diet. The leg of pork they were about to eat for Sunday dinner had been supplied by Mr Henderson. He paid far more for his bed and board than a lodger should, and he was entitled to consideration. She did not intend to grovel to the milkman any more, and she did not intend to hide from the Rent Man as she had done in the past. She had spent too many nights awake, worrying over bills. What had happened, she said, had been bound to happen some time or other, and Morris's father might go or stay; that was up to him. But if he stayed, he would have to put up with things as they were, and not go biting the hand that was feeding him. Only when he had begun to bring home enough money to keep his family properly would he have earned the right to decide how they should live, and with whom she could sleep. The life she had now was the only one she would get, and it was not going to be messed up by a man who farted in his sleep.

Morris's father opened the back door, and pushed past Morris. He went into the bicycle shed, and slammed the door. Morris's mother said, 'Your dad's left his bath-water in. You'd better have a bath. Then you can go to the pictures when you've had your dinner.'

Morris placed his school plimsolls in the hearth without first filling them with old newspaper, and went into the bathroom. As he closed the door of the bathroom, Mr Henderson crossed the hall naked, and went into his own room.

The water in the bath was lukewarm, and smelled of either pigs or cocoa: Morris could not decide which. The bath itself was small, and had two levels like a slipper-bath. Morris had to sit upright in it, and a cold draught from the window caught him in the middle of the back. His father had shaved while sitting in the bath, and black stubble floated on the surface of the water and clung to the grease mark round the sides.

Morris closed his eyes and remembered previous Sunday afternoons, and long walks taken with his mother while his father slept. They had picked blackberries, and eaten them on the way home, and when he had been very small they had picked rose-hips also, and sold them to a lady in the village. The lady had bought as many rose-hips as Morris and his mother had been able to collect, and she had sent them all away to be made into Rose-Hip Syrup, and this syrup had then been sent overseas to soldiers, to provide them with the concentrated Vitamin C they needed in order to finish winning the war.

At dinner, Morris pushed the pork on his plate to one side, and thought about his father who was still sitting in the corner of the bicycle shed. Morris had been sent by his mother to fetch his father in to dinner, but his father had looked away from him, and when Morris had taken hold of this father's hand, and attempted to pull him up from his sitting position, his father had squeezed tight on Morris's hand, and then let go, and used his own hand to cover his face.

Mr Henderson ate quickly, mopping the meat on his fork round in the gravy. Every so often, he looked at Morris, and smiled, and Morris looked away. Morris wanted to look at Mr Henderson, but he did not wish Mr Henderson to look at him. Nor did he wish him to smile.

'Don't you want that?' Mr Henderson pointed to the meat on the side of Morris's plate. Morris shook his head. Mr Henderson forked a large piece of pork from Morris's plate, and pushed it into his own mouth. Attached to the large piece of pork was some crackling, and on the crackling were strands of the dead pig's hair.

Morris watched the hairy crackling disappear, saw the gravy it left on Mr Henderson's lower lip, and remembered the naked body crossing the hall.

That afternoon he walked three miles to the cinema, and saw *Sanders of the River* for the second time in his life.

At various times during the afternoon, Morris's mother went out to the bicycle shed carrying a glass of milk, and attempted to persuade her husband to drink some of it, or to come indoors, and take food with which to soothe his ulcers, which were known to play up when his stomach was empty. But both milk and food were refused.

At ten past six (by which time Morris's father was in considerable pain), Mr Henderson carried a glass of milk out to the bicycle shed. He opened the door slowly, and peered at the body hunched up in the far corner. Carefully, and with short intervals between each pace, he moved towards the body, and when he reached it, he paused even longer. The body did not move. Bending slowly, Mr Henderson placed the glass of milk beside the body. The body didn't move.

After what must have been four minutes of complete stillness but seemed longer, Mr Henderson became worried, and placed a hand on Morris's father's arm. The body didn't move. He waited another minute, and then pushed his hand inside Morris's father's jacket, and felt about for Morris's father's heart. The heart moved, but the body didn't.

Mr Henderson waited another two minutes, and then undid the buttons of the shirt beneath the jacket, and began to massage where he assumed the ulcers to be.

After four minutes of massage, the body moved. And Mr Henderson began to massage more freely.

Learning

'There was once a king, whose queen had hair of the purest gold. She was so beautiful that her match was not to be met with on the whole face of the world.'

'Thank you, Dora. Next!' Dora Birtwistle sat down, and Janice Mottram stood beside Miss Addison, and began to read.

'When the queen felt that her end was near, she said to the king, "Vow to me that you will never marry again unless you meet with a wife who has golden hair like mine." ' Miss Addison raised a hand to the arrangement of hair on the top of her own head, and scratched vigorously.

Morris had found two nylon stockings lying over the end of his mother's bed. He had taken one of the stockings, and put it in his pocket. The stockings had been given to his mother by Mr. Henderson. Morris put his hand into his pocket, and felt the nylon. The moment the girl in front of him was called up to read, he would excuse himself, and go to the lavatory, and he would stay there until the bell rang.

'This will not do. The king must marry again, so that we may have a queen.'

'Don't rush, Margaret. Tell the story nicely. Make me want to listen.'

He had sat under the table, and drawn faces of women on the backs of old envelopes while his parents had played Dummy Whist with Mr Henderson. Mr Henderson didn't like Newmarket, which was the only game Morris could play. And he didn't like children playing for money. But Morris's mother had told Morris to watch and learn a thing or two, and his father had said, 'Lay your Jack on my Queen, and we'll see a few

165

tricks.' Then they had laughed and laughed, and been unable to stop.

'Why may I not marry my daughter? She is the very image of my dead wife.'

'Very nice, David. Next!' Four more children would read. Then he would leave the room.

If they had climbed into a train at Millbrook and travelled to Bletchley and Beyond, instead of spending the whole day in the Waiting Room, Morris's mother might have become a famous actress. Morris would have sat quietly at rehearsals, and watched. He would have waited in his mother's dressing-room every night until the curtain came down on the performance. Men with bouquets of flowers and huge boxes of chocolates tied up with silver ribbon would have pushed at the dressing-room door, but he would have kept them all out. One had given her a silver tea-set to use in the play. Others sent her nylon stockings. But only Morris was allowed to help her put the stockings on, only he was allowed to brush and curl her hair.

'His daughter was greatly shocked, and said, "Before I marry anyone, I must have a cloak made from a thousand different kinds of fur. Every beast in the kingdom must give part of his skin." ' Miss Addison lifted the pencil she was holding, and used the blunt end of it to scratch behind her ear. 'Who's next?'

Morris wiped his hand on the nylon stocking. In the lavatory, he would take it out and rub it over his face. None of the lavatory doors had locks any more, but he would lean his back against the door, and wait for the bell to ring. When two more children had read, he would raise his hand.

'When the cloak was ready, the princess wrapped herself in it, and besmeared her hands and face with soot. Then she threw herself upon Heaven for help in her need, and went away to journey the whole night.' Miss Addison considered the difficulty and improbability of anyone's actually being able to throw herself upon Heaven, since even if one could manage the jump, one would be bound either to bounce back or go through. Luckily the class was not accustomed to common sense in fairy stories.

Two weeks after he had picked beet for Mr Spark, his mother had said that it was wrong for a boy of Morris's age to sleep in the same room as his parents. A curtain had been made from the large chintz table-cloth, and Morris had helped his father to hang it from one side of the parental bedroom to the other. Mr Henderson was to sleep on the camp bed behind that curtain, so that Morris might have his own room back. Mr Henderson said that he didn't mind the smallness of the camp bed: he was used to it.

'Next!' That was Clive. When Clive had finished, Morris would excuse himself.

'The huntsmen's dogs came to the hollow tree where the princess was sleeping. They began to sniff, and then to bark. "Look sharp," said the king to the huntsmen. "See what sort of games lies there. If you can catch it alive, we will take it with us." '

'Morris, what are you doing with your hand in your pocket?' Miss Addison stopped Clive from reading any more, and stood up. 'Put it away, whatever it is, and come out here.' The rest of the class began to giggle, and Morris walked to the front.

'Please, miss, I want to be excused.'

'Well, you're not excused. Start there.' Miss Addison pointed to a line of print on the page, and Morris lowered his head, and tried to bring the print into focus.

The words merged into one another, and the letters inside the words danced up and down, trying to remind him what sounds they stood for. But not being able to make the sounds themselves, they had no way of really helping him.

'I . . . am . . . a . . . poor . . . ' His mother had licked her fingers and pressed down the hair on top of his head. She had wiped the corners of his mouth with her apron, and pretended to bite his nose off.

'Poor what, Morris?'

She had taken his left hand in hers, and shown him how to place it on his hip, and she had touched his shoulders, telling him that they were too round, and should be pulled back. But all this was a long time ago. His mother never touched him now. He wished she would.

'Child, Morris. The princess says she is a poor child. Read on.'

'I am a poor child . . . that . . . has . . . lost . . . both . . . '

They had moved all the furniture to one side of the living-

167

room, and pretended that the fireplace was the audience. She had placed his hand on his hip, and given him a pair of black gloves to hold. He had walked down the Strand with his gloves in his hand, and had walked back again with them off.

'I'm waiting, Morris. You're not making me want to listen.' Miss Addison lifted a strand of hair which was dangling over her ear, and placed it under the clip which held the arrangement on her crown in place. With the strand secured, she dug her fingernails below the clip, and scratched furiously at the scalp.

'I am a poor child that has lost . . . both . . . father and . . . mother.'

Morris's mother moved about their prefab more quickly now. He would follow her, and try to stand close to her, and sometimes he would reach out towards her. Once he had reached out, and touched her arm, and she had suddenly cringed, and had burnt her fingers with hot fat.

'Have . . . pity . . . on . . . me . . . and . . . take . . . me . . . with . . . you.'

Miss Addison examined Morris's left ear and the hair which surrounded it. Closely. The hair looked clean enough, but one could never tell. Someone in this class had infected her, and the itching was about to drive her mad.

'All . . . right, Miss . . . Cat . . . Skin. You can . . . sweep up and . . . do . . . things of . . . that . . . sort.'

She had bent down before the fire in her underslip so as to dry her hair quickly, and Mr Henderson had sat watching her. She had put lipstick and powder on her face. But she had not allowed Morris to wrap her hair in curling pins. She had sat in the chair, wearing her underslip, and Mr Henderson had watched her. Morris had been sent to bed.

' "Ah, . . . pretty . . . princess," . . . thought . . . she . . . "What will . . . now . . . " '

'Become.'

' "Become of . . . thee?" ' There would be too many boys in the lavatory at playtime for Morris to take out the nylon stocking, and even if the doors had locks, it was possible to climb up a door and look over. Morris never used the lavatory properly when he was at school.

'Thus . . . Cat Skin . . . lived for a . . . long . . . time . . . very . . . '

168

'Sorrowfully.'

'Sorrowfully but . . . when . . . '

'No, Morris. Look. What's that?'

'Full stop, miss.'

'And what do you do at a full stop?'

'Count three, miss.'

'Then why didn't you? At a full stop, you count three. And when do you count one?'

While Morris tried to remember, someone at the back of the class shouted, 'Comma, miss.'

'Good. Go on, Morris.'

Morris nodded his head three times, and counted under his breath before continuing, 'But when the. . . king. . . called. . . for a. . . ' He looked at the next word. It began with 'f' and had five letters. A sheet of smoked glass, like those found in bathroom windows, had descended between Morris and the five letters. He looked at Miss Addison's face, hoping that something about her expression might remind him how the word sounded. Miss Addison stared back at him. Her expression gave nothing away.

He slipped his fingers into the nylon stocking in his pocket, and felt the ladders his fingernails had made. He longed for his mother to touch him again. When he had slept in his parents' room, his mother had often woken him by tickling his feet. She had shaken the camp bed as if it were a cot, and then they had sat together on her bed, and discussed what they should do with the rest of the day. If she had been in a play, he had prompted her in her lines, for although he could not read the script she had marked with pencil, he had attended every rehearsal and knew everyone's lines off by heart. Today, when he had gone home from school at lunchtime in order to miss this Reading Lesson, his mother had ordered him back, and sent his father to follow and make sure he got there. And last night, when he had tried to climb on to her knee, she had pushed him away, and called him a nuisance, and Mr Henderson had laughed at him. Apart from that push, his mother had not touched him for three weeks.

Suddenly Miss Addison shouted, ' "Feast", boy! "Feast",' and grabbed hold of Morris's left arm, and tugged it. His hand came sharply out of his pocket, still holding his mother's nylon stocking. Miss Addison tightened her grip, and forced Morris's hand upwards for the whole class to see. The stocking covered his hand, and hung downwards, shaped like a woman's leg. His mother's leg.

As the children laughed, Miss Addison scratched her head. And the bell rang.

At the end of that term, Morris painted what he considered to be the best picture he had ever painted, but the Art Teacher told Morris that the picture looked a mess, and later he wrote on Morris's report, 'Morris's Art is just a mess of shapes.' No one asked Morris what the shapes in his picture were supposed to be. To Morris they were not shapes at all. They were his mother, his father and Mr Henderson.

First he had painted the bed with its white sheets. Then, before the white had dried (since he wanted to paint it quickly while he still remembered it), he had painted a pink woman lying on the sheets. On top of the pink woman, before she had dried, he had painted a blue man, and on top of the blue man, he had painted Mr Henderson. Mr Henderson was red. He had painted each of them in different colours so as to be able to tell one from the others, but by rights they should all have been pink, since none of them was wearing any clothes.

Both Mr Henderson and the blue man had faced the woman, and the pink woman and blue man had lain very still, so painting them was easy. But it was very important to Morris's picture that the lower half of Mr Henderson's body had moved up and down on top of the blue man, because that was what Morris had seen, and he wished to get it right.

But the red paint ran into the blue, and the blue into the pink, and the more he had tried to show that the red Mr Henderson was moving, the bigger Mr Henderson's body had got, and the more the red paint had run down through the pink and blue figures, and stained the white sheets under the pink woman. So that finally Morris had been forced to change Mr Henderson into a red eiderdown.

He had asked the Art Master, 'Sir, how do you make people move?' and the Art Master had told him that you could suggest movement in several ways. Then he had looked for a long time at Morris's painting, while Morris sat silently, and then he had

170

gone across the Art Room to the Art Room Cupboard, and taken from it a piece of blank paper and a tin of pastel crayons. He brought them to Morris, and said, 'Why don't you draw what you can see out of the window? Imagine it's playtime, and put one or two people in the playground. These pastels won't run.'

'Moving?'

'Yes. You try and make them move in your way, and then I'll tell you how I would have done it.'

Morris drew a mess of shapes on the white paper. This time none of the shapes moved. The blue shape was standing close to Mr Henderson in the bathroom while the pink shape was cooking breakfast. None of the colours ran. Out in the playground, it began to rain.

This was in 1951, the year of the Festival of Britain. If Stephen, years later, had been confronted in his Art Room by a painting like Morris's, since he had been to a Teachers' Training College, where he had seen reproductions of works by Jackson Pollock and Dubuffet, he would never have called it a mess of shapes: he might have described it as interesting abstract work. But he would not have known, any more than the Art Master did, who the shapes were, and what they were doing.

Offenders

On the afternoon of Thursday, May 3rd, 1951, the day on which the Archbishop of Canterbury, from the steps of St Paul's Cathedral, declared the Festival of Britain open, after which Sir Malcolm Sargent and Sir Adrian Boult led the people of Britain in singing 'Rule Britannia' and 'All People That on Earth Do Dwell', a day on which Morris Cowley (aged twelve) had been asked to keep an eye on Angela Richards (aged five) while Morris's mother and Mrs Richards paraded through the village on a float, giving away Festival of Britain mugs, a day on which Morris's father and his friend and lodger, Mr Henderson, stood behind a stall which had been erected in the school playground and filled those mugs with home-brewed beer, a day on which bonfires were lit all over the country, chiefly by Boy Scouts, in order symbolically to unite the young people of the nation, on this day Morris Cowley was discovered by Mrs Richards in the kitchen of the Richards home, pushing Ludo counters into the molehill of her daughter, the said Angela, during the course of a game of 'Doctor and Patient' instigated by Morris. And with this offence the said Morris was duly charged by due process of law, and duly appeared before the Juvenile Magistrates to answer it.

On the afternoon of Thursday, November 23rd, 1972, a day on which no mugs were given away nor bonfires lighted, Morris Stephen Cowley (thirty-four), a teacher of Art, was apprehended by the police, partially clothed, in the bedroom of Mary Whittaker (fourteen), one of his pupils, the said police being engaged at the time in a search for cannabis resin in pursuance of their duties under the Dangerous Drugs Act. Since no cannabis resin was found by the police on the person of the said Morris Stephen Cowley, nor was there any evidence of his being involved, either solely or in conjunction with any other persons, in the sale of cannabis resin, nor did he own or rent the property – i.e. the Whittaker home – in which cannabis resin was ultimately found, he could not be charged with any offence under the Dangerous Drugs Act; nevertheless the said Morris Stephen Cowley was duly charged by due process of law with the offence of having sexual relations with the said Mary Whittaker, she being a person under the age of sixteen, and did duly appear before the Magistrates to answer it.

Justice

The lion and the unicorn were fighting for the crown.

He was standing below a platform on which there was a long high desk. On the desk were three bottles of water, and covering each bottle, presumably keeping out dust, there was a glass tumbler. Behind the desk sat three people, one man and two women. The man sat in the middle behind the centre bottle of water. He was very fat, and had four chins. Above the chins, the man's features were small, and as he held his head back and studied the fanlight in the centre of the ceiling, the round pink swelling of each chin stretched to reveal the crease which separated it from its neighbour. This man was the Chairman of the magistrates. His name was Sir Ernle Freece.

The badge on the wall above the fat man's head was smaller than Stephen remembered it, and the tip of the unicorn's horn seemed bent.

The lion beat the unicorn all around the town

Mrs Richards had pulled Angela off the kitchen table, and beaten Morris about the head with her clenched fists. She had screamed at him, and her screaming had made Angela scream. Angela had screamed that the ludo counter inside her was hurting, but Mrs Richards' screaming hadn't consisted of words: it had consisted of high-pitched noises. Morris had tried hard to concentrate on ducking the blows which Mrs Richards threw at him, but the movement going on inside her nylon blouse had fascinated him. As her arms had swung, so had her breasts. They had swung, and wobbled, and he had imagined himself holding one breast in each hand, and burying his face in them.

'*I hope you like tongue, Stephen. Mary said you might. You don't*

174

*mind first name terms right away, do you? Mary made the salad. It
was good of you to come.'* That had been on the first visit.

The Chairman of the magistrates shook his head in response
to something whispered by the lady on his left, and his pink
chins wobbled like the contents of Mrs Richards' blouse. Mary's
breasts had been small, like air-bubbles trapped behind wallpaper. He had fingered those bubbles, and moved them about.

*'I have to go out soon. I hope you can stay. Mary hates being left
alone. We're both very upset about your experience with the fudge.'*
There had been four visits altogether, and each time Mary's
father had gone out. Mary hated being left alone.

Some gave them white bread, and some gave them brown.

He had waited in the corridor outside, and watched three
Pakistanis chain-smoke and offer each other pound notes with
which to pay fines for speeding. A large West Indian had chained
his Alsatian dog to the railings outside the court, and then asked
a policeman to keep an eye on it. The dog was howling. There
was no time now for race relations.

Some give them syrup of figs, and beat them out of town.

He had spent a long time in the lavatory. His stomach had
been upset, and still was. He had not slept, and had left the
house shortly after dawn. He had walked and walked, and
listened to his footsteps on the pavement. As he walked, it had
rained, and his shoes were now wet and tender like calves' liver.
He had gazed into shop windows, looking at knitting patterns,
hanks of silk for embroidery, Suntex underwear, carved effigies
of Bambi, boxes and boxes of sanitary towels and a great
number of Coseytoes Acrilan bedsocks. *I've tried not to need
anything else, but I find that I do.*

He had arrived at the court far too early, and had paced up
and down outside. Then he had gone to the lavatory, and sat
waiting for the pain in his stomach to go away. As he had
waited, he had read what there was to read:

'Psychiatry kills!'

'Police are fucking liars.'

'WOG SCUM OUT.'

'Is a plice cadett a facist Piglit?'

'Grass is the natural way of Seeking help.'

'Am I the only Queer in Accrington?'

He had taken a pencil from his own pocket, and written, 'GIVE ME A BIG CLAP. I LIKE LITTLE GIRLS.'

Then he had stood in the corridor until a man in uniform had opened a door, and called, 'MORRIS STEPHEN COWLEY' in a very loud voice. Stephen had walked obediently towards the man in uniform, and he had turned and shouted into the court-room, 'WE HAVE AN ANSWER, YOUR WORSHIPS.' (*Somewhere on the Admiration Ladder he must write his own name. The next question asked him whether he ever thought about the future.*)

There was a square green wrought-iron grille facing the magistrates, with a seat inside it. Stephen went into it, and stood with his hand on the rail, but the man with the loud voice took Stephen out of the grille and made him stand in front of it. Stephen thought that perhaps the grille was for dangerous prisoners. There was a woman sitting at a table below the magistrates' desk. On the table were piles and piles of putty-coloured folders. The woman asked Stephen whether he wished to be tried in this court or before a jury at a Crown Court. Stephen said, 'Here.' (*But does it have to be tonight, sir?*)

He had been instructed to plead 'Not Guilty', and he did. Stephen did not know any solicitors except Messrs Duckworth and Hanson, who had dealt with the house. Knowing that he was already breaking the terms of his father's will by allowing Uncle Leonard in the house, Stephen had been reluctant to go to them for help, but he had been welcomed by a new junior partner there, who had become excited and enthusiastic as soon as he had been told of what he persisted in calling 'your little difficulty'. He had been so delighted, and so unable to keep still, and so determined to make his name by his conduct of the case, that he had made Stephen nervous. He had asked Stephen many questions about whether anyone but the two policemen had been present in the room in which he had been discovered with Mary, and what the policemen had done, and none at all about what Stephen and Mary had done. Then he had instructed Stephen to plead 'Not Guilty'.

People shuffled about behind him, and doors were opened and closed noisily. Policemen wandered in and out. Some sat behind other policemen, and whispered. It was not like the films or television, where people spoke clearly because what they said was important. The noise from the rooms off this room was deafening. A policeman who had arrested Stephen climbed into the witness box, and said, 'These are the facts in this case, your worships.' He then looked down at his notebook, and became totally inaudible. The woman whose job it was to write it all down stopped the policeman, and asked him to speak more slowly, but no one asked him to speak more loudly. They were talking to themselves, and expecting Stephen to listen. (*We don't want to go into too many details, because it's only embarrassing for all of us, isn't it?*)

The Alsatian dog outside howled, and people in the corridor began to laugh. (*The slates beneath his feet were wet and slippery, and yet he laughed, and shouted, 'Morris!' 'Morris,' he shouted, but the boy who turned to look had no features, just a round pink blob, made up of curling brush-strokes.*) It was his trial, and nobody seemed to notice. He was standing in the centre of the room, and yet they ignored him. The facts which the policeman claimed to have in his book concerned him. They were his facts, yet he was not to be allowed to hear them.

The door at the side of the court opened yet again, and Sarah was directed to the three wooden benches reserved for members of the public. Stephen watched her walking sideways between the pew-like benches and then lowering her bottom on to the seat gently as though she were in church. He saw her attempt a smile, and that the smile, which started confidently, faltered for a moment, and then died completely as her eyes moved away from his to gaze at the magistrates and then at the policeman, still mumbling in the witness box. When Sarah looked towards him again, Stephen mouthed the words, 'Thank you,' and Sarah placed two tightly crossed fingers on the side of her face, and smiled again. This time the smile was more convincing.

He had asked her not to come, talked of newspaper reporters, and said that her presence would inhibit him from stretching the truth. He would not be able to lie well, he had said, if she were going to be there, and Sarah had said, 'Love, don't, whatever you do, assume that the police will tell the truth.' In fact there were no reporters. At least no one was sitting on the bench marked 'Press'.

Now he looked across at her face. She was not wearing make-up, and her coat was the oldest she possessed. He realized how nervous she must have been about coming, for if she had merely decided to ignore his request she would have been there already when his case was called, there since the court opened: she would have sat through all the motoring offences and the drunks and disorderlies to be present when he was put up, and give him comfort.

She must have spent all morning working hard on that smile, standing before a mirror, trying to make it look natural. The more she worked on it, the more uncertain of its credibility she would have become. Her reasons for deciding to wear old clothes and no make-up would not be simple. They would be complex, and would have taken time to work out. Not to gain sympathy for herself (if anyone there should know her), but to present herself as a frumpish slovenly wife whom anyone self-respecting would be right to desert. No that was not it. She would have done it for Stephen's benefit, not the court's or the reporters' (since it was most unlikely that anyone *should* know her), to show herself to him at her frumpish worst in case he should be tempted by the emotion of the occasion to trap himself into returning to her. (*Dear husband, I hope you'll forgive me for not being able to leave you to your little girls.*)

Well, her arrival *had* given him comfort: he was glad to see her there. And what was more, in thinking of Sarah, he had forgotten to think about himself.

He had asked his mother and Uncle Leonard not to come also, and they had not come. Uncle Leonard had grinned a very knowing grin, and crushed Stephen's hands between his own sweaty palms, saying, 'There's no gain without pain,' and Stephen's mother had contemplated the difference between a teacher's salary and unemployment benefit, and asked, 'What has he gained?' Whereupon Uncle Leonard had moved out of her line of vision, and tapped the side of his nose lecherously with the index finger of his right hand. (*Morris watched the hairy crackling being swallowed up by Uncle Leonard's mouth, and thought about his father sitting in the corner of the bicycle shed.*)

He had resigned from his job at the school. The junior partner had said that, if things did go badly, it would look better in mitigation if he had already resigned, but that he was to look on the bright side and not think of that. Nevertheless, Stephen did think of that.

Three thin ropes were tied to the wall just to one side of the witness box. They were like the ropes used to open and close the windows at school, and Stephen's eyes followed the ropes upwards to see where the window was. There was no window. The ropes were attached to ventilators in the ceiling. Just below the ventilators was a small balcony, and on it sat two young men with notebooks in their hands. So there were reporters, after all. One of them nudged his companion, who seemed to be in some danger of falling asleep, and pointed downwards towards Sarah. The sleepy cub-reporter looked, and then started writing something in his notebook. Stephen had seen him before. With Mary. In the park.

The mumbling policeman stopped mumbling, and looked towards the woman at the table, who rummaged among her putty-coloured folders, and found two copies of a letter which she handed to an usher in a black gown, who in his turn handed one copy up to the magistrates, the other across to Stephen's solicitor, who took it, read it quickly, and winked at Stephen.

Stephen knew what was in the letter. It had been taken from his trouser pocket, when this same policeman had snatched the trousers from the back of a chair in Mary's bedroom, and searched them for drugs. He hadn't mumbled then: he had shouted.

The letter said:

'Dear Sir, Mary has told me how kind you have been to her, and I would very much like to meet you. Since her mother died, I have felt the responsibility for her welfare a great strain. I would be most grateful if you could find the time to come over to the house for tea soon. A second opinion on what line of work Mary should persue on leaving school would be much appreciated. I'm sorry that it is not possibile for me to come to the school to have this talk. But I found my own school so depressing, and I fear the same may hold true of yours.

Sincere best wishes,
Mary's father.'

Mary's father had shown Stephen line-drawings he had made with a ballpoint pen while under the influence of hash. The drawings had reminded Stephen of Mary's doodles. As the three of them had looked at the numerous drawings, Mary had wrapped her fingers around Stephen's fingers, and squeezed them tight, and Mary's father had said, 'She's her father's girl. Since her mother went, we've been very close. I never wanted sons. I hope you like tongue. It's a weakness of mine.'

Three weeks and three visits later, the policemen had followed Mary's father home, and burst in to search the house. By this time Stephen had lent Mary's father a total of thirty pounds with which to buy food until he found a job. It was also, they both agreed, to help him to stop trafficking in hash and pay off the money he owed his contact.

'My problem, you see, is one of finance. Although I believe that hash is useful in our constant search for self-knowledge, and certainly no more harmful than alcohol or cigarettes, I should never have started to sell it had I not been financially embarrassed.' Mary had leaned her weight against Stephen, and he had rubbed his thumb along her tiny fingernails and felt the disc of her identity bracelet against his wrist. (*Twenty-five shillings and six cracked eggs did not make up what she considered a proper weekly wage. . . Her life wasn't going to be messed up by a man who farted in his sleep—a man who had lied to her about what he was earning all those years, and saved money to buy a house—a man who had sat on the roof looking out for fires, while she lay between utility sheets in an underslip wet with warm pee!*) 'I hope you can stay for an hour or two. I'm afraid I've got to go out, and Mary hates being left alone.'

One policeman had struck him across the jaw, while the other had grabbed Mary and thrown her down on the bed. ('*It says here that you let other boys hit you, and you won't hit back, and yet you complain. Is that true?*) The policeman who had thrown Mary down put his hand up her underslip, inserted a finger, and said, 'We've got to search you. This is one of the few perks I get, you filthy little beast. You could have stuck the stuff up here, and we'd never know.' ('*Morris, it says here that on the afternoon of May 3rd you interfered with Angela Richards, and that you were found in the act of interfering by Angela's mother. What do you say to that, Morris? Is it true?*)

The junior partner from Duckworth and Hanson had risen from his seat at the solicitor's table, and now confronted the mumbling policeman. 'You have told the court that you and Sergeant Franklin surprised my client with the girl, Mary Whittaker, in the bedroom, is that correct?'

'Mumble.'

'I beg your pardon.'

Sir Ernle Freece moved his four chins fretfully, and said, 'Tell him to speak up. I've heard very little so far.'

'His worship would like you to give your answers clearly. Did you and Sergeant Franklin—'

'Yes, we did.'

'In her bedroom?'

'That's right.'

'Was there a chair in the room?'

Silence. (*Angela had stood on a chair at the sink, wetting pieces of old newspaper under the tap. She had torn the newspaper into shapes resembling fish, and her intention had been to sell the newspaper fish to Morris. She had climbed down from her chair, and slapped the wet pieces of newspaper on to the kitchen table with a cry of, 'Look! They're lovely!' She had pushed them under Morris's nose, saying 'Aren't they fresh? Smell my kippers,' but Morris had shaken his head because her kippers were not fresh, and she had climbed back on the chair, and bent over the sink to wash the newspaper fish again, and Morris had looked up and noticed that Angela was not wearing knickers.*)

'Do you not remember? You have been using your notebook up to now; I am sure that their worships would allow you to refer to it, if you should be in any doubt.'

'There may have been.'

'There may have been a chair. Was there a desk?'

Silence. (*He had bought the newspaper fish with two Ludo counters, and Angela had placed one of the counters in her mouth, and tried to break it with her teeth.*)

'A table? A small table on which homework might conveniently be done?'

'Mumble.'

'What does he say?'

'He seems, your worship, to be unable to remember whether there was a small table or desk in the room.'

A police sergeant, sitting on a bench at the side of the court, cleared his throat sharply, and the mumbling policeman said, 'May have been.' This sergeant was unknown to Stephen; he was not Sergeant Franklin, who would be waiting outside.

'There may have been a desk. Books?'

Pause. 'I can't remember.'

'You were conducting a thorough search for drugs, and you cannot remember whether there were any books in the room?'

Pause. 'May have been.'

'There may have been books. Was there a poster on the wall? Gramophone records? A record-player?'

'May have been.' (*She had dropped a Ludo counter down the front of his shirt, and rocked herself from side to side over his knee, bumping her head gently against his shoulder.*)

'There may have been a gramophone and records. Were there pictures of singers—Donny Osmond, David Cassidy and David Bowie in particular—cut from magazines and sellotaped to the walls?'

The mumbling policeman had begun to sweat. Since all Stephen had found himself able to say when he was apprehended had been, 'I'm sorry; I'm sorry,' over and over again, which had been taken as an admission of guilt, and duly recorded as such in the notebooks, the police had not been expecting this case to be defended. If the magistrates in their wisdom were to decide that Stephen's offence was so heinous that it was beyond their powers to punish adequately, and were to remit the case to a Crown Court, that would be another matter; counsel would have to be briefed and the mumbling policeman properly coached, or at least not put up first simply because Sergeant Franklin had been engaged until late on other business. Now he was having to sweat it out.

'Did you, in the course of your thorough search for drugs throughout that small council-house, find any other room in which a schoolgirl might keep her books and records. . . the bits and pieces she needed for her school work. . . her private possessions, in short?'

'Beg your pardon.'

'Did you—'

Sir Ernle Freece said, 'I think he heard the question.'

'I can't say.' (*Morris had pulled the front of his shirt out of his*

182

trousers in an attempt to find the Ludo counter. Angela had placed three of her dolls on the kitchen table, and Morris had examined them, and given them medicine from a teaspoon. Now it was Angela's turn.)

'Well, no doubt if you could remember, you would be able to say, so we may assume that there was no such room.'

Sir Ernle Freece said, 'All right. We take your point.'

'Thank you, your worship.' The junior partner explained to the policeman, who was staring at him in baffled hostility, 'His worship means that it is not a question of your finding my client and the girl in her bedroom: you merely found them in her room—the room in which she kept her personal possessions and anything which might concern her work at the school.'

The sergeant sitting on the bench at the side of the courtroom cleared his throat again, and the mumbling policeman said quickly and clearly, 'There was a bed in the room. Undergarments of an intimate nature,' and the junior partner replied pleasantly, 'Yes. She kept her clothes in her room. You would not expect to find them in the kitchen. Now. . . this letter you say you found in my client's pocket. . . '

The junior partner was rapidly able to establish the innocence of the letter. (*Morris placed a tea-spoon in Angela's mouth, and told her to say, 'Ah!' He ran his hand over the front of her dress, and felt her stomach. He turned her over. He examined her behind. That evening Boy Scouts would light a bonfire on a cleared bomb-site behind St Paul's.*)

'Were they dressed when you and the sergeant burst into the room?'

'Undressed.'

'Naked?'

'They were in a state of undress.'

'Wearing nothing at all?'

A pause. The mumbling policeman looked about him for help, but the rules of the court had not allowed Sergeant Franklin to be present while his subordinate was giving evidence, and the mumbling policeman could not know what Sergeant Franklin would say. 'I wouldn't say that.'

'They were wearing some clothing?'

'Underwear. They were in a state of partial undress, clothed only in underwear.'

'Now, I want to get this clear. Your reason for following the

183

girl's father home and for bursting into that room was not that you expected to find and to apprehend my client and the girl together in a state of undress? That was not your intention or your expectation in coming to the house?'

'Beg pardon.'

'You were searching for drugs?'

'That is correct.'

'Was the girl's father present?'

'What?'

'When you burst in, and discovered—'

'He was downstairs.'

'So nobody else, except yourself and the sergeant, actually saw my client and the girl in a state of partial undress?'

'No.'

'Otherwise the police would no doubt be calling the girl's father to give evidence?'

A pause. 'I can't say as to that.'

Sir Ernle Freece said, 'I don't think that's his business, is it?'

'I beg your pardon, your worship. I just wanted to make that quite clear.' The junior partner turned again to the policeman. 'You searched everywhere? The books. . . ? the desk. . . ? the bedclothes. . . ? the various intimate possessions. . . ? clothing. . . ?'

'We conducted a thorough search, and did in fact discover in the house certain substances which have since been submitted to chemical analysis.'

'That is not an issue in this case. Has my client been charged with possession of dangerous drugs?'

Pause. Reluctantly. . . 'No.'

'You found no dangerous drugs on the person of my client?'

'No.'

'Or in his clothing?'

'No.'

'Nor does he own or rent or lodge at the premises at which you say you did find dangerous drugs?'

'No.'

'And how did you search his clothing?'

'We. . . searched it.'

'The pockets? The linings? A thorough search?'

'Yes.'

184

'How could you search the linings without taking his clothing off?' Pause. 'His jacket and his trousers—how could you search them thoroughly without taking them off?'

'We were not required to take them off. They were already off.'

'But would it not be true to say that both in the case of my client and the girl, you could not make a thorough search of their garments without removing those garments?' A silence. The policeman looked at him. Sweat breaking out all over the mumbling policeman's face, and running down his chin. The junior partner had conducted cross-examinations of this sort before over and over again, in his head, in the bath, in bed between sleeping and waking. 'Would it not be true to say that, whether they were discovered only partially dressed or not when you and the sergeant burst into the room, or whether they were in fact fully dressed, they would in any case be only partially dressed by the time you had finished your thorough search?' The question was of such complication that the mumbling policeman could not begin to answer it. 'Would it not be true to say that, whatever happened, you yourselves were bound to undress them? And that there was nobody else present to see whether you did or not?'

Sir Ernle Freece said, 'We take your point.'

'Thank you, your worship.' The mumbling policeman seemed to be about to leave the witness stand, but that happy time was not yet come. 'And the girl? Did you have her medically examined?'

'Beg your pardon.'

'After you had finished conducting your thorough search, you allowed my client and the girl to dress, and required them to accompany you to the police station, where they were charged. Did you have the girl medically examined at the station?'

Silence.

'Was she medically examined in order to discover whether she had recently enjoyed sexual intercourse?'

'No.'

'You did not think that necessary?'

A wild glance around. 'As to that, I can't say.' This time it was Sir Ernle Freece who cleared his throat, and one of the lady worships poured herself a glass of water. 'It's not my responsibility.'

'No, it's not. Indeed it is not. But to your knowledge, the girl was not medically examined at the police station to see if—'

'There was no need. Being as evidence of intimacy had already been established.'

'Oh, I wouldn't say that. That's under dispute, you know: that's why we're here. And in any case, she'd already been examined, hadn't she?'

'Sir?' The mumbling policeman had not used this word to the junior partner before, but even before the sword goes in, a bull may sense when he has been defeated.

'You had already examined Mary, had you not? You had already thrust your fingers into her vagina, had you not? You had thrown her down on the bed, put your hand inside her underslip, and thrust your fingers into her vagina, had you not?'

It was very silent in the court room. Stephen could hear pencils moving over the pages of notebooks from somewhere above him near the ventilators. But the local papers would never print such stuff.

The junior partner said, 'I know that the police, out of a natural sense of delicacy, are not calling the girl, Mary Whittaker, as a witness in this case, and I would also rather spare her such an ordeal, but you do understand that it is still possible to call her?'

The sitting sergeant's cough said, 'Deny it. Brazen it out. They will take your word against the girl's.' But the mumbling policeman misread that signal, and said, 'We are required to search for dangerous drugs, sir, wherever they may be concealed.'

'Even in the most. . . private. . . ?'

'Yes, sir.'

'Bodily recesses?'

'Yes, sir.'

'Ah! In that case, no doubt you turned my client round, and placed those same fingers up his—'

An anguished clearing of the throat from Sir Ernle Freece.

'No, sir. I did not.'

'And the sergeant did not?'

'No, sir. He did not.'

186

'You were a little selective, then, in your choice of bodily recesses to search for dangerous drugs. I have no more questions.' (*Morris cupped the fingers of one hand, and put them to his eyes. Looking down the tube his fingers made, he said, 'This is the largest telescope in the world, and it can see all the way to Australia.' Angela giggled, and Morris picked up a Ludo counter, and placed it on its side next to the little finger of his other hand in the cleft of Angela's molehill.*)

After that, the cross-examination of the sergeant came as an anticlimax, since he was only asked whether the words, 'I'm sorry, I'm sorry,' might not as easily have been the words, 'I'm sorry: I don't know what this is all about.' This was both astute and daring of the junior partner for, if he had asked Sergeant Franklin whether his constable had searched Mary's recesses for dangerous drugs and the Sergeant had denied it (which was probable), the police evidence would have been altogether discredited, but the junior partner felt that enough was enough, and he feared a backlash from Sir Ernle Freece, and he had also, even as he spoke the words, 'No more questions,' begun to wonder whether any triumph was worth incurring the lasting hatred of the police.

What he now did was to request their worships to dismiss the case for lack of evidence. There being no police solicitor to object, Sergeant Franklin objected. The junior partner said, 'With respect, your worships, we have heard evidence that my client visited this girl at her father's request and with his approval, that my client was with her in her room, as one might expect him to be, and that two police officers burst in to that room, and proceeded to conduct a search for dangerous drugs, in the course of which it was necessary for them to remove clothing from my client and the girl. There is no direct evidence of any form of intimacy, and no corroboration of the police evidence that my client and the girl were only partly dressed when they burst into the room. As to the way in which the search was conducted, well I am sure I do not need to draw your worships' attention further to that.'

Then the three magistrates gobbled together up on the bench in low voices, and then Sir Ernle announced that they would retire. And everyone stood up, and the magistrates retired, and Stephen sat where he was before the green wrought-iron grille.

★

Child Care Officer's Report: May, 1951. Morris is a shy, inarticulate boy, almost always in a dream. His physical appearance is hard to describe because it is somewhat ordinary. Mouse-coloured hair. Hazel eyes, deeply set. Nose a little too broad. Sallow greasy skin. Height a little above normal for his age. Round-shouldered. I think Morris needs a shock to bring him out into the real world. On the estate, children call him 'big baby' and adults 'little gentleman'. He cries very easily. He is watchful of me, and I think he knows more than he is prepared to let on. His ears are large and a little unclean. I have visited the home on several occasions. The lodger, Leonard Henderson, has now moved out, owing to the publicity caused by the case. The father was unwilling to talk about Morris, and tried to move the conversation on to his own lack of good health. He believes that their living in a prefab is to blame, and also the sort of neighbours they have been forced to mix with. He had never spoken to Morris about sexual matters, but had once found him drawing 'the dirty bits' on to the figures in a Buck Ryan cartoon, when he had snatched away the paper, struck Morris on the head, and called him a 'dirty-minded little beast'. He had not thought it necessary to tell Morris 'the facts of life' because, 'You can't tell them anything these days.' The mother said, 'I wish people would stop interfering with us. We are a happy family.'

Housemaster's Report: October, 1951. After starting badly, and having been assessed as a poor academic specimen, Morris has suddenly found his feet. The subject at which he excels is Art, and he paints five pictures while the other boys are trying to think what to draw. This gives him a little status, and a bit more confidence, so that his other work has also improved. His pictures are very lively, though crude and colourful: he seems to be fascinated by cats and blood. His appearance has improved, and he is quiet and well-behaved. Rather cowardly at games.

Housemaster's Report: October 1952. Morris continues to improve, and his painting has become skilful and more varied in subject. He signs his pictures 'Stephen Cowley', and has crossed out 'Morris' and written 'Stephen' on all his exercise books. I have requested the other teachers to fall in with this preference, since 'Stephen' is his second name. Welfare Officer feels Stephen should stay with us. He continues to be well-behaved and obedient. Still rather cowardly where sport is concerned.

Housemaster's Report: October, 1953. Alderman Hargreaves, Chairman of our School Board, has paid ten pounds for one of Stephen's pictures, a watercolour of Birley Wood, the money to be spent on books and painting equipment. The picture will be hung in the Public Library. Well done, Stephen! What next? 'O' Levels?

In fact, when Stephen returned to his parents in the north, where his father had held a regular job for the last two years, he did study for 'O' Levels at Night School, to his father's approval, and duly obtained his GCE.

A small door opened behind the magistrates' desk, and their worships returned. Everyone stood up, and then sat down again when their worships sat. Stephen was instructed to remain standing. Sir Ernle said, 'We find there's no case.'

Nobody applauded. Nobody cheered. Nobody came from the body of the court to embrace Stephen. Even Sarah did not seem to know what to do. The junior partner said, 'I don't want to push it, your worship, but there's the question of costs.'

Sir Ernle said, 'No costs. We'll get on.'

The junior partner gathered his papers together, came over to Stephen, and said, 'That's it. We can go.' Stephen said, 'Thank you very much.' They moved out into the corridor. Sarah came from the public benches to join them. Stephen said, 'Thank you very much,' again to the junior partner, who replied, 'Not to worry. We'll be sending you a bill, I'm afraid. Care to quaff a noggin?' But Stephen did not think he would be able to quaff a noggin in a public house with everyone watching, so he said he wasn't feeling very well, and the junior partner went off down the corridor, and Sarah took his arm, and the Alsatian dog continued to howl.

If the fire in the grate were still alive, she would heat some curling tongs, and wave her hair. She would paint her legs yellow with a permanent dye from Woolworth's, and sit in her underslip before the fire while Uncle Leonard watched. While his mother and father had argued about money and debts, he had sat and watched an old man spit blood into a stainless steel basin.

Sarah said, 'Come on love.'

He would walk down the Strand with his gloves in his hand, and walk back again with them off.

Sarah said, 'Come along, eh, love?'

His father had stood outside the bedroom door, and said, 'Don't go in there.' He remembered for a long time the closeness of his father's face to his.

Endings

Mary's father was sentenced to five years' imprisonment. For those five years he would have no financial problems.

Mary was taken into care. Under section 44 of the Act of 1933, she was removed from undesirable surroundings, and proper provision was made for her education and training. She was placed in an Orphanage for Girls, run by a strict Anglican order. She was no longer harassed by the lustful attentions of older men, yet her freckles, her often-chewed lower lip, and her straw-coloured eyelashes continued to be admired, and many hands fingered and moved about the breasts which were like air-bubbles trapped behind wallpaper.

Uncle Leonard became a barman at the Traders' Arms, and Stephen's mother would spend every evening sitting close to the electric fire, listening to it squeak and spinning out two bottles of brown ale and a packet of crisps, as she watched the coloured globules on the fruit machine joining and breaking apart and joining up again.

Stephen and Sarah made a joint application to work as house-father and housemother at an Assessment Centre and Community Home in Staffordshire. Sarah's previous experience with handicapped children had been the deciding factor in their favour. They lived on the campus, and looked after thirty-five boys aged between twelve and fifteen.

Stephen finished reading the document in the putty-coloured folder before him, and looked across at the boy who was emptying his pockets and placing the contents on the desk.

'So you damaged some gravestones? Broke into a woodman's hut? Stole a macintosh and wellingtons? Bored holes in the side of the hut to see who was coming? And now you can't explain where you got this RAC First-Aid Kit?'

'No, sir.'

'Fourth time you've done a bunk.'

'Yes, sir.'

'Why?'

'Don't know, sir.'

'All right. Go and get a shower, and try to calm down. Have you taken your pills?' The boy nodded. 'Well, you're back home with us now, so everything's ended happily after all.'

Nothing ends unhappily. Everything ends happily.